The Equestrian's Embrace

BOOK #1 IN EMBRACING THE LOVE SERIES

LAUREN L. MOON

The Equestrian's Embrace

LAUREN L.
MOON

The Equestrian's Embshow Book One of Embracing The Love Series Copyright ©
2026 by Lauren Moon
First Edition | Paperback Publication Date:
ISBN: 979-8-9891528-6-5
Copy Editing by: Melony Ann
Paperback formatting by: Gabbie Dixon
Cover design by: Gabbie Dixon
Published by Lauren Moon

To my dog, Bosco, I miss you beyond words. This way you can live on forever in my stories... I will never stop telling our story. Thank you for everything.

To my cat, Saint, I love and miss you so much. Thank you for the countless smiles, and the amazing memories. You were taken from me too soon. Thank you for being the best kitty.

IN LOVING MEMORY

SAINT

August 15th, 2020 to February 15th, 2024

Chapter One

SKYLAR

My sneakers squeak against the floor as I head down the hallway. I'm late. I'm always late. I shove my phone in my purse. Ale said that I wouldn't have any problems getting through security.

Everything will be fine.

Everything will be fine.

Last time was an accident. No one is going to grab me again. But I should get my ID out, just in case. Did I remember my wallet? I bite my lip. I'm tempted to turn around. Call my brother, and just go back home.

When I see the security guards, I start digging through my bag, trying to find my stupid wallet. *Everything is fine Skylar. Don't panic. Everything is fine.*

"Fans aren't allowed back here," one of the guards tells me.

I swallow. He already seems mad.

"I..." I shake my head. "I'm not a fan. I mean... I am one, but..."

"Exactly. You're a fan. Turn around. The game will start, and you'll get to see the players then," he snaps at me.

Yeah, I'm calling Ale. I can't do this. I turn on my heel

wanting to head back the way I came, but I hear someone yell at the end of the hallway.

"Babe! Wait!" a male voice calls out.

That's not my brother or Leo. I stop and turn to watch the man running from where the locker room for the team is. When he gets to the security guards, I scrunch my nose.

I don't know who he is.

"This is my girlfriend. She's good to come back," the guy tells them.

The guards look at me, before turning to look back at him. "If you say so," the one who snapped at me says.

Ale isn't going to like any of this. I don't like any of this. I rub my bare arms. I just want my brother. This guy is wearing a jersey, so he must be one of the new players.

"Come here, babe. I've missed you," he turns to look at me.

I have to look up at him. He's about a foot taller than me. I don't say anything. I just walk to his open arms. He wraps his arms around me when I get close enough for him to grab me.

"I would've come out here if you would've texted me, babe," he tells me, keeping his arm around my shoulder as we turn and walk down the hall.

I can't bring myself to say anything. All I can think about is how I just wish I'd gone home. But I promised Ale I'd come. I got distracted.

Really, I don't know how I remember to do everything for my horse, River. Which reminds me that she needs new shoes, so I need to call the farrier.

When we get close enough to the locker room, the guy lets me go.

"There you go." The guy smirks as he looks down at me. "You're a fan? Who's your favorite player? I could get you an autograph. Maybe even a picture with him."

This guy really doesn't know who my brother is?

"My favorite player?" I repeat his question.

He leans over me, backing me against the wall. My heart skips a beat as I feel the brick press against me.

"That's what I asked, beautiful," he says, his green eyes stare into mine. "Maybe later after I win this game, I can take you out for a drink."

I squeak when I hear the door open, this guy's bicep is in my way so I can't see who's there. I hope it's my brother... Or Leo. It has to be one of them.

Chapter Two

BRAXTON

Before I even have a chance to react, I'm shoved away from the beautiful blonde in front of me. Is she a player's girl-friend and no one told me?

"And what do you think you're doing?" Alejandro, the team captain, growls at me.

Oh, yeah, they're probably dating, and I'm going to get myself fired. The woman moves to stand behind Ale. Hmm... If they were dating, he would've said to get my hands off his woman. He didn't.

"I was just flirting. She's hot," I tell him, shrugging off where I hit the opposite wall.

Ale's body stiffens. I really need to learn to keep my mouth shut.

"How many times do I need to say that my sister is off limits?" he growls at me. I straighten up.

I didn't know that was his sister. They look nothing alike. She has long blonde hair, tan skin, and beautiful, crystal blue eyes. Even knowing that's his sister, I'm still going to flirt with her.

"First off. I didn't know she was your sister. You guys look nothing alike. Blonde hair. Blue eyes. Tan skin. And let's be honest, not ugly," I tell him. I just can't help myself.

It's too much fun riling him up.

"You keep your grubby hands off of her. She's off limits. She's wearing my jersey, our last name, and she has a pass that says she's the Captain's sister. If you touch her one more time, I'm going to break all of your fingers," he threatens, turning on his heel and ushering his sister in front of him.

I rub the bridge of my nose. It would be just my luck that she's the Captain's sister. How are they even related? I'm not asking. I brush off my jersey before heading into the locker room. We're practicing for a game coming up, but since it's the last practice before the season starts, the coach thought it would be a great idea to sell some tickets.

"His name is Braxton Vance. I don't want you anywhere near him. He might be a good player, but I don't trust him. He sleeps around. He's not a good person. He doesn't ever get seen with the same girl twice. So, don't be alone with him," I hear Ale say, presumably talking to his sister.

I can't help but roll my eyes. I'm not saying that he's lying. I like sex. But everyone I've ever slept with knew that I wasn't looking for a girlfriend. I'm still not.

"Oh, you stop that. I forgot my wallet, probably in my car. He was just helping me get through," Ale's sister tells him.

Her voice is sweet. Innocent. I shake my head. Off limits. Spain is a new start. I can't screw things up here.

"Why didn't you call us?" Leo asks. He's sitting on the couch with his wife, Celia.

"I was about to get my phone, but he came out. It's fine, really. I promise nothing happened." Her cheeks are pink.

I smirk. I saw the way she was looking up at me. I'm hot. I know how to get a woman to want me. But something about her is different. I walk over to my locker, not planning on saying anything to anyone. I haven't made friends with anyone yet.

"You try flirting with Skylar?" Another new player, Max, is getting into his locker beside mine.

"Yeah. Why? She taken or something?" I ask, pulling out my cleats to slip on.

"No. Single. But she's an absolute prude, won't flirt with anyone, won't go on any dates. She's like a nun, a major turn off," Max tells me.

I ball my fists, before taking a deep breath in. Max is an idiot. Everyone hates him.

"Ale keeps her under lock and key. He's a control freak." Max just won't shut up.

I slam my locker shut before grabbing him by his collar and getting in his face. All of the talking in the locker room stops immediately.

"I don't know you, but I'll let you know one thing about me," I say through gritted teeth. "I'm not afraid to start over in a new country. Keep your mouth shut about Alejandro and his sister."

Max nods quickly as I let him go. I don't look at anyone. I just grab my cleats and head to the door. "I'll meet everyone on the field."

I don't wait for an answer. I just need to get away from Max before I lose it on him.

Chapter Three

SKYLAR

Ale leans down in front of where I was sitting on the couch. He kisses my forehead.

"It won't be longer than an hour. Feel free to stay in here, or you guys can come out and join us on the field. Whatever you want." Ale smiles at me. "Are you hungry? I can have someone get you something."

I smile up at my brother. He always makes sure I'm eating.

"I'm okay. I thought we were going to be getting food after practice." I tilt my head up at him.

"Of course. Anything you want. Okay, I need to get out there," Ale tells me before heading to the door.

Celia crosses her legs and turns to look at me. "So, Braxton started flirting with you?" she asks.

I knew that she was going to ask me that. I cover my face. I don't know if that could be considered flirting. I didn't even speak to him. He was making all of the moves, and I stood there... Frozen. I'm used to having my own space, and then he was there. Staring at me with those beautiful, green eyes.

"Come on, Skye! Tell me! What happened?" Celia continues on before pulling my hands away from my face.

"Nothing happened. I swear. I was late. I forgot my wallet, so I didn't have my tag or ID or anything. The guards weren't going to let me through. He came out and said I was his girlfriend and brought me down here. He just had his arm around my shoulders, and that's it.

"When we got to the door, he kind of pressed me against the wall and asked who my favorite player was," I say before Celia starts laughing.

I don't know what I said that's so funny.

"That is the most pathetic pickup line. He definitely has more game than that." She giggles before covering her mouth. "Keep going. I'll shut up."

"Nothing happened. He said he could get me an autograph, and maybe he could take me out on a date. Ale opened the door, and that was it. I know I haven't been around much, so I didn't think he would know who I was. But I at least figured that he'd know considering the whole number and last name thing." I rub the back of my neck I don't know why I'm so anxious about telling her this.

She's one of my only friends, my aunt, really.

"Well, at least he didn't say anything else. He's really sweet when you get to know him. He has a hard shell, trust me... But I think you'd really like him." Celia pulls out her phone before looking up at my face.

I scrunch my nose. "Are you close with him? Does Leo know about this?"

Leo is protective of Celia... I wouldn't imagine him being okay with her talking with Braxton.

"That's a long story, and not something that I think is my place to say. Just... Ale is protective of you. It's alright, but don't let him keep you from getting to know Braxton if you want to know him..." Celia grabs my hands and gives them a squeeze. "Now. Tell me about River and your travels. I want to know everything."

I smile, my cheeks turning pink. I want to know more... I want to ask questions about what she means that it's a long story. Maybe she'll tell me when she's not around Leo. Or maybe I could ask Braxton. But Ale wouldn't like that.

I don't know what to do.

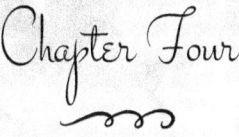

Chapter Four

BRAXTON

I roll my shoulders before opening my locker up. Practice was fine, the same usual thing. Running drills. Passing balls. Hearing Ale yell at me more than anyone else.

It took everything in me not to ask him why he takes his anger out on me.

I know why. It has to be because I stepped foot near his precious princess. But it's not like anything happened. I helped her get into the locker room.

The little devil on my shoulder snickers. She's attractive, but she's off limits. I need to get that through my head.

Off limits.

I squeeze the bridge of my nose before pulling on my hoodie. I take an ice cold shower, but the image of her big, blue eyes staring up at me won't go away.

I groan before slamming the door shut. I hate myself. I entirely hate myself.

"Hey, Vance!" Leo calls from his side of the locker room.

I pocket my phone and wallet before turning to look at him. "What's up, man?" I ask, tilting my head.

"A few of us are getting together at my house. You should come." Leo pulls on his shirt as he walks over to me.

He's got to be messing with me. I'm being invited over to the inner circle's house? Leo snaps his fingers in front of my face.

"I'm talking to you. Are you going to pay attention?" Leo chuckles.

"Sorry. I thought you were messing with me." I smirk, shoving him softly. "I'll come. You gonna text me your address?"

"Gosh, you act just like her." Leo shakes his head as he walks out of the locker room.

I quickly follow after him. I'm not going to turn him down if he wants me to come to his house. I'm too new to turn down anything that they ask.

"Act just like who?" I question, following him down the hallway.

I run a hand through my wet hair before shaking my head.

"Skylar. 'Text me?' 'What's the address again? I can't remember.' 'You need to text me'," Leo mocks, but I can tell it's not to be mean.

"You do realize that I've never been to your house, right?" I remind him.

I've heard rumors of where they live. They allegedly bought a lot of land and started to build houses together. It's like a compound with a gate and everything. No one gets invited there except for the inner circle.

"Oh," Leo stops and looks at me. "Uh. You can just follow me. I have the yellow sports car."

I snort. That sounds just like him.

Leo smirks before he starts walking again. "My wife is the one who bought it for me. She says it matches my flashy personality." He grins.

I don't know him well enough to agree or disagree with him. I don't answer him. I just follow him to where our cars are parked. I still have a stupid rental. I haven't found a car I like enough to buy. I haven't even found a house either. I'm renting a flat in the city.

"Vance?" Leo randomly says, his hand going to the driver's side door of his car.

"Yeah?" I answer him, opening the door to my sedan.

"I hate your car. If you're going to be in the inner circle, you gotta match our style." He winks before getting in.

I'm left standing there and staring at him. If I'm going to be in the inner circle? Match their style? I know I'm starting to over-think this. I jump when I hear a car horn honk in front of me.

"Get in, Vance! I don't like keeping my wife waiting," Leo shouts from his window.

I shake my head before opening my door and getting in. I didn't think that anyone liked me on the team, let alone being a part of the team for only a couple of weeks and then getting invited to the inner circle.

I might have a panic attack, but I don't have the opportunity to think more about it because Leo speeds off in front of me.

I'm forced to get out of my head and drive after him so I don't get lost.

Chapter Five

SKYLAR

Ale has been in a mood since we got home from practice. I know he just doesn't like Braxton. I've tried to reassure him that nothing happened, but he just keeps telling me that he doesn't trust Braxton. He doesn't want him anywhere near me.

I just don't understand why it's such a big deal. It's not like Braxton is even interested in me. I'm not his type. I'm not in the spotlight. I stick to myself. I'm in no way his type. Why doesn't Ale see that?

I sit cross legged on Celia and Leo's counter watching as Ale makes spaghetti.

"Can I do anything to make you feel better?" I ask, watching him move swiftly.

"No. Braxton knows you're off limits. Everyone knows it. It's fine. I'll deal with it if Braxton comes near you." He shrugs.

I shake my head. I love my brother more than he could ever know, but I think he should calm down. He's going to give himself a heart attack.

"Doesn't it make you feel better that I typically don't spend time at practice? That I'm usually busy with River?" I ask, trying to make him realize that everything is going to be just fine.

Ale laughs, before looking over at me. "No, because I would one hundred percent choose to have you around rather than Vance. He's cocky; kind of annoying. I don't like him."

Before I have the chance, Celia walks to me with my drink. I smile and take it.

"Everyone on the entire team knows that you hate him," Celia laughs. "I'm pretty sure even more people know than that. Braxton isn't as awful as you make him out to be."

"And how do you know?" Ale questions, before tilting his head at her.

I shrug. It's not like anyone is asking me for my opinion right now.

"Wouldn't you like to know?" Celia grins, before hopping onto the counter beside me.

"I would. I don't care if he's an angel. He's not good enough for my sister." Ale glares playfully at Celia.

"I'm not dating him," I say, trying to interject.

"Good. I'm so glad that you're not. He's gross. Pretty sure he's got skin issues." Ale smirks as he dumps the noodles in the strainer.

"No, I'm pretty sure they're called tattoos," I tease.

Celia laughs. "Would you look at that! The kid's got sass! I've never been more proud."

Ale groans dramatically. "I hate you. I really do. You stop trying to teach her to be like you. I don't need two of you. I wouldn't make it." He sighs and leans on the counter as looks at me.

"So, how do you like the updated stable?" Ale smiles at me.

I'm happy that he seems to be calming down now. "I love it. River loves her bigger stall, too. I do think that I should maybe think about getting her a friend so she's not lonely. Or opening the stable up for our friends to board their horses if they want to," I think out loud before I fidget in place.

I thought it was a good idea, but then I'd also have to hire a stable hand or someone. River wouldn't be able to be around any

Stallion. I mean, eventually, I'd love to have a mini her. But right now, that would ruin all of our plans. I need her in top shape.

I feel someone boop my nose, and I flinch. "What?" I squeak, before rubbing my nose.

"You were getting in your head. Stop that," Ale says, smiling softly at me.

He's not wrong. I most definitely was getting in my head. I can't help but laugh.

"I really was. I'm sorry." I hop off the counter. "I zoned out there for a minute."

"I know you did. That's why I brought you out of it. Dinner is ready," Ale tells me, handing my bowl to me.

"Thank you." I move to head to the living room. I thought the plan after practice was supposed to be us watching a movie. So, I sit in the loveseat that I always do. It's very comfortable. I have the same couch at my house.

When I hear the door shut, I look around. I thought everyone was here already.

"What's he doing here?" Ale whines.

I can't help but laugh. Just by his reaction I think I already know who's here.

Chapter Six

BRAXTON

I rub the back of my neck as I follow after Leo. He leads us away from the city, and I can't help but think that this is some joke. Some twisted form of messed up comedy where Leo leads me to a prank instead of what everyone calls the inner circle.

My heart stops as I look at the gate that's coming up. What is this team? This literally looks like a compound. The gate is metal with a symbol of the moon in the middle. Hm... Interesting.

Leo stops in front of me; reaches out and punches in a few numbers before leaning back in his car. This is a bad idea. I should turn around. Ale hates me. He'll hate that I'm coming here.

I let my foot off the brake, letting my car roll through the open gates. My car doesn't make a sound as I press down on the gas and speed up after him.

We drive down the road before turning into a long driveway. I hate that I'm here. I hate that I want to be here.

He parks in the garage, so I park my car outside. I still have a chance to back out and leave. But they'd never let me live it down, and I refuse to look like I'm scared of them.

I turn my car off, waiting inside of the car for him to walk closer to me. There's no way I'm walking in his house without him. I unbuckle myself before taking a step out of the car.

"You ready to die?" Leo grins, before laughing.

My face must show that I'm nervous.

"I'm just joking, don't get your panties twisted. Cee said she wanted me to invite you. So, are you ready to join the inner circle? We're a tight knit bunch." He smacks my back before walking up the sidewalk to the door.

I don't say anything as I follow him. I won't stay for long, maybe an hour. Then, I'll say that I need to leave because it's a drive to where I live. Probably about thirty minutes, which isn't anything, but that's going to be my excuse.

Leo opens the door, and I immediately hear Ale.

"What is he doing here?"

He whines. He actually whines, and I smirk in response.

"Breaking your heart one hour at a time." I wink.

"Why did you invite him?" Ale questions, glaring right at Leo.

Celia walks up to Leo, before giving him a kiss. "We decided to invite him. We get to invite whoever we want to the inner circle. That's the deal," Celia tells him.

So this inner circle thing is true.

"No. We get to vote," Ale sighs.

I turn my head and look at Skylar as she leans against the doorway to what I assume is the living room.

"I remember the deal being that if we like someone and trust them enough, that we can invite them to the inner circle." Skylar smiles at Ale.

I cross my arms, my eyes slowly drop down her body. She's gorgeous. She's in a pair of black and purple shorts, and a baggy cropped hoodie.

I need to turn away. I really don't want to. I don't need to be getting hard right here. Especially not in front of her brother.

"If it's that big of a deal, I'll leave," I offer, tilting my head as I look at Leo.

He's an inch taller than me. I think he might be the biggest person on the team. In height and weight.

"Nonsense. Ale will take the stick out of his butt and be just fine. We have food.We're really just watching a movie tonight. Nothing else," Celia tells me.

She moves away from Leo so she can push me into the living room. It's got gorgeous, giant, comfortable couches. It's honestly beautifully decorated.

Skylar comes back into the room, sitting down on the love seat and pulling her blanket on top of her again.

"Apologize to her if you want to. I'll take Ale into the kitchen." Celia winks at me.

I feel my cheeks heat. I don't know why I'm so flustered around this woman. Skylar has a tablet beside her. Before she grabs it, I sit down beside her.

"Hey..., I was wondering if we could talk for a second?" I ask quickly before I can talk myself out of it.

Chapter Seven

SKYLAR

I nod at him and move over so that he can be more comfortable. He moves back, putting his back to the couch before turning to face me.

"So about earlier..." He trails off, his eyes darting down to my chest before they go back to my eyes.

About earlier? Nothing happened.

"What about earlier?" I ask. I hope he knows how confused I am.

"I wanted to apologize. I'm sorry for making you uncomfortable... I didn't know you were off limits to talk to before. I mean, I knew Rodriguez had a sister, but no one would tell me any information about you," he tells me, making sure to look me in the face.

I look away. I'm horrible with eye contact.

"You don't have to apologize, I promise." I smile before looking back at him. "You didn't make me uncomfortable. You helped me. I forgot my wallet, and I also forgot that they hired new guards that don't know I'm Ale's sister." I rub the bridge of my nose. "I'm very forgetful... So really, you don't have to apologize. Everything is fine, nothing happened."

Braxton nods, listening to everything I say. "That wasn't what

I was aiming for. I just thought you were..." He stops himself from talking, but I know he has something else to say.

"You just thought that I was what?" I question.

A part of me wants to know what he has to say. The other part of me is terrified of his response.

"I can't say it." He looks away from me for a second.

"It's just me and you in this room. Tell me what you want to say. I won't say anything to my brother," I tell him, hoping he can see how serious I am.

Although, I can't promise anything. If it's bad, I'm going to tell my brother. Braxton looks around, making sure I'm telling the truth about us being alone before looking back at me.

"I just thought that you were hot. I wanted to flirt with you. I wanted you." He shrugs it off like it's nothing.

Wanted to? Wanted me? There's no way that he isn't messing with me. Mr. Sleep Around himself? He could have anyone he wants.

"Thank you for being honest with me." I smile at him.

I want this conversation to be over.

"Thank you for not having Ale kick me off the team," he chuckles before throwing his arm on the back of the couch.

"Why would I have Ale kick you off the team?" I turn to sit on my side so I can better look at him.

His laugh is like music to my ears. I take the time to look over his face. His strong jawline, his olive skin, there's a slight scar underneath his eye. It seems really old. I want to know what happened to him.

"You could get him to do whatever you want. I can tell by the way he looks at you. He literally growled at me in the locker room after practice when someone mentioned your name. You hold all of the power in your hands." He smirks.

I can't help but stare. He's so handsome... I don't know how he can exist and look like that.

"He's just protective of me, that's all," I tell him. "I don't think I hold all of the power. I can't pick and choose who goes on the team."

If I had that power, I would've requested that Max get traded to a different team. He makes me uncomfortable.

"Don't sell yourself short, Sunshine," he tells me with a wink.

Before we get to talk anymore, Ale, Leo, and Celia walk into the living room.

"Aw! Look at that. Skye's making a friend!" Leo teases before Ale smacks him on the back of the head.

"She has more than enough friends. He's going to move," Ale tells him.

But Braxton shakes his head. "Nope, can't do that. I'll only move if Sunshine wants me to."

I snap my head over to look at him. "What did you just say?"

"I said, I'll move if you want me to. Only if you want me to. But if you don't want me to move, then I'm not," he tells me as I lock eyes with him.

I look away from him, turning to look at Ale to gauge his reaction. I don't want to upset him or Braxton. It wouldn't be great to have another person on the team to make me uncomfortable to be around. Celia and Leo are smirking at each other before they sit on the couch together.

"It's fine. Really. He's not bothering me," I promise.

Ale groans as he moves to sit on the big chair in the room. "Hands above the blanket. I'll break them," he threatens, causing me to giggle.

"I'll put my hands wherever I want," Braxton huffs.

"Do not start anything in my house, Alejandro." Celia glares.

Maybe letting him sit beside me was a bad idea.

Chapter Eight

BRAXTON

I inhale before trying to stretch. I must've fallen asleep after dinner. I blink slowly before realizing that I have a weight on my chest. Did I go to the bar last night after leaving Leo's house? I look down at my chest and see blonde hair.

I took home a blonde?

No. I would've remembered going to the bar. Wouldn't I? I'm on a couch.

I'm on a loveseat. No way. I'm still at Leo's?

"I don't want him sleeping with her!" I hear Ale's loud whisper.

Skylar's sleeping on me? I look down again, seeing a purple, tie dyed blanket over the top of me and her. But I can feel her leg over my waist. She's curled up against me perfectly.

"Didn't you say she can't sleep through the night most nights? Well news flash, Ale. She fell asleep at nine last night and is still sleeping now," Celia snaps at him.

"It's not like Braxton did anything to her." Leo tries to calm Ale down.

I don't even remember falling asleep. I remember feeling Skylar slump against me, and then I remember waking up. I groan, before I wrap my arms back around her. This is the best night of sleep I've had in years.

The smell of vanilla and jasmine rolls up my nose, and I can't help but smile. She smells amazing... I press my nose gently into her hair and inhale. My heart slows, and I close my eyes.

If this is only going to happen once, then I'm going to bask in this feeling. It's different from waking up after sex with someone. This feeling is... Different.

It's Better.

I feel content at this moment, like no matter what happens I'll be fine.

"He could hurt her. I can't let anyone hurt her," Ale whispers, but his voice sounds pained.

When I looked down at Skylar, I can't think about waking her. She looks peaceful... She looks like an angel.

When I feel her hand slip under my shirt and rest on my abs, I bite my bottom lip. I'm not making a single sound to let them know that I'm awake.

"I know Braxton... I actually know him, Ale. Do you really think that I would ever let anything bad happen to her? I love that kid. She's my niece," Celia whispers back.

My heart squeezes. Celia was the only one who ever put in an effort with me when we were in high school... She saw through the act I put up and wouldn't let me push her away.

I can't believe that she would stand up for me to Ale... I smile slightly. I guess this won't be awful... being in the inner circle. Celia has my back.

"I know... Okay? I know. Are we going to wake them up to go get breakfast? Or are we going to bring it back here?" Ale asks. I can tell he just wants this conversation to be over.

"We. Me, you, and Leo are going to go get breakfast and bring it back here so they can still sleep," Celia tells him, leaving no room for discussion.

She's probably the most bossy person I've ever met. But she knows how to get us to listen.

Leo and Ale don't respond to her. When I hear them start walking over here, I close my eyes and pretend I'm still asleep.

"We'll be back soon, Ale. Nothing is going to happen," Leo promises as they walk out of the door.

When I hear the door shut, I open my eyes and look at Skylar.

I know deep down in my heart I'm screwed.

Chapter Nine

SKYLAR

I move so I can scratch my nose, but when I try to lift my hand, it's trapped. I feel someone underneath me. Did I fall asleep on Leo or something? Hands tighten around me, and I don't feel trapped. I feel content.

When I open my eyes, I see I'm still at Leo and Celia's, which isn't out of the ordinary, we'll sometimes spend the night over here. But when I see who I'm laying on, my heart skips a beat.

There's no way I fell asleep on Braxton. We're all tangled up together, too. Ale didn't flip out? He didn't wake me up and move me? That's weird.

Another weird thing is that I slept all night. I actually slept all night without waking up. I don't really know what's going on.

"I know you're awake, Sunshine." Braxton's voice rumbles through his chest.

I would do anything to hear his deep voice every morning. My goodness, that's hot.

"I am," I tell him, even though I don't need to.

I don't make a move, though, I'm comfortable here. I'm warm. I feel safe.

"Well, good morning. How'd you sleep?" Braxton asks me as he gently runs his hand through my hair.

I smile and close my eyes again. I feel like this is a dream.

"Good morning. I slept really amazingly, honestly. How'd you sleep?" I ask, placing my hand back on his warm skin.

I'm a little sad that this will probably never happen again.

"I slept like a baby. Gosh, I've never slept that good in my entire life." He groans, and it takes everything in me not to giggle.

"I don't think I've slept that good since I was a child," I tell him as I reluctantly sit up.

Braxton pouts. He actually pouts at me.

"I was comfortable." He frowns, but he sits up with me.

"So was I," I grin at him. "But you know how my brother is..."

"He loves you. It's more than fine. He just doesn't want anything bad to happen to you," Braxton tells me. I nod in response.

I know how much he loves me. I don't blame him.

"He does... he also really doesn't like you," I tease him softly.

Braxton laughs, standing up so he can stretch.

"I don't blame him. Ale, Leo, and Cee are out getting breakfast. I'm sure that they'll be home very soon," he tells me before sitting down again.

Oh, well. Yeah, that makes sense.

"So, Cee really likes you," I say, awkwardly.

I haven't had to talk to someone outside of my family in so long. I don't know what to say.

"She was my best friend years ago. We lost touch due to some family stuff I had going on. But yeah, she's super great," Braxton tells me, smiling to himself.

He obviously likes her, too.

"That's nice, though. She's like an aunt to me," I try to explain, bringing my legs up on the couch so I can turn to look at him.

"Like an aunt to you?" he repeats..

"Yeah. I knew Leo before Cee. Leo is like a brother to Ale. So, therefore, my uncle, making Cee my aunt. It's a whole adopted family type thing." I shrug, it's always been hard for me to explain this to outside people.

"Hm," Braxton hums. "I like it. It's sweet. Found family is better than a biological family..." He trails off.

His body language changes. I know what it's like to feel overwhelmed with a conversation topic. I grab his hand before squeezing it. This causes him to snap his focus back to my face. There we go!

"Topic change, yeah? Seems like a good idea. Okay, tell me your favorite color," I ask him. I smile when I see he smirks at me.

"Bossy. I like it. Red, what's yours?" he returns the question.

"Purple. I'm surprised you didn't know from my purple SUV out there," I laugh.

My car matches the theme out there. Bright colors and expensive cars.

"I thought that was one of Leo's." Braxton laughs. "Okay... So, the next question. What do you do as a job?"

"I'm a professional show jumper. My horse is The River's Song," I tell him, taking my phone and pulling up a picture for him. "Ale got me River when I was in high school because he thought it would help me get more confident."

"And did it?" Braxton asks, taking the phone out of my hands and scrolling through my pictures.

"Well... I can control a one thousand pound animal with my legs, so pretty confident, I think." I grin when his cheeks turn pink.

He's so easy to get flustered. It's cute.

"I can't exactly ask you what you do for a job... So, what made you pick Spain?" I ask next as he gently takes my hand and intertwines our fingers.

Is this actually happening?

He doesn't let my hand go. He's just staring at our fingers intertwined. The feel of his thumb swiping against my skin brings a smile to my face.

"I wanted a change of pace. I wanted something different.

Spain felt like that move for me," Braxton tells me before looking up at my face.

That makes a lot of sense, actually. Spain is home, even with traveling and everything. I always want to come back here. I can't imagine living somewhere else.

"Well... good! Spain is nice. It's really a lot of fun. There's a lot of book stores in Barcelona," I tell him.

I've wanted to go to the bookstore for a while. I wonder if Ale would come with me. I should probably text him before I forget.

"So, how about it?" Braxton asks, causing me to shake my head.

He was talking to me? I wasn't listening to a single word he said.

"I'm going to need you to repeat what you just said," I tell him.

I can't believe I wasn't listening. He laughs before squeezing my hand again.

"I asked if you would come with me to see the sights and everything sometime," he repeats. "Just as friends, of course."

I laugh when he adds in the part of just as friends. He might think I'm attractive, but I know he'd never want to be with me. I'm not his type... I'm nothing like his type.

"Of course, I would love to. It would be fun, I think. For all of us. Ale, Leo, and Cee."

Braxton grins at me, pulling out his phone so we can exchange numbers.

I know I shouldn't give him my phone number... I know I shouldn't, but at the same time, I can't tell him no.

Chapter Ten

BRAXTON

I wake up late the next morning. I couldn't fall asleep or stay asleep. I don't know why. This work out session is going to be awful. I hike my gym bag up higher on my shoulder. I was told we were meeting at the gym that Leo owns. Powerhouse Athletics.

Only the most popular gym. Most people can't even get a membership. Probably why it's insanely packed here now. I head back to where it says "VIP Room Gonzalez".

I should've skipped. I could've said that I was still hungover. I don't want to have to deal with Ale's attitude towards me. Before I can even open the door, it opens before me.

Just my luck, it's Ale. He just groans as he looks at me. "Leo invited me," I tell him.

"I thought you were my sister." Ale rolls his eyes before heading back into the room.

I shake my head. I need to remember he's my captain. He's my captain. If I do anything to tick him off, he could very easily get me booted off the team.

I walk into the room and toss my bag down in the corner. Everyone else has some fancy brands, I'm just glad mine holds up.

"You need to be nicer to him," Celia complains to Ale. "He hasn't done anything to you."

"He annoys me," Ale tells her.

I laugh. He finds me annoying just because I've talked to his hot sister. I shake my head before I start stretching. I don't need to injure myself right when I just started my job.

"I don't think you're doing that right," the sweetest voice says to me.

I look up, and I'm stunned to see Skylar standing there. She's working out with us? I should leave. I'm not going to be able to focus with her standing there looking like a model for a gym outfit place. I can't think straight.

This outfit looks like it was made for her. The leggings hug every curve, and her sports bra? Kill me now. Ale's going to murder me and make sure no one ever finds my body.

It would be worth it. I'd die a happy man. I can't stop myself from looking over her entire body. She's gorgeous.

"I can show you how I stretch before cardio," she offers.

Was she talking this entire time? What has she been saying? I didnt listen at all. Crap. I stand up fully now so she has to look up at me instead.

She's probably a foot shorter than me. I can't help but love it.

"We're doing cardio today?" I swallow thickly. I shake my head. Nope. I'm not going there.

"Yeah. At least that's what Leo said. It's to help get your endurance up." She shrugs like it's no big deal.

"Why would you be here then?" I blurt out before I can stop myself. She just stares at me. "That's... no. That did not come out right at all. I mean you don't run for your job, right? So why would you need to get your endurance up?" I try to save myself. It's not working because she looks like she might be upset. "I have a problem with not thinking before I speak," I laugh nervously.

Skylar smiles softly at me. "No... I get it. I'm not upset. But for what I do, cardio and strength training helps a lot. It helps with balance, stability, endurance, keeping control of the horse since a lot of my control has to come from my legs. I mean, I can keep going about it. Horses are unpredictable. So, I like to be on the top of my game," she explains to me like I'm five. "I've always worked out with the team since Leo owns the gym. He lets me join in."

I nod. "That makes sense. Leo brags about this place all the time. I didn't really look at anything other than looking for the VIP sign. Since Leo told me that's where we'd be training," I tell her.

Skylar brings her left leg up behind her and pulls it to her butt. Okay. She's flexible. I'd probably fall if I went to do that. I look behind her and see the line of treadmills.

"Who's ready for the competition!" Leo announces loudly to the room.

Skylar turns around, and I look directly at Ale, who looks like he's one second away from breaking my neck. I'm not going to push it, so I stand by Cee.

"Ale's not going to hurt you," she promises. "He's just protective of Skylar."

I can't bring myself to reply to her, so I just nod. I don't even know if I want to stay here. "What's the competition?" I ask, looking between everyone in the room.

My eyes connect with Diego's, and I groan. I can understand Ale's hatred for me. But how can he even stand Diego's presence around Skylar? That guy makes me angry.

"Every time we train cardio, we all get on a treadmill, and whoever can run on it the longest wins. We typically go to get food afterwards, so they get free food or whatever else they want," Diego explains to me.

I clench my fists. They let this prick hangout with them for what I see as no reason. I shake my head. "Let's do it. I can at least run longer than you, I know that." I glare at Diego.

He smirks, and it takes everything in me not to punch him.

"Want to put your money where your mouth is?" he taunts.

"Ten Gs to the winner. That includes anyone here. Whoever wins gets ten grand. Are we all good with that?"

Everyone seems to nod in agreement. "How about ten grand to a charity in whoever's name?" Skylar offers, and Ale smiles so brightly at her.

I don't think I've ever seen him smile. Let alone smile as big as he did at her. "Perfect. I brought your water bottle," Ale tells Skylar before handing her a purple water bottle.

"Wait? I thought I was grabbing her one?" Leo asks, holding out another purple one.

"Okay... I didn't think anyone else was going to remember, so I grabbed her one, too," Celia says, holding out a water bottle to Skylar.

I'm half expecting Diego to be holding one, too, but he just shrugs. "I didn't know that we were supposed to be grabbing extra water," Diego says. "But I'll take one!"

"NO!" I shout before I can stop myself.

Everyone turns to look at me, and I shift my weight from foot to foot. "I just mean let's get this started already. What are we waiting for?" I say with a grin.

Celia is staring so intently at me. I know she knows something is up. But I'm hoping that she will keep her mouth shut and not say anything. "Yeah, sure. Let's do this thing," she agrees with me.

I breathe out a sigh of relief before climbing on one of the available treadmills. I expect Diego to come beside me, but no. It's Skylar.

Of course it's Skylar. I'm never going to be able to win this if she's running beside me.

At least it's not Diego. I see her start running on the treadmill, and I push start next before I start jogging to warm into a full run.

I need to win this. Or at the very least last longer than Diego.

Chapter Eleven

SKYLAR

The hum of the treadmills and the feet thudding against the belt gives me something to focus on. I forgot my earbuds at home, but I can focus without music. I can, at the very least, make sure I'm not the first one to get out of the competition.

"I think we should go to The Andalusian Courtyard for lunch. Their Cordero Asado sounds delicious." Diego practically moans at the thought.

I don't eat out a lot, so I have no idea what he's talking about.

"Cordero Asado?" Braxton repeats beside me. "Lamb? You eat lamb?"

"What, Braxton? Are you a vegetarian?" Diego asks. "I like meat. Popcorn... Skittles. Skittles sound good right now. I enjoy working on my car... I could keep going if you want to know more about me, Braxy. I knew you'd come around to liking me eventually. Everyone does! I'm irresistible!"

Someone is really cocky. That's for sure. I don't know how he does it.

Braxton groans and shakes his head. "I regret even responding to you," he huffs.

I steal a glimpse at Braxton. He, at some point, took his shirt off. He looks... down right delicious. His muscles are so defined. I focus back on the wall in front of me. I can't stare or I might fall and break my leg.

"Mile six. Anyone looking to give up? Or is everyone still good?" Ale calls out.

I hear someone click a button. Celia is the first one to get off. "I don't see how you guys do this for fun. I'm all for being healthy and working out, but that's just awful," Celia complains.

I laugh. That sounds just like her. She typically walks more than anything else. "Anyone else want to give up?" Ale asks.

"Diego will," Braxton coughs out.

"More like Braxton will so that he can watch your sister," Diego taunts.

I look over to Ale to see his reaction. He stumbles but manages to catch himself so he doesn't fall off. "You'll pay for that comment, Diego," Ale growls.

I don't respond. I don't think I need to. Ale might actually fall off his treadmill if I do.

"I'm shocked Ale let you talk like that without wanting to come and punch you," Leo joins in. "If that was Braxton making those comments about his precious sister, he'd be off that treadmill and grabbing Braxton off of his in the blink of an eye."

Diego laughs. Ale groans. But Braxton remains silent. They always act like this.

"Hey," Braxton randomly says to me.

"Hey," I repeat.

I spare him a glance. He's holding out one of my waters to me. "Make sure you hydrate. Running this much will make you get dehydrated," he reminds me.

I smile and take the bottle from him. "Thank you," I tell him before I open it and take a large gulp.

I need to get better at training cardio. I've definitely been slacking.

"Noooo! Come on, Ale!" Leo whines as Ale pushes stop on his treadmill. "I was going to win!"

Celia laughs. "Don't poke the bear. Especially the papa bear," she teases from somewhere behind us.

I inhale through my nose. I think I'm doing pretty well. Maybe it'll be easier to win now that Ale isn't calling out the miles. I don't have to look to see how long we've been running.

I know if I do that, I'm going to get bored and lose all focus. Running. That's what I'm doing. That's what I'm going to continue to do until someone tells me I have to stop.

I feel good. Running is good.

All I hear is the footsteps and the treadmill hum.

I breathe out. I can do this.

Nope. Nope. This is so boring. I look beside me and Braxton and Diego are still there.

"You going to get off? We haven't even hit ten miles yet?" Diego tells me with a smile.

Braxton visibly cringes. "I hate this guy," he mumbles.

I don't know if he knows I heard him. He doesn't say anything else. I turn to look at Diego right as he's rushing off of the treadmill and heads right to the trashcan before he throws up.

Braxton starts laughing. His laugh is so contagious, I can't help but giggle, too. "I'm not even sorry. He should know not to chug water while he's running or he'll throw it all up," he laughs. "Oh, it gives me such happiness."

I laugh harder. "You really don't like him?" I ask before looking straight ahead again.

"He pushes my buttons more than I like to admit," Braxton answers.

That is definitely obvious. Ale comes up to stand beside my treadmill where I can see him without turning my head. "Do you want me to cheat? I'll make Braxton get off. He'll listen to me cause he's scared of me," Ale tells me with a smile.

"I am not scared of you," Braxton chimes in.

"You don't have to cheat," I shake my head.

That wouldn't be fair. I'd like to win fair and square if I can. Braxton does this for a living. So, I don't know.

"I know I don't have to. But what if I reallllllly want to?" Ale grins. "It would make my day. It would also make your day because you won!"

I laugh. "It's okay. I've got this," I promise him.

Ale nods and replaces my water with the one he brought for me. "I tried," he tells the group behind me.

"How much longer are you planning on running for?" Braxton asks.

Does he already want to stop?

"I will run for as long as I can," I tell him.

I won't stop running. It might be boring. But winning will be worth it.

Braxton's treadmill stops beside me, and there's cheers from behind us. "Princess Rodriguez WINS!" the group cheers.

I shake my head. Why did he stop? I push stop on my treadmill and see that it says I almost ran nine miles. I look at Braxton as I hop off the treadmill. "Why'd you stop?" I ask.

Ale hands me my towel, and I wipe the sweat off of my face. Leo has the air blasting in here, but that was definitely a workout.

"I couldn't do it anymore." He shakes his head. "I'm starving. I didn't eat this morning. I honestly thought that if I ran for much longer I was going to throw up."

"What charity do you want him to donate to?" Diego asks me.

I tilt my head. "Equine Hope?" I offer.

"What's Equine Hope?" Braxton asks me.

"Equine Hope is my rescue..." I tell him with a smile. "Well... me and Ale's rescue."

"I'm not taking any of the credit for that," Ale corrects. "It was all Skye's idea. She built it from the ground up. It's Skye's rescue."

"That's amazing, Sunshine," Braxton praises. "I didn't know you had a rescue."

Before I have the chance to even respond to him, Diego is cutting in. "Let's gooooooo! I'm starving! Let's hit the showers and go get some food," Diego cheers and heads out of the room with his gym bag.

"I hate that guy. I don't know why you guys even like hanging out with him," Braxton complains as we all head to get our stuff.

"I didn't ask him to join in," I tell Braxton.

His face lights up at my words, and I can't help but smile. He looks so cute when he's trying to hide how happy he is.

"I thought we were going to work out more than that," I tease Leo. "Are you that hungry, too?"

"Yes. I'm starving. But I also want to get everyone home before the storm rolls in," he tells me before motioning to the window behind us.

I nod. I didn't know that it was supposed to rain today. "Is Braxton coming to get food with us, too?" I ask.

Celia smiles at me before handing me my bag. "Don't let your brother hear you say that. But yes, he is."

My cheeks warm. I'm getting out of this room before she corners me.

Chapter Twelve

BRAXTON

I really, really need to buy an actual car. I hate driving around that rental, so I ubered to the gym today. I didn't know that we were going to get food afterwards. I look down at my phone to see how much longer I'm going to have to wait for my ride when a purple Range Rover pulls up in front of me.

The black window rolls down, and I see the blonde ponytail before I see her beautiful face. "Do you need a ride?" Skylar asks me.

I stare at her for a second. Even this far away from her, her eyes are so beautiful. The bright blue, crystal eyes are going to haunt my dreams for the rest of my life.

"No... No, that's alright. I ordered a ride," I tell her and show her my phone in my hand. "I can wait."

Skylar shakes her head. "Everyone is waiting," she tells me. "I'll give you a ride."

I swallow the lump in my throat. I can't tell her no. She's being so nice to me even without knowing me. I find myself opening the passenger door so I can get in.

When the door shuts, her perfume fills my nose, and I close my eyes. It's vanilla and roses. The sweetest smell for honestly one of the nicest people I've ever known.

That's saying something because I don't know her.

"You can turn the temperature to whatever you want," Skylar tells me. "Or change the music. Pretty much you can do what you want."

Skylar pulls up behind the rest of the nice, fancy cars. I really need to buy a car.

I chuckle. "It's your car, Sunshine. I'm not going to mess with anything. I'm comfortable," I tell her. "Maybe a little cold just because of the rain."

Cold because I took the iciest shower I could handle to calm myself down. Watching her run today? She kept up with all of us without hesitation. Her smile. Her laugh. Her everything.

It's like she's my own personal ray of sunshine.

The ride to the restaurant is short. Before I know it, we're there and in the parking garage. Skylar parks in-between Ale and Leo's cars.

"Thank you for giving me a ride," I tell her.

The smile she gives me is the brightest one I've seen yet. "Of course. I would never just leave you out in the cold," she promises me.

We get out of the car and head to meet with the others. "Ugh. I thought he drove his own car," Ale grumbles.

He doesn't even look at me. He's looking right at Celia. "Why are you looking at my wife like she knows what he's supposed to be driving?" Mr. Territorial asks.

"Because she stands up for him all the time," Ale responds.

Skylar shakes her head and walks right past them. "I'm hungry. Stop arguing. I wasn't going to just leave him in the cold like you all did," she practically snaps at them.

I bite back a laugh as I follow after her. I think everyone else is following us, but I don't care to look. Skylar's in front of me and that's all that matters.

"I don't think I've ever been here before," Skylar tells me as I open the door for her. "So, I don't know if anything is good."

I smirk at her. "I've never been here before either. So, it looks like it's going to be an adventure for the both of us." I wink, and she rolls her eyes at me.

"Oh! Can I sit by Skylar?" Diego asks loudly from behind us.

I groan, which earns a laugh from Skylar. "No thanks," she answers him before tapping my shoulder gently.

The outside of the restaurant is brick. It looks like it belongs in a story. But the inside? This place is gorgeous. Vaulted ceilings with beautiful artwork in between the skylights. Sparkly marble floors. Old wood tables shine almost like they're brand new. It almost looks like we should be dressed up to be here.

But we're not. Everyone is in t-shirts and jeans or shorts. My eyes trail over Skylar's bare skin. She has a few tattoos across her arms but none on the back of her legs.

"I'd stop staring before Ale catches you," Celia tells me, which causes me to snap out of my trance.

Good idea. I don't want to die today.

Chapter Thirteen

SKYLAR

"You need a table for six?" the hostess asks me while she's looking at her tablet.

"Yeah. Anywhere you want to sit us is fine," I tell her with a soft smile.

"Follow me right this way, Ms. Rodriguez." The hostess speaks loud enough so the rest of the group hears.

We follow her to one of their bigger tables, and we all take our seats. I think the sky lights are one of my favorite parts of this place. It would look so pretty with the moon above.

"I really want to eat by Skylar," Diego complains. "Ouch!" he then whines.

I look over, and he's rubbing the back of his head. "Stop complaining," Ale commands.

Braxton chuckles beside me before pulling out my chair for me. I take a seat beside him. "So, your rescue? That's really cool," Braxton tells me. "What made you start a charity?"

I look down at the menu in front of me. I don't even know what I should order. I look back at him. "I've been obsessed with horses for as long as I can remember. Ever since I was really young, Ale would bring me to the local stable. They helped me get started on a horse, and due to our situation at the time, they let me ride there for free," I explain.

They used to watch me while Ale went to go work a shift. It was a lot of fun.

"Ale makes such a good girl dad," Braxton says with a soft smile on his face.

He doesn't sound like he's teasing.

"Well, he's my brother," I corrected him. "But yeah, I wanted to open something like that. A safe space for people to come and spend time with no worry for anything. We have free food, drink, and shelter. It's something I'm insanely proud of."

"We worked on it together, but it was mostly Skye. She gets all the credit," Ale adds. "I'm so proud of how far Skye has brought it. She has a stable in Barcelona, Sitges, Girona... And has plans for more to be added in."

My cheeks warm at his compliment. It's gotten so popular that people are contacting us all around Spain wanting one in their city.

"Are you trying to talk her up to Braxton?" Leo gasps playfully. "I'm pretty sure you don't have to do that. Braxton already reallllly likes her."

I turn to look at Braxton, and he just rolls his eyes, but I can see the tint of pink to his cheeks. It's barely noticeable underneath the lights.

"I could make you sit out of the next game," Ale threatens.

"No you won't. You want to win just like everyone else," Leo laughs.

Braxton just shakes his head before turning back to look at me. "They fight like an old married couple," Braxton chuckles.

"Sometimes, I feel like they've been married longer than we have," Celia joins in. "Skylar is always looking for donors for her charity, though."

"Oh my gosh, you don't have to do that!" I quickly tell him. "The charity is doing amazing. Honestly."

"Well, a bet is a bet, first off. I'm a man of my word. I'll donate the money to your charity, and if you need any other help with it, I'm more than happy to," he tells me with a grin.

I look down at my menu again so I don't have to look at anyone else. I can't tell if he's being nice to me because he wants to be nice, or if he's only doing it because my brother is his captain.

Honestly... if he is how everyone seems to think he is, it's probably the second option, and that's going to suck.

Chapter Fourteen

BRAXTON

I lay there in my bed just staring up at the ceiling. It's been a week since I accidentally spent the night with Skylar, and I can't sleep. When I do, it's restless. I rub my face as I sit up. Today is the day that I'm supposed to meet everyone in town to explore.

I want it to be just me and Skylar, but I guess the group will be fine, too. Or I could cancel. That sounds like the better idea.

I hear my door open. Who's here? I didn't think anyone knew where I lived.

I didn't want anyone to know where I lived. It's just easier this way...

"Oh, Braxton! I know you're home. Your stupid rental is in the parking garage," Celia sing-songs as she walks through my flat.

I smirk. I wonder if Leo is with her. I don't say anything. I know she'll find me. She always did when we were younger.

"Ah ha. I found you." She rolls her eyes at me before throwing me a donut. "You could've told me where you were."

"What would you have done if I had a woman in here?" I can't help but question.

Celia smirks at me.

She smirks.

At me.

"Please. I might not go out with the team, or hang out with everyone all of the time, but I hear things. You haven't taken a girl home in... a week." Her grin makes me want to throw a pillow at her face.

I won't, though. I shrug, not wanting to admit to her that that's true. I've been off my game for a week. I don't know what's wrong with me. Every time I go out, women flirt with me, but when I look at them, all I see is bright blue eyes, blonde hair, and a woman who hasn't left my mind since I laid eyes on her.

"Not true." I refuse to look her in the eye.

She knows when I'm lying. She'll call me out on it.

"Oh yeah? Do I need to call my husband to tell you what he told me? That you're all grumpy and sit alone at the bar when you guys go out together?" she questions me as she plops down on my king-sized bed beside me.

"No. Don't do that." I've heard enough razzing from him for a lifetime.

I don't know what's wrong with me. I can't get Skylar out of my mind...

"So, are you going to tell me why you haven't taken a girl home? Or do you want me to start guessing until I guess the answer?"

I know she won't stop until I tell her, but I don't want to admit it. I can't even bring myself to say it out loud.

"We both know the reason why. We don't have to talk about it," I groan, laying back on my mattress to look at the deep red ceiling.

She's in my mind. Everyday and every night.

I can't complain, though...

"Oh, we're talking about it. Whether we talk about it now, or we talk about it later. You know as well as I do if you get inside your head, everything will implode later on," Celia scolds me.

I cringe. She's always acted like some mother figure to me, even though we're almost the same age.

"I can't admit it, Cee... I've never had this happen to me before. It's terrifying." I shiver at the thought.

I've never had a crush. I don't even know if it's a crush.

I've always been the one people have a crush on. Being on the opposite side of it is weird. It's different. Just the thought that she wouldn't like me back... It freaks me out. She has all the power in this situation, and I don't like it.

"She's in my head, and she hasn't left. When I go out, I want to get laid. But when women come up to me...," I groan as I rub the bridge of my nose. "It's not fair. I want sex, but I can't seem to get that woman out of my head long enough for it with anyone else. Just the thought of her."

I'm doomed. I've never felt this way about anyone before.

Celia lays here beside me, quietly listening to what I'm saying. It would never work out between us. Skylar and I? She deserves better. She deserves more than what I can give her.

"Stop doing that," Celia snaps at me.

"Stop doing what?" I ask, even though I know exactly what she's talking about.

"Telling yourself you're terrible. Telling yourself you don't deserve Skye. It doesn't even have to go anywhere. She's a great friend to have. She's sweet. She'll do anything you want," Celia trails off, and I smack my forehead.

"Don't phrase that sentence like that," I groan.

Get it out of your head, Vance. Don't think about it like that. She didn't mean it like that. Celia starts laughing.

"It's true! You do like Skye! Oh, this is hilarious. This is going to be great. I can't wait for this," she giggles, smacking my abs.

I grunt, but move my hands away from my face anyway. "You can't wait for what?" I question.

"You. Being miserable because you won't make a move on the precious Princess Rodriguez." She grins like she's thinking of some evil plan.

"Cee," I warn. "Don't do anything. She's off limits. Off limits.

I don't want Ale to castrate me. He would find a way to do it, too."

"So, you're saying you're not going to flirt with her. She's totally off limits, and you're never going to touch her, think of her, or talk to her ever again?" Celia asks, but she's not looking for an answer. "That you're going to leave her completely alone? What if Diego tries to be with her?"

We both know that answer. I sit up and smirk at her. Also, I hate that guy with every fiber of my being. He just gets under my skin.

"You and I both know that I won't be able to stop myself from doing that." I smile before standing up.

If I'm actually going to go to hang out with everyone, I need a shower. Preferably an ice cold one.

"There's the Braxton that I've missed!" Celia gets up. "Now, I'm leaving because if my husband finds out that I saw you naked, he'll kill you and not think twice about it. Wear something... nice. Add a jacket! It might be cold!"

I roll my eyes before heading to the bathroom that's connected to my room. "Okay, mom! I'll text you when I leave so you don't think I got kidnapped!"

"Good boy!" Celia laughs, before shutting the front door to my flat.

Ew.

Ew.

I gag.

No. That's disgusting. Good boy? Ew.

I shake that off before looking in the mirror.

Today's going to be amazing. I'll make sure of it.

Chapter Fifteen

SKYLAR

I tap my foot against the floor of Ale's sports car. I don't really like going out. People crowd around me, and I don't like my personal space being invaded.

"Everything will be just fine. You'll have Leo, Celia, and me here. We also will have a small security team to help with the crowd. So, you don't have to worry about anything. I've planned out everything," Ale smiles softly, looking at me before looking at the road.

Realistically, I know it'll be okay. I just get overwhelmed very easily.

"I know... Really. I'm just overthinking," I try to explain.

We don't add people into the 'inner circle' often. The last time we did, it was Leo, and then Celia. I rub a hand down my face. I just have to stop. I close my eyes and take a deep breath.

I'm fine.

Ale will leave with me if I want to leave.

I think I might've zoned out for a minute because when I open my eyes again, we're parked in the parking garage close to the mall.

Leo's car roars in the enclosed building as he parks beside us, then what I assume is Braxton's car beside his. Braxton drives a sedan? That's a little surprising.

Ale chuckles, turning the car off and grabbing his wallet. "That stupid sedan makes him look so out of place."

"Maybe he just hasn't found a car that he likes yet," I offer with a shrug.

Ale doesn't respond to me, he just gets out of the car so he can open my door. I grab my phone and step out of the car when Ale opens the door for me.

"What're we coming here today for?" Leo is already whining.

Celia smacks the back of his head. "It's called getting out of the house, babe. Stop with the whining, or no pretzels."

Leo gasps. "No pretzels. Just tell me you want a divorce."

I laugh at his comeback. "A divorce over pretzels. Did someone wake up on the wrong side of the bed today?" Braxton teases, walking up.

I swallow as I look over what he's wearing. It's simple, but he looks amazing. He's wearing black, ripped, skinny jeans and a deep red hoodie. His hair is brushed back out of his face, and I need to stop looking at him before someone notices.

When I turn my attention to Celia, she's smiling at me. I feel my cheeks flame before I quickly look away from her.

"Are we ready to get this show on the road?" Ale asks, stretching with a slight groan.

I expect to hear agreement, but Celia shakes her head.

"No. We're waiting on one more," Celia tells us.

"One more?" Braxton asks.

"Yup. One more." Leo nods in agreement.

"One more. Who?" I ask, not understanding.

I thought they had their pick, but I guess Braxton could've been Cee's or Leo's pick. Not just the both of them.

"Okay. Whatever, I'm not fighting it today." Ale rolls his eyes before shoving his hands in his pockets.

That's weird. What did Cee say to him to get him to not say

anything? Does he know who's joining us? He would've told me, right?

"He better not make us wait, though." Braxton rolls his eyes and crosses his arms.

"Don't worry, Vance. I'm not going to make you wait any longer. Wouldn't want you to have a meltdown in front of Skylar, now would we?" We all turn to look at who just walked up.

Chapter Sixteen

BRAXTON

Why am I surprised at this point? They probably invite him along just to irritate me. He's smirking like he knows he gets on my nerves.

I'm bigger than him. I'm stronger than him. I could take him in a fight. I close my eyes for a second to breathe deeply. If I assaulted him, I would be kicked off the team without a second thought. I'd like to be here for a little bit longer, at least.

Diego is staring at Skylar like he can't wait to take a bite of his favorite dessert. I'm not going to punch him. No matter how tempting. All I can think about right now is I really can't stand that guy. I should've known something like this was going to happen. I ball my fists and grumble.

I can't stand him. There's no real reason other than I think he's one of the most annoying people I've ever met.

"Oh, Vancey!" Diego calls out to me as I turn to walk to the mall.

I should've just asked her to spend time with me alone. That's what I really wanted. I know Ale would never allow it, but she's an adult. She can make her own choices.

"I like you more and more everyday." Ale laughs behind me.

I'm leaving. I'm leaving. If I have to stay with this group, I might deck Diego. But then I feel a soft hand slide across mine, and my body stiffens.

"They're just teasing you... I'm sure they don't mean anything by it," Skye's soft voice drifts into my ears.

I'm stunned. No one has ever been so nice to me.

"I know, Sunshine." I give her a soft smile.

Doesn't mean I wouldn't like to punch Diego for the way he's staring at you.

I should let her hand go. I should. Skylar gives my hand a soft squeeze before letting it go. I hate myself for missing her touch. I need to get a grip on myself.

This girl has more control over me than I have over myself.

"Where are we going first? Or are we kind of just splitting off?" Ale asks, cracking his knuckles.

I guess when I started moving, the group followed right after me. I'm surprised Skylar was the first one of them.

"We could split off. There's six of us. Three and three? Or three sets of two?" Celia offers.

Two. Please pick two. Please pick two. I chant inside my mind. Ale grumbles.

I don't want to be closer to Diego than I have to.

"No. We should just all stick together if it comes down to it," he huffs.

"You're such a whiner," Leo chuckles.

I push the up button to the elevator.

"No, he isn't. He's looking after his sister. He has every right to want to keep her safe," Diego says, standing up for Ale.

I find myself punching that button even more now. I need to get away from Diego. He's making me hate him even more. Ale's security team circles around us. My heart starts to beat faster. *Get me out of this situation.*

I can't pass out in front of them. My career would be over. Everyone would find out. It would be across the internet in a matter of hours.

Everything would be ruined.

"I like this guy more and more. What's your name again?" Ale asks. I know he's turning to Diego.

When one of the elevator doors opens, Ale and them are ushered by the security team to get on the elevator. Ale's in the back of the elevator before he notices that Skylar is standing right beside me as the doors close.

Her blonde hair falls in curls around her face. I can't help but rub at my chest, she's... breathtaking.

So breathtaking... It's almost like she doesn't see it.

See that she's the most perfect woman in the entire world.

"Everything can be a little much," Skylar tells me, filling the void of silence. "They really are amazing when you get to know them. Are you feeling okay?"

I shake my head to snap myself out of my head. "Huh?"

"Are you feeling okay? You're rubbing your chest," she tells me. "And you kind of kept punching that button like it stole your car."

So matter of factly. How can someone be so adorable? I notice we're alone. I must not have gotten on the elevator. How could they have not noticed she wasn't with them? I could see them not seeing I wasn't with them. But how can anyone not notice her?

"Yeah, Sunshine, I'm fine," I tell her.

I don't even believe myself, so I push the up button again and shove my hands into my jeans pockets.

"Well..." Skylar trails off before placing her hand on my forearm and tugging at my hoodie.

I look down at her and cock my head. "What's up?" I ask, giving her a smile.

"I knew if I touched you, you'd smile and calm down a bit. You've been on edge since Diego came up," she tells me, and I can't hold back the laugh.

No one has ever been so observant with me. I don't know how to feel about it. At least I know she won't make fun of me.

"What's funny?" Skylar asks me before walking onto the elevator.

The only thing I can think about is I have to keep my hands to myself. I can't touch her. I inhale deeply before blowing it out. I need to keep my hands to myself.

"Nothing..." I follow after her, keeping my hands in my pockets and giving her her space.

The elevator music starts to get louder. Selena Gomez's voice filters in.

"Can't keep my hands to myself
No matter how hard I'm trying to
I want you all to myself..."

I smirk. Those words are going to haunt me. I know that for sure.

"You're... just something special," I say, giving her a wink.

She giggles, brushing a piece of her hair behind her ear.

Chapter Seventeen

SKYLAR

When the elevator doors open, Ale is standing there and tapping his foot repeatedly. Before I can even take a step, Ale grabs my hand and pulls me into him. He's acting like he hasn't seen me in days.

"Well... hi," I smile as he wraps his arms tightly around me.

"Did he touch you? At all?" Ale almost demands.

Braxton rolls his eyes, walking out of the elevator next. "I didn't. Not a single hair on her head. I had my hands in my pockets the entire time," he promises.

Ale looks down at me, and I can't help but laugh. "We stood on opposite sides of the elevator. Besides, not my fault because you're the one who left me behind," I tell him with a teasing smile.

I don't want Ale to actually think I'm upset. He won't let it go. I see Leo, Celia, and Diego huddled up together, so they're definitely planning something. I don't want any part. I want to get new shorts. Maybe see if I can get a new laptop, because I don't know where my charger went.

I don't realize I'm even walking until I feel a hand gently grab my arm and stop me. "Hey there," Braxton tells me. "We're all going this way. Your brother has been calling your name."

I tilt my head. "He has?" I ask. I didn't hear anything. "Why didn't he come over here?"

Braxton shrugs, hesitantly letting my arm go. "Cee told me to go and grab you. You know her. Everybody listens to her," he smirks, before laughing.

I don't understand what's funny about that comment. "I don't know why that's funny, but she has a way about her. Everybody always listens," I say with a shrug.

Braxton nods, leading the way where the group went. "Cee has a strong personality. That just kind of happens. You know Ale would never forget about you, right?" He bumps my shoulder gently, making me look up at him.

"Oh, well... yeah of course. Ale cares so much about me. I know he'd never forget about me. I guess I'm just slightly off today, sorry." I rub the back of my neck.

With traveling for shows and stuff, I feel like my days are off. Being home... Not having to take care of River and worry about being late to something...

"Hey, you don't have to be sorry. We all have off days." Braxton tries to make me smile. "At least you're beautiful, so that should take the sting off of bad days." He winks.

I bite my lip, and look away from him. I don't know how to take compliments. My hair falls around my face. When I feel his finger under my chin, I tilt my head up to look at him.

"You don't have to hide away from me...," he whispers, his green eyes looking much brighter with this lighting.

I swallow. I open my mouth to say something, but I don't know what to say. My body is screaming but calm all at the same time because he's touching me.

"I like you just the way you are," he tells me.

His voice sounds like it has so much truth. I can't help but lean into his touch. His presence alone calms me down.

"Thank you..." I say softly.

Braxton smiles wide enough, it shows his dimples. How does he just get more attractive?

I look over at the book store, and Braxton follows where I'm looking. "Do you want to go there?" he asks.

I go to shake my head, but he just grabs my hand and pulls me along. "You don't have to come with me," I try to tell him, but he just shakes his head.

"I don't mind, let's go," he says as we're already walking into the book store.

I didn't even know that they had one here. I haven't been in the mall in ages. "I should at least tell them that we're going to the bookstore," I tell him before digging for my phone in my pocket.

"Where's the fun in that?" Braxton teases, but he lets my hand go.

We stand just inside of the brightly lit book store. I don't think it's a big branded book store. It looks like it's new to the mall.

"Ale will worry." I look up at him. "I know he's protective. He does mean well, though."

Ale has worked really hard to get us where we are. I think he deserves to be a little protective.

"I know, Sunshine, I really do. I just like to tease him a bit. He's funny when I ruffle his feathers," Braxton assures me. "I know he just loves his sister so much. You deserve it."

I laugh and shake my head before typing out a quick message to Ale about where I am. "I know he needs to relax a little bit." I head deeper into the book store. "I've never been to this store before... It's so pretty here."

Chapter Eighteen

BRAXTON

Watching Skylar walk through the bookstore, carefully looking at every single book that they offer is the highlight of my week. She looks so calm here. Before, she seemed stressed, but it's like the moment we walked in here, something switched off in her, and she fully relaxed.

"What type of book is your favorite?" I ask.

I want to know everything I can about her.

"My favorite genre? I'm between Romantasy or Rom-coms," she tells me before showing me the cover of one.

It's light purple, has flowers on it, and a beautiful font. "I'm pretty sure you just spoke a different language to me," I chuckle.

I have no idea what she just said to me, but it was cute coming out of her mouth.

Skylar laughs. "Romantasy. It's romance and fantasy. So romance elements with the fantasy genre. Shifters, vampires, witches, and stuff like that. Rom-com is a romantic comedy, just like the movies. Have you ever seen a rom-com movie?" she asks.

I reach over to take the small pile of books that she's carrying. I don't want her to fall and hurt herself.

"I don't think I have," I tell her honestly. "Mostly just super-hero movies and action movies."

Skylar moves to the next aisle over and bends down to look at the bottom shelf. My eyes trail over the curves of her body before I catch myself and take a step away from her. I'm not going to stare.

That's rude.

"Superhero movies are good. I watch them with Ale all the time," Skylar agrees with me. "*Wonder Woman* is pretty good."

I bite back a laugh. Of course she would love *Wonder Woman*.

"I agree. I like her movies," I tell her.

Skylar stands up and places a giant box on top of the ones I'm holding. I tilt my head when I look at her. How often does she read?

"This is a complete set of books." Skylar taps her fingernail against the top of it. "I think there's seven."

"Do you need to ask your brother before spending all this money?" I ask.

Skylar laughs. "Why would I have to ask him? I make more than enough money to be able to spend it on my books," she tells me. "I make a lot from my shows."

I chuckle. "I wasn't sure. I didn't know if you had to ask him anything since you live with him," I tell her.

Skylar shakes her head no. "No, I don't. I make my own money. He doesn't care what I spend it on." She laughs again like it's the funniest thing to her. "Ask my brother if I can spend my own money. I'm a grown adult."

"I know you are," I laugh. "I was just wondering how that all worked."

"We live together. He doesn't control anything I do," she explains. "It's very easy to get confused. I don't blame you. Especially with just getting into the mix of everything."

"I'm a slow learner." I nod towards the books. "Is there anything else you wanted?"

We should probably head out before Ale really freaks out about us being together.

"I don't think so," she answers me.

"We can always come back," I tell her and she looks up at me with the brightest eyes I've ever seen.

"You'd come back to the bookstore with me?" she asks before leading me to the front of the store where the registers are.

"Of course I would. Why wouldn't I?" I ask.

It's a lot of fun being here with her. Just us. No one is rushing us for being famous or anything. It's quiet and it's nice. I would, for sure, do it again.

"I don't know. No one really has ever come to the bookstore with me," she explains.

"Hi!" an employee says cheerily to us.

"Hi," Skylar says with a smile. "How are you doing?"

"I'm doing good! Did you find everything okay?" the employee asks, before smiling brightly at me.

"I don't know." I shrug. "I just came here to spend some time with this cutie right here." I turn to look at her, and Skylar is blushing.

Score.

"We found everything okay," she answers the employee before looking through her purse for her wallet. "Crap."

I'm already getting my wallet out of my pocket so I can pay. "The total is two hundred and twenty one euros," the employee tells us after she's bagged up everything.

I don't give Skylar an option to speak. I insert my card into the machine. "You didn't have to do that," Skylar tells me, and I smile.

I didn't have to. I wanted to. There's a big difference. I put my card back into my wallet and put it into my pocket. "Thank you, have a great day," I tell the employee.

I grab the bags before grabbing Skylar's hand in my free one. "I wanted to. I know I didn't have to," I tell her. "I wanted to do something nice for you."

"Thank you," she tells me almost shyly.

I just want to hold her and never let go. I don't know how I could be so obsessed with someone.

As we walk out of the store, I'm about to ask what she wants to do next. "Oh, Braxton," a male voice says, and I feel my body stiffen. "I didn't know you had a girlfriend."

I immediately shove her behind me. There's no way I'm going to let her get mixed up with him.

Chapter Nineteen

BRAXTON

When I hear his voice, my body stiffens. I can't believe he found me. That he's actually here and confronting me in public.

"Aren't you going to introduce your girlfriend to your big brother?" Brody, my estranged brother, asks me.

No. Absolutely not, because he doesn't need to know anything about her.

"No. I'm not. You're not going to even look at her." I hear the growl in my own voice.

Skylar is small enough to be hidden by my body. She won't speak up. I, at least, can be calm about that. She holds onto the back of my shirt, and I force myself to take a deep breath. Nothing matters as long as she's protected.

"Oh, come on now," my brother complains. "I just want to see the pretty blonde."

"No. We're leaving. You can go back to the hole you came from," I snap, turning on my heels and turning Skylar with me.

She's scared. Something about her being scared makes my body prepare to fight. I'm prepared to do whatever it takes to get her out of this situation.

Then, I hear the words, "I will get what I want," and I see red.

I turn around and grab him by the collar of his shirt. "If I ever see you within ten miles of her again, I will put you so far down in the dirt that you will be Satan's roommate. Don't touch her. Don't think of her. Don't come near her. You'll learn your lesson if you mess with what's mine," I spit in his face.

I'm shaking. I see the fear in his eyes, and I just don't care. He's made me feel this way more times than I can count. He deserves to feel the pain; the fear I felt for years.

I'm older now. I know how to protect myself. I won't hesitate to protect Skylar. I throw him away from me, turn around, and smile down at Skylar.

"It's okay, Sunshine, I promise," I tell her, wanting to reassure her that everything is going to be just fine. I tilt my head down at her. Her eyes water. I frown, wrapping my arms around her and holding her tightly. "Everything's okay, Sunshine, don't worry." I soothe her, rubbing my hand down her back. She nods, not saying anything to me just yet. I need to get her mind off of it. "Let's get something to eat," I tell her, leaving no room for discussion.

I grab her hand, intertwining our fingers and lead her to the food court. When we get there, I'll send Cee a text and tell her that we're there. If she still doesn't feel well, I'll take her home. I don't care about what Ale has to say.

I'm over being here already anyway. The only reason I came was because I wanted to see Skylar. I don't know how Celia managed it, but I'm thankful when I see her beautiful face.

She's still silent, and it's eating away at me. "Want my hoodie?" I ask, giving her hand a squeeze before stopping to give her my full attention.

"Huh?" she asks, shaking her head before looking up at me.

"Want my hoodie?" I repeat, letting her hand go.

I guess I'm not really asking, I'm hoping it will give her comfort. I tug it off over my head before she lifts her arms. I put it on her. When the hoodie goes down her torso, I have to bite my lip to prevent the groan that's threatening to come out.

This is a bad mistake. I'm... I'm not going to be able to

control myself with her wearing my hoodie. I take a big deep breath in before exhaling.

I'm completely fine... I'm fine. It will be just fine.

Skylar smiles up at me. I reach behind her neck and gently lift her hair free from the hoodie. "There's that gorgeous smile I always love to see. I'm sorry you had to see that. Are you okay?" I ask, brushing my hands along her body.

I know nothing happened to her. But I just need to make sure... I need to make sure she's fine. Skylar nods, stepping closer to me. I smile at her closeness. "I'm okay... Nothing happened. Are you okay?" she asks, and I laugh.

"Nothing happened to me, Sunshine... But it wouldn't have mattered even if it did," I tell her confidently. "Do you like my hoodie?"

"I do," she blushes, and my heart skips a beat.

I need to keep my heart calm. I'm not going to pass out here. Not in front of her. I can get a hold of myself.

"Good. You can have whatever hoodie of mine that you want. Do you want to get something to eat?" I ask, leading her to the food court again.

Her stomach rumbles, and I grind my teeth. Did she not eat today? I shake my head. We're not going to do this. We're just going to get her something to eat.

"Will you share it with me?" she asks, walking right beside me.

I throw my arm around her shoulders and pull her into me. I might just knock someone out if they come up and talk to her. "Yeah, that sounds great. Pretzels? We could get a fruit bowl," I offer next.

"Both?" she requests.

"Your wish is my command." I wink.

I only let go of Skylar long enough to grab my phone and type a quick text to Cee letting her know where we are, but I'm quick to hold onto her again. If this is the only time I get to hold her, I'm going to soak it up while I can.

Chapter Twenty

SKYLAR

I smile before taking a bite of my pretzel. "Thank you for buying this for me... I wasn't expecting anything from you."

I'm not used to anyone outside of Ale, Leo, and Cee caring enough to buy me anything, let alone food to make sure I eat during the day. Braxton rolls his eyes at me, and I giggle.

"You never did tell me about your horse. Is she at your house?" he asks, sticking a fork into a piece of strawberry.

I can't help but watch as he brings the piece of fruit to his mouth. I blush before grabbing the lemonade in front of me. "No, I don't have her at the house with me. She has her own stable. I'm actually looking into getting her a friend so she's not alone. Horses are social creatures. She's almost done with her quarantine. So, I'll be able to look after then."

"Why is there a quarantine?" he asks, reaching over to get a pretzel bite from my cup.

"I didn't need to quarantine her. But we travel a lot. I'm not always one hundred percent sure who she's stalled beside, so I like to be safe about it. I don't want to risk losing her," I say, trying to explain the thoughts inside of my head.

I know I'm a little overprotective of River, but we've been through a lot to get to where we are today. A lot of training. A lot of riding. I'm not ready to give her up. I honestly don't think I ever will be.

"Stop that," Braxton tells me.

Huh? Stop what? Did I just say that outloud?

"I can practically see the wheels spinning in your head. Is this about Ale?" Braxton asks me.

Did he say something about Ale? How much did I zone out?

"I'm not going to lie to you, I have no idea what we're talking about." I laugh nervously.

But he grins at me, before taking a sip of my lemonade. "That's alright, gorgeous. I'm sure your brother and everyone will be coming this way shortly. Is there any place you wanted to go? Or was it just the bookstore? I'm happy to go wherever with you."

He actually actually wants to spend time with me. Like he's not messing with me?

"Oh yeah, bookstore. I was maybe thinking about getting a new laptop or something, but I'm getting a bit over being here," I tell him honestly, rubbing the fabric of Braxton's hoodie between my thumb and pointer finger.

"That's alright. We can always come back. Or order everything online. That seems like the better option. Malls are bad luck for me." He chuckles, moving his head to look behind us.

I scrunch my nose. Malls are bad luck? I mean, it's a lot to handle that's for sure. But how are they bad luck?

"Malls are bad luck for you? Why?" I ask. It's not like he has to tell me.

But I'm curious now, and it's better to ask then forget what I wanted to say. Is it just because of that one guy before?

"Oh, Sunshine..." He chuckles, leaning back in his seat and crossing his arms. "You're just getting to know me. I don't want to ruin my image with you already."

"You're something else... I wouldn't think of you any different." I try to tell him, but I doubt he'll believe me.

Braxton grins at me, placing his elbows on the table. "You are like a breath of fresh air, Sunshine..."

I smile at him, looking down at the bowl in front of me. "Thank you. I appreciate it."

"Ooohhh, is little Braxton actually flirting with Skyeee?" Leo laughs, smacking Braxton on the back with an audible slap.

I cringe. That had to hurt, but Braxton didn't flinch or make a single move. "I have been perfectly behaved." Braxton winks at me.

I smile, biting my bottom lip as I eat another piece of fruit. "Well, would you look at that? He's got you smiling and eating. He's going to be perfect in this little group of ours. Cee, Diego, and Ale want to go to the movies. I was tasked with coming to get you guys. Are you guys ready to go? Have you been here the whole time?" Leo asks, raising an eyebrow at Braxton.

I laugh as Braxton grins up at Leo. "We've been sitting here. The pretzels are just that good. Not to mention the company is even better." He winks at me again. I giggle at the way he looks at me.

"The pretzels *are* just that good. You're right. Anyway, yeah, we're heading to the movies if you want to come with us. Or I can make up an excuse if you guys don't want to," Leo tells us.

I refuse to say anything. I don't have to. If everyone wants to go to the movies, we'll go to the movies.

"And Diego is coming to the movies?" Braxton asks, causing Leo to nod in confirmation.

Braxton looks at me. "If you're going to the movies, then I am, too." Braxton rolls his eyes. "I can't stand that guy. So, what do you want, Sunshine?"

"Oh..." I say, not really knowing. Watching a movie at home sounds a lot better, but it's fine. "Oh, everybody else wants to go to the movies. So, we'll go there. It's alright," I tell Braxton. I don't want to go.

But I don't want Ale to be upset either.

Braxton's quiet for a second before he stands up and holds his hand out to me.

"We're not going to the movies. I don't want to go. So, I'll take Sunshine home," he tells Leo, causing him to nod.

"If you make her cry, I'll break your legs," Leo tells him before kissing my forehead. "See ya soon."

I take Braxton's hand so he can lead me out of the mall.

"I could tell you didn't want to be here anymore, so how about we leave? We don't have to go to get your laptop. I could just take you home," he tells me before tucking me under his arm.

"I didn't mind going..." I try to explain, but he just shakes his head.

"I don't care about what they want to do. I only agreed to come here today because I wanted to spend time with you," he tells me.

His words make my heart beat faster. Part of me wants to believe him.

The other part... the other part feels like he's just messing with me.

I like being here with him. Maybe I might just be willing to take this risk with him.

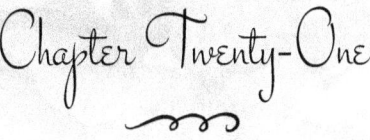

Chapter Twenty-One

BRAXTON

After I get her into my car, I start it and pull out of the lot. She's silent for a moment, and I don't like it.

"I'm planning on getting a new car," I offer, wanting her to talk to me.

Her voice is like music. I'll never get tired of hearing it.

"Huh? Why should that matter to me?" she asks, tilting her head in the cutest way.

I just thought she would've been used to the expensive luxury cars that Ale and them drive around. I mean, she was riding with Ale in his car.

"I know it's not the most fancy car. I really haven't had the time to go and look at the car lots to see what I like," I tell her as she nods.

"Well... yeah. Makes sense. All the practicing. Games. Then partying," she teases me, and I chuckle. "Car shopping is a lot. Aren't you wanting to stay here for a while?" she asks me, sitting cross legged in the passenger seat.

I want to put my hand on her thigh, but she's not mine. She deserves better.

"Well... my contract is for five years. So, I'm staying here for at least that, unless they decide to keep me longer than that. Or potentially trade me," I shrug.

I've never thought about buying something here... I've never thought about staying in a place long enough to warrant buying something instead of renting.

Skylar tilts her head, looking up at me with those gorgeous blue eyes of hers. "Well... you're a really great player. So, I'm sure they won't want to give that up. I've seen practice, and if you get in with Leo and Ale? They won't let you get traded," she reassures me.

I lick my lips slowly. Her trying to make me feel better makes my heart warm.

"Well..., that's sweet. But I wouldn't expect them to do that for me," I tell her.

I'm not expecting them to like me. I think Ale might have a brain aneurysm when he knows we're hanging out right now. Not that this is us hanging out.

Skylar fills the silence. "Do you want to talk about what happened at the mall?"

I could groan. I haven't spoken about this to anyone besides Celia. I give her a quick look. She looks so concerned. "I..." I swallow.

It's okay to make friends...

"Sure, maybe when we're at your house," I tell her, and she nods.

"Okay... I just want to make sure you're safe," she speaks softly and I swear I feel my heart tighten.

No one has ever cared about me before. I don't know how to handle it.

"Do you know the code for your gate?" I ask, slowing to a stop at the gate.

The number pad lights up purple, and I grin. I know that Ale must've done that for Skylar.

"Nope. But push the ring button. The security guard will answer," she tells me.

I don't ask questions. I reach out and press the phone button. Sure enough, it starts ringing.

"Hello?" a male voice rumbles through the speaker only a second after I press the button.

"Hi, Salvator!" Skylar says, speaking loud enough for him to hear.

"Oh, hi, Ms. Rodriguez! Do you need me to let you in again?" he asks. It must happen pretty often.

"Yeah, I didn't drive my car today. I should've sent you an email. I forgot. I'm sorry. But yeah, if you could let me in, that would be great. Ale and the rest of them will be home in a couple of hours, I think. They're watching a movie right now," she says, smiling like the guard can see her.

I have to force myself not to grumble. My chest hurts knowing she's smiling at someone other than me. I've never been jealous before. For any reason.

What's wrong with me?

"That sounds like a plan! Thanks for letting me know, Ms.Rodriguez. Will you be ordering in today?" he asks, and everything in me has me wanting to yell at him.

"No, we're going to make something at home. Thanks for checking, Salvator." She leans back in her seat as the gate in front of us opens.

Good. I can move away from the thoughts inside of my head. I don't want to think about why I'm feeling this way. I don't want to have to deal with this right now.

"Have a nice night, Ms. Rodriguez!" the voice shouts as we pull through.

His voice gives me a headache. If they have a security guard, where is he located?

"There's a house down the road slightly. Ale didn't want them on the immediate property, but there's cameras and different stuff," she tells me.

I snap my head over to her for a second. "Did I just say that out loud?" I ask her.

I really thought I was just thinking it, but by the giggle I hear, I already know the answer.

"Yes, the whole thing. He's really nice!" she says, putting her stuff back in her purse.

I don't respond. I don't want to have to get into it. I pull up her driveway slowly before parking and shutting off my car. I'll walk her to the door, and then head back to my place.

"Happy to be home?" I ask, opening my door before I head to get her door as well.

"Yeah, the mall ended up being more than I thought." She shrugs, stepping out of my car and walking up to her house.

I follow after her. I want to make sure she gets inside her house. She digs her keys out of her purse before unlocking her front door.

"Malls can be like that," I tell her with a soft smile.

Skylar laughs before she opens her door and takes a step in. I'm about to tell her I hope she has a good day.

But she talks first.

"Do you want to come inside?" she asks, looking me in my eyes. "I'm sure they're going to be gone all day, and I don't want to be alone," she tells me honestly.

I close my mouth. I wasn't expecting that.

"Yeah, of course." I grin at her, walking into the house.

I'll stay for one movie. One movie. That's it. Then I'm leaving.

As I walk into her living room, I know I'm not leaving until she tells me to.

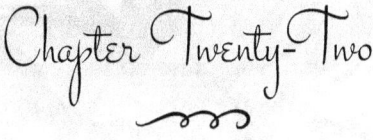

Chapter Twenty-Two

SKYLAR

I walk into the kitchen so that we can start making dinner. Braxton shoves his hands in his pockets before he leans against the fridge and just watches me. I pull out two pots before turning to look at him.

"The quickest thing to make is spaghetti," I tell him. He nods.. "It's one of my favorites."

"I can see that," he tells me before he fidgets just slightly.

It's barely noticeable. "You know you don't have to tell me anything, right? I'm not going to make you talk about it if you don't want to," I explain as I finish getting all the ingredients out. Before I have a chance to get everything out I'm suddenly lifted up and placed on the counter.

"I don't have a problem telling you... It's just really personal so you can't tell anyone. Not even Ale," he tells me with so much seriousness in his voice.

"Why not Ale?" I ask instinctively.

"Well, you see, he has this precious princess that he doesn't want anything to happen to. So if this secret gets out, he'll want me as far away from her as possible," Braxton teases.

I roll my eyes playfully at him. "He wouldn't just get you fired without a reason why," I promise him. "He can keep his personal feelings about someone aside when it comes to business."

"I'm not so sure about that when it comes to you," he chuckles. "I think he would do anything to protect you."

"Are you okay?" I ask.

He rubs the back of his neck. "I guess that's... Debatable. I'm okay for now... The guy who came up to us was my big brother Brody," I sigh as I take the big pot and move to the sink to fill it with water. "Brody and I were never close..."

I think I might know where this is going, but I want him to tell me at his own pace.

"I'm years younger than him, so he was super close with our father by the time I was born. My mother was never supposed to have another kid. They told her there was a big possibility of her dying..." I see his Adam's apple bob, and I just want to hug him.

After he puts the meat in the next pot and turns the stove on, I reach over to him and squeeze his arm gently. "You're safe..." I tell him.

He gives me a gentle smile. "She got really sick after I was born. Some sort of cancer, but she fought as long as she could," he tells me, staring intently at me. "They both blamed me for her dying, so it didn't take long for them to start taking their anger out on me after she passed away..."

My mouth falls open before I quickly shut it again. "B..." I hop off the counter and wrap my arms around him as tight as I can. "That's not your fault..."

Braxton inhales sharply. "It has taken me a really long time to learn that," he tells me before wrapping his arms around me. "I left home when I was sixteen and I never turned back. They've tried to reach out to me a few times, but I've always ignored them." He lets me go a few minutes later before he turns to continue cooking our dinner.

"Are you worried they're going to come after you here?" I ask, fidgeting with my ring.

Is he in danger because of his family? Would he tell me if he were?

"If you want me to be honest with you... I'm not entirely sure. My brother likes to go off on his own and do his own thing that my father doesn't approve of. So it's a possibility that they will, but it's also a possibility that they won't," he tells me like it's no big deal.

I watch as he moves to put the noodles in the boiling water. "If it gets to that point, will you tell me?" I ask.

Braxton snaps his gaze up to me. "No, Sunshine. I don't want you involved in this in any way. If it gets to that point, I'll be dangerous to be around me. I'm not going to put you in a situation where you could potentially get hurt." He shakes his head.

I nod as I listen. "Will you tell someone at least? Since you don't want to tell me."

Braxton closes his eyes and inhales. "If I'm still on the team... I'll consider telling Ale, okay?" he asks, turning to look at me. "Is that good enough of a compromise?"

I smile at him. "I will take that and be okay with it. We want to make sure you're okay, that's all," I tell him.

He chuckles. "I know sunshine, I know. But I've been dealing with this for a really long time. I know how to handle it," he puffs out his chest. "I'm a strong man."

I laugh. "Strong men know how to ask for help when needed," I tease.

He smiles as he puts the sauce into the drained meat. "I'm sure everything will be just fine... It's better to be positive. Maybe they won't come after me," he offers with a shrug before he's silent for a moment. "Hey," he says randomly.

"Yeah?" I ask, tilting my head at him.

"What movie did you want to watch?" he asks.

I shrug. "I'm good with whatever you want to watch."

He's opened up a lot to me, so I want to make sure he's comfortable and can calm down.

It must've been hard for him. I know that it sucks having to talk about what's happened to you.

He helps me off of the counter. "Do you want to go pull up something while I finish up here?" he asks.

I nod. "I like that plan. Good team work!" I say.

He laughs. "You learned from the best captain."

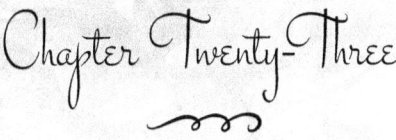

Chapter Twenty-Three

SKYLAR

The next morning, I see Braxton and I fell asleep on the couch together. I'm surprised that Ale didn't wake us up, but then again, Celia might've been there. She would've never let that happen. But Braxton had to leave early to head back to his flat to shower and change before practice, so I was left alone.

I figured I'd finish eating breakfast and get a tea before heading to the stable to be with River. I hate that she's so alone, but that'll change soon. I'll look later tonight about getting her a friend. I should maybe get two so that when I take River for shows the other horse won't be alone.

It makes sense to me. I'm just cleaning up from breakfast when I see a pile of my things on the end of the counter. I head over to look at the purple sticky note on top.

"Don't forget these, love you, I'll be back later tonight! - Ale"

I smile, taking my phone, wallet, and keys and holding them in my hands so I don't put them down. I'm not forgetting anything, at least I don't think so.

If I forget anything, I'll just come back home early. It's fine.

I slip on my flip flops before walking out of the door and making sure to lock it behind me. I have my boots at the stable. I always make sure to leave them there. I head to my Range Rover. I open the door before getting in.

Phone. Keys. Wallet. That's all I need. Nothing is left on. I'm ready to go.

I open the garage door, and back out of my spot. I make sure to turn around in the driveway. I hate backing up so much.

It doesn't take long before I'm pulling out onto the main road and heading into town. My mind spirals back to Braxton staying over, him wrapping his arms around me and keeping me tight against him.

I haven't slept that good in an extremely long time. I honestly don't know when the last time I slept that good. I rub the side of my face. I don't know why he's being... so...

Present with me?

I want to believe that this isn't some sort of joke, but I'm worried. I don't want it to not be real.

When I pull onto the motorway, I notice the same black car behind me that's been following me for quite a while. Okay... That's weird. Really weird.

Maybe it's a coincidence. Maybe they're just going to get food or something? The small shop that I get tea from is right by a few food places. I'm not going to worry about this unless I absolutely have to.

My phone is connected to my car, so calling someone would be super easy.

Everything is fine. Everything will be just fine. I turn on my signal, before slowing down so I can go through the drive-thru. And sure enough, the car pulls through with me. Okay... I think I need to call my brother. This isn't good.

I don't even stop to order. I keep driving through. The car keeps up with me.

Yeah. Definitely not good. I tell my car to call Ale. Ringing almost immediately fills my quiet car.

"Please answer.. Please answer...," I repeat quietly.

But he doesn't. I called again. Same thing. Okay that's even weirder. Why isn't he answering? He always answers.

When the car behind me starts to speed up, I do, too. I'm not letting him rear end me.

I call Braxton next, and of course he answers on the first ring.

"Braxton!" I say quickly before he can even say anything.

"Hey. Are you okay? Why do you sound so scared?" he asks quickly, and I keep frantically looking in my rearview mirror.

"No. No, I'm not okay. Ale isn't answering me. I don't know why. I thought he would. But that's not the point. Someone is following me. They've been following me since I left my house. I don't know what to do," I wheeze out.

Not now, asthma. Not now. My asthma has been under control for the longest time. Of course it chooses now for it to start being annoying again.

"Okay, Sunshine, take a breath for me. Everything is going to be okay. I'm at the field right now, so come to me. I'll be waiting outside. No one is going to touch you, alright?" he tells me. He sounds so confident and strong.

I feel calmer already.

"No one is going to touch what's mine," his voice rumbles through my car.

"I'm close," I tell him. I'm, like, maybe five minutes away from the stadium.

"I know, Sunshine. I can see your car. I'm waiting outside. Don't be afraid to speed up a bit," he tells me, and I listen.

I know I'll be okay because he's right there for me.

He won't let anything bad happen to me.

Chapter Twenty-Four

BRAXTON

Time slows while waiting for her to pull up to me. Finally, I see her car. It's purple and a Range Rover. It's not hard to spot coming down the road. She takes a sharp turn into the parking lot, speeding right towards me. My heart beats faster, my vision blurs. But I refuse to let myself pass out.

There's a time and place for that, and right now... Skylar needs me.

Her tires squeal against the pavement. She's quick to park the car and open the door. I'm right there. grabbing her out of the car and holding her to me.

I kiss her forehead, my arms tightening around her. She's shaking, and everything in me wants to make her feel better.

"You're alright, Sunshine. I've got you," I assure her, kissing the top of her head.

She holds onto me tightly, her fingernails digging into my back, but I won't move. If that helps her feel better, I'll let her do it, no matter what.

"Why don't you go inside? Go straight to the locker room. If Leo is there, tell him what's happening, but tell him that I want him to stay with you. I'll take care of everything out here," I tell her, reluctantly letting her go.

"O-okay...," she says softly, walking away from me.

I want to be with her. I want to protect her. But at the same time, I don't want her to see me like this. Not yet. Maybe not ever. I shut Skylar's door gently, moving to the trunk as I see a car pull up behind it.

I cross my arms as the man sticks his head out of his window. "Hey, man! Have you seen the woman who drives this car? She's my girlfriend. I was trying to surprise her with a drink. Is she with her brother?" the man asks, putting his car in park and stepping out.

I walk closer to him. "Did you say she was your girlfriend?" I ask. Something about that statement alone makes me want to put his head through a wall.

I could.

I could put his head through his window. That would feel nice. For me at least.

"Yeah, it's new. But we're having fun with it, taking it slow and all that." He leans against his car, crossing his legs in front of him.

"Are you so sure about her being your girlfriend?" I question, crossing my arms against my chest.

Jail wouldn't be fun. Jail would not be fun at all.

"Yeah, why wouldn't I be?" he asks me, starting to glare at me now.

"Well... here's the thing," I tell him, taking a few steps closer to him so I'm in his personal space. "I know for a fact that you're not dating her." I dig my fingernails into my palms.

I'm hoping the slight pain will calm me down, but it doesn't. Thunder claps, and the skies start to slowly darken. I guess the storm is coming in faster than I thought.

The man in front of me rolls his eyes. "You're wrong. That woman is mine. No one else can have her," he tells me, getting on his tippy toes to try and reach my height.

I chuckle darkly. I'm quick with my movements. I grab his arm and pull him to the front of his car. Before he can do anything in return, I slam him against the hood. Gripping him by the back of the neck, I pull his right arm back enough to get him to start screaming in pain.

"I wouldn't do that if I were you," I laugh as he starts to struggle. "One wrong move, and your shoulder will dislocate."

"I'll sue you! Get your hands off of me!" The man's screaming like a dog in pain.

I twitch his arm just enough, and he starts to cry. "Never, and I mean never... come near my girlfriend again. Feel free to let everyone know that she's under my protection. I won't hesitate to put you six feet under." I reluctantly let him go when I hear the security guards coming up behind me.

"Is everything okay, Mr. Vance?" the new security guard calls out.

The guards take him after I let go. "Everything is alright. He didn't touch Ms. Rodriguez. He was just following her, and then pulled in here like a madman. Is Ms. Rodriguez in the locker room with Leo?" I demand, crossing my arms.

If she's alone... I might just lose it on Leo for no reason. I inhale deeply, before letting it out.

Skylar is fine. She's safe. She called me.

"Yes, sir. He was the one who called us to come out here and check on you. We'll deal with him," they tell me.

I nod, turning around and heading into the stadium. I want to see Skylar. I want to know who this guy is. Does Ale know about this, or is this the first time this has happened? I have a million questions, but the first thing that I want to make sure is that she's okay.

As I'm walking down the hallway, my vision blurs enough that I stumble. I grab onto the wall, but I fall to my knees. I feel like my heart is beating too fast.

The world goes in and out, but I hear an angel's voice drifting towards me.

"Braxton!"

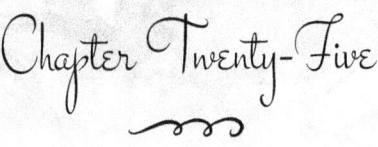

Chapter Twenty-Five

SKYLAR

My flip flops squeak against the ground as I run to him. Did something happen outside with him and whoever was following me? I fall to my knees beside him.

"Braxton! Honey?" I ask, but he's dazed.

I don't know if he's awake or not. His eyes seem unfocused. I gently place my hand against his cheek.

"Braxton... Sweetheart? Please... Wake up. Look at me," I beg. I don't know what's happening.

I place my hand against his chest. His heart feels like it's beating way too fast. I contemplate calling for help, but he groans. I can't leave him, and I think Leo has my phone. I bite my lip before looking back at him.

He doesn't seem beat up... His face is still the same. His hands don't have any bruises on them. So, no obvious fighting happened. I don't move, though. It seems like my hand being on his face is helping his heart to calm down.

"S..Sunshine?" he slurs, blinking his beautiful green eyes up at me.

"Ryder?" I say, cupping his face gently. "Ryder, are you

alright? Is everything okay? What happened? Why did you pass out?" I spit out questions. I'm worried.

I need to make sure he's okay. Braxton smiles tiredly at me, before I'm yanked into his lap and held against his chest.

"I'm okay now...," he mumbles. "Now that I have an angel in my lap."

I laugh, but let him keep me here anyway. "I don't know if I'm an angel."

"You are. You're my sunshine," he tells me. "The sunshine to my darkness."

I smile, biting my lip gently. My ear is pressed to his chest, so I get to hear his heart slowing down. I don't think I've ever heard a heart beat that fast before.

"Are you going to tell me what happened?" I ask again I know I'm pressing about it.

But... he was walking just fine, and then randomly fell to his knees. I think he passed out, but I want to know from him. Braxton grumbles, his chest vibrating with his voice.

"Nothing happened outside. I let the guy know that he's not going to come anywhere near you anymore. The security guards took care of it, and then I came in here. Does this mean that you're going to tell *me* what happened?" he teases me, purposely skipping out on the information I was asking about.

"And you came in here and passed out," I tell him, reluctantly sitting up from his lap and looking him in the face. "You passed out, but you said nothing happened. So, it's not about the fight or anything."

Braxton grins, his dimples showing as he reaches up and brushes a piece of my hair behind my ear. "You're beautiful. Did I tell you that today?"

I smile at him, cupping his face again and leaning closer to him. "Stay focused. I want to know why you passed out."

Braxton groans. "I don't wanna," he whines, but he's so adorable when he whines. I can't help but laugh and move out of his lap. "I was comfortable." He pouts, and I laugh again.

"If you tell me why you passed out, I'll sit in your lap again," I tease with a bright smile as I stand up.

Braxton gets up after me. "I don't want to talk about it here. I don't want anyone else hearing about it."

I swallow, but nod anyway. Maybe I shouldn't have pushed as much as I did. I don't want to make him uncomfortable.

"Leo has my phone. I left everything else in my car. Did you put it in a parking spot?" I ask, tilting my head up at him as we walk down the hallway.

"Nope," he tells me like it doesn't matter.

My mouth falls open. What if my car gets stolen?

"What if my car gets stolen?" I frown, repeating my inner thoughts. I really love that car.

"I'll buy you a new one." He shrugs again like it's no big deal.

"Do you know how expensive my car is? It was custom painted, too," I tell him, wanting to get my point across.

"I don't care. Not at all. You're worth all of the money in the entire world, Sunshine," he tells me, before opening the door to the locker room. "Yo, Garcia! Give Skye her phone. We're leaving."

Leo looks up from the couch and gets up to give Skylar her phone. "You doin' alright, Skye?" He looks down at me before pressing a kiss to my forehead.

"Yeah... I'm okay. I was just a little shaken up, but I feel better now. I'll have Braxton drive me home so you don't have to worry," I say, giving Leo a tight hug.

Leo wraps his arms tightly around me. He looks at Braxton. "Make sure she's okay before you leave, okay?"

"Of course," Braxton tells him.

Leo reluctantly lets me go. "I'm only a phone call away, alright?" he tells me. "I'll finish up paperwork, and then I'll be home."

"Okay. Maybe pick up some dinner on the way home?" I ask, and he grins.

"Of course," Leo tells me. "I love you."

"I love you, bye," I tell him, Braxton places his hand on my lower back and leads me back out into the hallway towards the main doors.

"I will tell you whatever you want to know when we're in private... You just can't tell anyone," Braxton explains, opening up the outside doors and letting me walk out first.

I breathe out a sigh of relief when I see my car sitting in the same spot. "I'm so glad that my car didn't get stolen," I say.

It took me a while to pick out the car I wanted, but this is what Ale got me for my sixteenth birthday, and I never want to lose it. Braxton laughs, opening up the passenger door for me so I can get in.

"How about we pick up lunch, and then we can go back to your place?" he offers when he sits in the driver's seat.

"That sounds like a really good idea," I tell him with a nod. "And then you'll tell me everything?"

Braxton laughs. "I would never hold anything back with you, Sunshine. This I promise you."

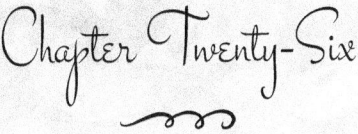

BRAXTON

I don't want to tell her about why I passed out... I can't risk it getting out in the world. Something like this could easily break my career if anyone besides me knew. But something in me knows that I can trust her. She's been nothing but nice to me.

"Thank you for driving... I'm sure driving a purple car isn't the most manly thing," she tells me, but she's so serious about it.

It breaks my heart. I would've driven her home if her car was neon pink and the definition of girly. I would do anything for her, and that scares me.

"I don't think color defines if you're a man or not. If it did, I don't care. It's just a color." I shrug.

It's not a big deal to me. Purple is her favorite color. That's definitely obvious. I look over at her for a split second. I just want to see that gorgeous smile on her face. It always warms my heart.

"This time when we pull up to the gate, the security will just open the gate. I only have this car, so they don't need to identify me or anything," she tells me, opening up her glove box and pulling out chapstick.

That's pretty cool. She has things stashed in here. I like it.

"That's actually really great. It would make things a lot easier on you," I tell her, pulling down the sun visor. A purple sticky note falls out.

I keep my eyes on the road, but reach down and grab it so it doesn't fall on the floor. "What's this?" I ask, handing it over to her.

Her fingers gently brush against mine, and I swear I feel a spark on my fingertips. She grabs the sticky note away from me.

"Oh, this is the note I have the gate code on. I forgot it was up there! When we pull up to the gate, you should put it back," she tells me, but she doesn't move to do it herself.

I might've had a heart attack if she tried.

"I will. If they just see your car and open the gate. Why do you have the number written down?" I ask. There's something about her voice that just makes me feel better.

Skylar fidgets, before bringing her one leg underneath her other one.

"Well, that was from before. I've had to call Ale to tell them to let me in. He got pretty upset about it. So, he told them that I only have this one car, and I'm the only one who drives it. So if they see this specific car, to let it in without any issues. It was kind of interesting to see. I don't think I've ever seen him that mad before," she tells me before pulling out her phone and quickly typing on it.

"Will there be a problem since I'm driving and you're not?" I ask. I know her window tint is dark.

But we're getting really close to the gate, I want to know what to expect before we get there.

"No, I don't think so. I don't think they can see you through the tint anyway. If there's a problem, I'll just say that it's me." She shrugs like it's no big deal. My chest begins to ache.

I force myself to take a deep breath. I need to calm down before I make myself pass out again.

"Well, I guess that makes sense," I tell her, slowing down as I turn to pull through the opening gate. "I guess they really learned their lesson, huh?"

Skylar laughs. "Most definitely, Ale can be really scary when it comes to me."

I smile at the thought. She deserves to have someone who would go to bat for her. Ale is obviously a really good big brother to her.

"I can see that. But you're his princess, so of course he's going to be protective," I tell her, pulling down the road before turning into her driveaway.

I know I can trust Skylar. That's what scares me. I've never been this close with someone in a long time, and that's what freaks me out. I don't want to have to leave Spain... I just got here, and I'm really liking it so far.

Or more specifically...

...I'm really liking this one part of Spain.

Chapter Twenty-Seven

SKYLAR

After Braxton parks in my spot in the garage, we walk into the house. I slip off my shoes before following him to the backyard. It's not boiling hot outside. There's a nice breeze.

"I really need you to know that it's important that you don't tell anyone about this. It could ruin my entire career," he tells me, before he sits down on one of the outside chairs we have around the firepit.

I sit in the large swing chair before folding my legs up. He seems worried about telling me. Maybe I shouldn't have pushed him so much.

"You know... you don't have to tell me. I'm not going to make you tell me whatever it is if it makes you stressed out. It could be a little 'if you tell me, I'll tell you' situation?" I try to tell him, but he immediately starts shaking his head.

"No. I'm going to tell you. I told you I would tell you. I don't want to go back on my word. I just want you to know that the coach can't find out. He'll force me out of my contract if he finds out," Braxton tells me, fidgeting in his seat before cracking his fingers. "And if you want to tell me stuff, great, if you don't want to tell me, that's also fine, too."

I shake my head. This is what we do for friends, right? Tell them personal information, they share personal information. I wait until he starts talking again. I don't want to push him, so I'll just be his listening ear for now.

"I would never do that to you. Whatever you want to tell me, I promise that it will always stay between us," I promise him, crossing my heart for an extra measure.

Braxton smiles at him, licking his lips slowly before bringing his eyes to mine.

"I have cardiomyopathy. I'm not supposed to play any sort of sport with it, but I've always wanted to play. I was good at it. I am good at it. My mom knew I had talent, so she pushed me to follow my dreams. I made it big. Some stuff happened to me in Italy, and it affected my heart. I wasn't born with it, but yeah. If I get too worked up by something, my heart starts to beat a lot faster. If I don't calm myself down, I pass out. Typically, I can just shut it off." Braxton starts to ramble, and I can't help but think it's the cutest thing.

He doesn't have to be ashamed with me. I'd never make fun of him for something like that. I nod at him.

"But when you play, you don't feel like you're going to pass out or anything?" I ask. I'm typically at most of the games.

Or at least every game I can be. Maybe I can watch out for signs so I can get him to come sit down before he passes out.

"No. I'm focusing on the game, not anything else. Sure, my heart beats faster, but nothing to make me feel like I'm going to pass out. I can feel it and sit down before anything happens." Braxton leans back in his chair, crossing his legs at the ankles and watching me.

"Well... yeah that makes perfect sense to me. As long as you're able to tell before you pass out, then that's great, right?" I ask, tilting my head slightly.

I wouldn't want anything bad to happen to him. He's really nice. Honestly, one of the nicest people I've met. He's way nicer to me than I deserve.

"Yeah, it's easy to notice. My vision starts to get blurry. I've figured out that that's one of the tells." He laughs. "It used to happen randomly. That wasn't any fun for me."

I laugh before shaking my head. "Well, passing out in general isn't a lot of fun, so I don't blame you."

He looks over at me, almost like I've grown two heads.

"What?" I ask.

"You've passed out before?" he questions.

"Well..., yeah. I used to have really bad panic attacks when I was younger. Plus, riding isn't the safest option. I've fallen and stuff before. I always wear a helmet, but if you hit your head hard enough, you'll get knocked out," I explain to him.

Braxton gets up and moves to sit in the chair directly beside me instead of across.

I look over at him, and he just smiles at me.

"What? I forgot we're all alone. I don't have to not sit beside you because your brother hates me." He winks, causing me to laugh.

"I don't think he hates you. I think he just hates you being near me," I tease him.

Braxton nods and rubs his chin. "That's a smart thought right there. I think it's both. I'll just randomly look at him sometimes, and he's looking at me like he wants to kill me."

I giggle. "At least you can rest easy knowing that he won't actually kill you," I tell him with a laugh.

Braxton smirks, getting up to sit beside me on the loveseat swing chair. I move over so he has enough room.

"I'm not sure about that. If he realizes how much we've been spending time together, I'm sure that he'd start planning my murder immediately." He sits down, before pulling my legs over his. "I might as well get all my sunshine time in now, right? While I'm still alive?" he continues.

I laugh and shake my head. "He'd never actually murder you, but I don't mind you spending more time with me."

My cheeks flame. I've never spent this much time with

anyone. They've always left me before I had the chance. I guess it might be something that's stuck in the back of my mind.

"So, your turn, Sunshine, what's the stalker for?" he asks.

I laugh at the way he words it. "I'm really good at my job, so I win more than I don't. I often see the same people at shows and everything, so I show against the same people. This one guy, who I assume is the guy who was following me today, he's gotten obsessed with me because of it. He really sucks at his job, though," I tell Braxton. I see anger flash across his features.

"Has he ever hurt you or anything?" he asks.

I shake my head. "No..." I say. "No, we started getting a security detail for when Ale couldn't be with me at shows. So, he hasn't gotten anywhere near me recently."

"So, Ale knows," Braxton says.

"Yes."

"So, Ale is taking care of it."

"Yes."

"So, Ale will know if I need to help?" Braxton won't stop.

I laugh and grab his hand to help calm him down. "Yes, he will know. He knows everything. Ale takes my safety very seriously. So he is aware of everything, and he will know if you need to help. But I'm safe. I'm okay. I'm not worried or anything," I tell him with a big smile. "Are we calm now?"

"NOPE!" he says dramatically before reaching over and grabbing my waist to lift me into his lap.

"Now calm?" I ask.

"Yes," he agrees and leans back into the swing. "Perfectly calm. It was like I was never worried in the first place!"

Chapter Twenty-Eight

BRAXTON

After we talked all day and I made sure that she ate dinner, we went back outside until it got dark. I made her a fire and we sat there together. It... it was nice. It has probably been the nicest time I've had in a while.

When I sat with Skylar on that swing chair thing she has, I didn't imagine she would fall asleep curled into me. I didn't want to move, I would've sat there holding her until the sun came up. But I had to...

I couldn't be weird like that, even though I didn't want to leave her alone since Ale was out on a date last night. She didn't ask me to stay, and I didn't want to overstep her boundaries. So, I stood up. I took her to her bedroom, and I tucked her in.

I went home. It took me a minute to tell myself that she's going to be fine. I don't know why I'm so protective of her... There's just something about her. Something I can't shake.

So, when I went home, I worked out to try and tire myself out, but I knew it wasn't going to work. I've been having a hard time sleeping since I fell asleep with her on the couch that first night. I run. I lift weights. I try to do so many things to make me pass out. But nothing works.

Laying with Skylar works, apparently.

After taking a cold shower, I climb into bed and stare at the ceiling. She swirls through my mind.

Her bright eyes.

Her beautiful smile.

How she asked me so many questions about my heart condition so she could better understand how to help me.

The smell of vanilla and roses...

She's the definition of perfection. There isn't one thing about her that I would change. I groan before covering my face.

I'm screwed. I don't know what I'm going to do. I know Ale hates me near her, but I can't not be near her.

I rub my face before I sit up. Forget trying to sleep. I'll go and just... check on her. Yeah. I'm just going to check on her, and make sure she's okay. Maybe I'll see if I can spend the night at Leo and Celia's if I suddenly get tired.

I get out of bed quickly. I slip on my hoodie and slides before grabbing my keys and phone.

I really need to get my own car. I hate this rental. Maybe Skylar would want to come with me to the car lot. That would be a fun day together.

This time, I'd make sure it was just us. I run a hand through my hair before heading to the elevator. I open my phone, pull up the notes app, and type a reminder to myself that I need to pay next month's rent on my flat. I also leave myself a note to contact a realtor. I might be staying in Spain a lot longer than I thought.

The elevator dings to alert me that I've reached the parking garage. I jog to my sedan. My body feels like it's vibrating. I'm quick to get in the driver's seat and start the car.

I just want to see if Ale made it home... That way, Skylar isn't scared if she wakes up. The storm rages outside. Rain is pouring down. Lightning strikes randomly as thunder claps. I pull out of the garage and head out of town to where Skylar lives.

If she's not awake, I'll just head to Leo and Celia's house.

Chapter Twenty-Nine

SKYLAR

The sound of lightning striking wakes me out of my sleep. I look around. I don't remember even coming to bed. I rub my eyes before rolling over to grab my phone. It's dark out. I know it's late.

But before I have the chance to look at the time, I hear something crash downstairs. That doesn't sound good.

I tell my phone to call my brother before placing it against my ear.

Please answer.

Please answer.

I silently beg, but after countless rings... I'm sent to voicemail. My heart starts to beat faster. What if someone got through the gate somehow? What if they got in the house?

Wouldn't the alarm sound if that happens?

I call Ale again, but the same thing happens. He doesn't answer. Is he home? Maybe it's him. Something in me tells me that I shouldn't go down there. I scroll through my phone, heading to Leo or Celia's number. But I stop when I see Braxton's name.

He'd come over if I ask... right?

Maybe he'll stay with me if Ale isn't home. I look at my texts, but Ale hasn't sent me anything... Okay. That's just weird.

I tell my phone to call Braxton. The phone rings once before he answers.

"Well, hello, gorgeous," he sing-songs to me.

I smile before biting my bottom lip. "Hi... What're you doing up?" I ask, covering myself more with the blanket.

"I couldn't sleep. What are you doing up, beautiful? You seemed pretty out when I laid you in your bed," Braxton tells me before falling quiet.

"I thought I heard something downstairs. I was wondering if you maybe wanted to come over? You can say no, of course..." I trail off. Maybe this was a bad idea.

He's going to tell me no. Then it's going to be super awkward. This was such a bad idea.

"Of course, gorgeous. I'll be there in ten. I'll make sure to look around downstairs before I come up to you," he tells me but still keeps me on the phone.

"Ten?" I ask, rubbing the side of my face.

The city is at least twenty minutes away from where we live. How is he ten minutes away? Braxton chuckles, and I find myself smiling at the sound.

"I might've already been on my way, but I'm speeding up now, so I'll be there in less than ten now." I can hear the smile in his voice.

"You were already on your way to me?" I repeat.

"Yeah, I couldn't sleep. So, I thought a drive might help. I haven't been able to sleep well since I fell asleep on the couch with you," he tells me so matter of factly that I freeze for a second.

He's telling me the truth... I mean, I can't lie. I haven't slept that well in a really long time.

"Sunshine? Are you still there?" he asks.

I shake my head to bring me out of my thoughts. "Yeah! I'm still here!" I quickly say. "I have to agree with you... I don't think I've slept that well in a long time."

"Well, I can always stay with you tonight if you want..." He swallows, and I can't help but giggle.

He sounds so anxious. It's adorable.

"I was actually going to ask you if you wanted to stay over... If you'd be okay with that," I tell him, tucking my feet into the blanket.

"Ugh, sounds like heaven. Like actual heaven." I hear the sound of the gate opening. "Looks like I'm almost there, beautiful. Want to stay on the phone with me?"

"Yeah... I think so. I haven't heard anything since before I called you. So, maybe it was nothing, but I don't know..." I trail off and turn my TV on.

"Hmm...," he hums. I hear him get out of his car before heading inside. "I'm looking around now. Ale's car isn't outside. I could start yelling, 'honey! I'm home'!" he calls into the phone. I hear him from downstairs. I laugh. "Baby! I've missed you! I've been gone for too long!" he yells again. "I'm not seeing anything, so I'm coming up to you."

"Okay." I smile, not moving from my spot on the bed.

One minute later, he opens my door and ends the phone call. "I should've stayed. I kind of wanted to," he tells me as he toes off his shoes and pulls off his shirt.

"Why didn't you?" I wonder aloud.

"I didn't want to overstep." He shrugs. He gets onto my bed and moves to lay beside me. "I didn't want to make you uncomfortable."

"Well..." That makes a lot of sense actually. "That makes sense. Thank you for that. It means a lot to me," I tell him before opening up the blanket to him.

Braxton quickly moves underneath it and pulls me into him. "What're we going to watch?"

"*Lady and The Tramp*?" I ask, tilting my head up at him.

"Anything you want," he promises me.

I snuggle against him, handing him the remote so he can play it.

Chapter Thirty

BRAXTON

The next day, I'm planning on heading to the gym, but as I'm driving, I find myself heading to Skylar's stable instead. I rub the back of my neck, I don't know what's going to happen with us, but I can't seem to stay away from her.

As I pull down her long driveway, I see her walking outside with a beautiful black horse walking behind her. That must be River. She must see me coming, so she stops and waits as I park beside her car. I turn off the engine and step out.

"Well, hey there, Sunshine, what're you up to?" I ask, noticing that she only has a bridle on and nothing else.

"We were just going to go on a ride," she tells me with a grin. "I thought it would be a good destressor."

"Destressor?" I repeat.

She nods. "Just to get away from everything for a bit," she tells me. "Do you want to come with us?"

"Do you have another horse?" I ask, and she shakes her head no. "How would we both go?"

"We could ride her together. The field I was planning to go to isn't that far. Or we could walk and she can follow after us," Skylar offers. River snorts at me.

I bring my hand up to her so she can sniff me. "She's beautiful," I compliment. "Maybe it would be better if we just walk. That way nothing happens to your horse."

Skylar nods. "I wouldn't have suggested it if I thought that it was going to hurt her," she frowns slightly. "But yeah, it's probably a good idea."

I follow her as she leads the way down the path going into the woods behind her stable. I like the sound of River's hooves hitting the ground. It's almost calming. Skylar is grinning at me.

"The sound is mesmerizing, right? Almost hypnotizing?" She asks.

I chuckle. "It's insanely calming, I'll give you that," I move so I'm walking side by side with her. "I can kinda see why you spend so much time here."

"That and the fact that I hate most people," she teases me, bumping into me gently.

"Well, people are annoying. So, I don't blame you, and I'm the same way," I grin as I look around at the scene around us. "Do you ride here a lot?"

She shrugs. "Uh... Kind of. More leisure than anything. I have to practice and train in the arenas by the stable," she tries to explain. "This is my favorite part, though... It reminds me so much of when I first started to ride when I was younger."

"Yeah? Why is that?" I ask.

She sounds so proud of it. I want to learn more. Just talking about riding seems to make her happy.

"After Ale adopted me, he met someone who was running a free training group for the teens in the city. We qualified because of how much he made. He immediately signed me up after we went and toured the stable. Everyone was so nice. After the group was done, they still let me come around and ride whenever I wanted," she tells me with a beautiful smile. "We rode through woods similar to these and they let me talk and feel like I was really accepted with them."

I smile as she tells me her story. It's a good thing she had somewhere safe to be around. "What happened to them?" I ask. I just want her to keep talking.

"I'm not sure... They thought I had talent in show jumping, which turned out to be true. So, I started professionally doing it. Ale met Coach, and we moved, and I haven't heard anything from them since. Or about the stable," she tells me before unclipping River's line.

"Sunshine, why did you just let go?" I ask, worried that she's just going to randomly take off.

"Because I trust River," she says, and sure enough River is keeping foot with Skylar like she's still being held.

"Wow..." It's a great relationship that they have with each other. "That's incredible."

"They're the ones who helped me find River, and we've been inseparable ever since," she tells me. It's like River almost knows we've gotten to our destination.

River trots ahead of us, and I'm stuck staring at how beautifully she moves. The purple bridle sticks out against her dark coat. She's gorgeous.

"She's amazing," Skylar says before taking my hand and leading me towards a big tree that has a box sitting beside it.

The field is full of tall grass and random wild flowers. I see why she says this is peaceful. Skylar pulls me to sit down as she sits in front of the trunk of the tree.

"This... is amazing," I tell her.

She sighs. "I know... It's peaceful and quiet..." She doesn't let my hand go.

"Was racing always your dream?" I ask her as I watch River graze in front of us.

Skylar nods. "Yeah, it's always been what I feel is my calling," she tells me. "But I don't know if it's what I want to do for the rest of my life..."

"Tell me more."

Is she wanting to quit racing? Or does she want to do something different?

Skylar shrugs. "I love racing. I do. It's my favorite thing. But I guess it's getting a little... Boring almost? Like easy. It's not challenging anymore," Skylar explains. "Does that make any sense?"

"Yeah, I get it. You want something new. There's nothing wrong with that," I assure her.

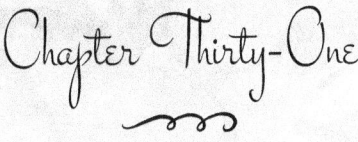

Chapter Thirty-One

SKYLAR

"Something new. I still want to show jump. But I've always wanted to open a charity to help with the less fortunate. Just like Ale and I when we were younger," I look down and see him rubbing his thumb across my hand.

I smile. I never thought that he would want to come out here with me.

"That's really sweet of you. Don't you have the horse rescue already?" he asks me and leans back against the tree beside me. "What happened for you guys to be... a family?"

I turn to look at him, he looks almost uncomfortable asking me that. "Well, first, yeah, of course I do. But I want it to be more... I want to help not just horses, but people and small businesses. And about us being a family? I don't know much other than what Ale has said to me. I was four when we first met," I explain.

I obviously know he adopted me, but it's a little broken up to that part since I was so young.

"That's alright. You can just tell me however much you want," Braxton closes his eyes as the sun beats down.

He looks so comfortable.

"Well, I was left at the school when I was four. No one could calm me down but him. I had to go to the hospital to get checked out and still wouldn't let him leave me," I try to remember it's been a while since we've talked about it.

It's been so long since Ale has talked about it with me. "Our aunt originally took me in because his parents didn't like me very much."

"So, Ale moved in with your aunt?" Braxtons asks.

I nod. "Yeah, we were always together. Anyway, some stuff happened and she passed away. He was left everything and took the right steps to being able to adopt me," I continue. "We moved once... We met Coach. That's kind of the short version of everything. I could ask Ale, but he'd ask why and well... that would be a whole thing."

Braxton laughs. "No, yeah, Ale doesn't like me and would probably have a heart attack if he knew I was asking." He chuckles at the thought. "You guys had a wild ride to get to this point huh?"

"Yeah..." I pick at the grass beside me. "Ale went through most of the trauma though... He fought every day to make sure I was allowed to stay with him and no one could try and take me away."

Braxton brings my hand up to his lips and kisses it. "He fights for his family. I barely know him, and I already know that about him. Besides, you're pretty amazing. Who wouldn't want to do everything they could to keep you safe?" He winks.

I snort and shake my head. "You're pretty good at that, aren't you?"

"Pretty good at what?"

I look back at River to make sure she's okay. She's rolling in the grass. She loves the field almost as much as I do.

"Flirting. Saying compliments as much as you can," I say, and then motion to his face. "Looking at me like I'm the best thing that you've ever laid eyes on."

Braxton smirks. "With you? I'm good at complimenting someone so amazing..." he starts. "Beautiful, kind, sweet, caring..." He ticks his fingers. "Someone who goes out of their way to make sure I'm okay. Do I need to keep going? I can count pretty high."

I shake my head and smile at him. "No... No, that's perfectly fine. You can stop." I feel my cheeks turning beet red.

I'm not great at accepting compliments. Braxton moves to lay his head in my lap and looks up at me. "As long as I'm around, I'll always compliment you. You're the best person I've ever met," he tells me as I place my hands on my stomach.

Before I have a chance to respond, his phone rings, and he groans. "I swear if this is your brother..." he huffs before answering it. "Hello, Captain Alejandro Rodriguez!" he says dramatically, and I want to laugh. "Nah, I'm with your sister. What's up?"

He actually admitted that he was with me? I keep quiet as I let him talk on the phone.

"We're at the stable," he says after a few minutes. "Yeah, I can take her back to my place. She can stay as long as she wants."

I look down at him. "What is he saying? Put him on speaker," I tell him.

Braxton nods. "Princess Rodriguez wants to talk," he says before pushing the speaker button.

"Skye, we found your stalker, but I don't want you to go home yet. I want to wait to make sure the restraining order goes through before then, okay? Im not sure why he got released, but I'll figure it out and take care of it. If you really want to stay at the house, that's fine. I'll make sure we have more security," he says quickly. I hear a woman in the background.

"Oh... Okay..." I say, I don't know how to feel right now.

"I'm getting us a place to stay until things settle down, so you don't have to stay with Braxton forever. If he touches you in a way you don't want, tell me, and he'll run until he passes out," Ale threatens.

I laugh. "It's okay. He's really nice. We'll head to his place now," I tell him. "I love you."

"I love you, bye." Ale hangs up.

Braxton groans. "I was just getting comfortable," he complains and stands up. "Let's go, Sunshine." He pulls me to my feet.

River trots back over to us saying that she's ready to go, too.

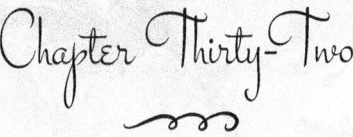

Chapter Thirty-Two

BRAXTON

Once we're back to the stable, I watch as Skylar grooms River. She's so gentle with her, easily switching between the different brushes and things. I don't know how she keeps track of everything. It all looks the same for me.

"You are really good at that," I tell her. She smiles at me.

"I've been doing this for as long as I can remember," she tells me. "Can you hand me the shine spray?"

I push off the wall and look at where she's looking. Shine spray. I look at the bottle hanging off of the side of the grooming container she brought out. "Is it this?" I ask and grin when she nods yes. "Look at me. I'm slowly learning what everything is." Skylar laughs and holds her hand out for it. I give it to her. "What's it used for?"

"A couple of different things. I mainly use it to help keep the flies away from her. But it's good for conditioning the coat, it helps the mane to detangle it, and at shows, it's good to have a shiny coat. I don't use it typically at shows unless the flies are bad," she explains it to me like I'm a child.

I chuckle. "Thank you. It seems to help, though?"

She nods. "I make it myself," she tells me. "It took me a while to find a recipe that I liked."

"Why don't you sell it?" I ask.

She shrugs. "I don't know. I never thought of it," she tells me before unclipping her from the cross ties and leading her back to her stall.

"Why do you stall her at night?" I ask next.

Skylar opens her door, and River walks in. "This is my answer only, not everyone does it for my reasons. But it just gives me comfort knowing that nothing is going to spook her. Nothing will make her jump and hurt herself. She's safe and comfortable and protected in here," she explains before closing the door and taking the bridle off of River. "She has access to food and water. So she has everything she needs."

"I like it. She doesn't get hurt and nothing gets to her," I agree. "You're great at this."

Skylar laughs and leads me out of the barn. "It took me a while to get to this point. I had a lot of things I needed to learn, and I'm still learning." She waves at a girl that walks up to her.

"Hello, Ms. Rodriguez!" the young woman says.

"I've told you, you can call me Skylar," she tells her. "River is all taken care of and locked up for the night."

"Thank you, have a great night, Skylar," the young woman says before carrying her bags into the barn.

"Who was that?" I guess I'm full of questions now, but she seems to not mind.

"She's one of my employees," she tells me as I open the door for her.

When she gets in, I'm quick to go to the other side and get in. We're taking her car. I don't care about leaving mine here.

"She stays here overnight so she can keep an eye on River," she has this adorable blush on her cheeks. "I don't trust crazy fans to not come up here and try to do something to my horse."

"I mean it's a valid concern," I assure her. "I think it's a good idea. A good thing to do just in case anything bad happens."

Skylar smiles. "Thank you... I appreciate it."

"Appreciate agreeing with you?" I don't think I understand what she means.

"Appreciate you not thinking I'm crazy or paranoid because I go through all these extra measures to make sure River stays safe," she tells me before pulling out her phone. "Which reminds me, I need to make sure she's still coming with us to the show next week."

"You have a show next week?"

"Yeah, it's to raise money for at-risk teens to come and be at if they need somewhere to sleep. I don't remember what it was called. Ale has it written down," she starts to mumble as she scrolls through her phone.

It's almost like I feel her stress levels rise. I reach over and grab her phone as I drive down the driveway and head back to my house in the city. Skylar stares at me, and I shove her phone under my leg. I know she won't go and get it there.

My phone buzzes a few times, and I know Ale, Leo, and probably Celia all texting me. I'm driving, so I don't go and reach for it.

"That's my phone," she tells me.

"I know that," I chuckle. "But you're stressing out."

"No I'm not," she says.

At a stop sign, I turn to look at her. She smiles innocently at me. "No?" I repeat.

"Okay, maybe a little," she tries to cover herself.

"A little?" I repeat, I know it's a lot.

"Maybe a lot," she finally tells me.

I nod. "Good girl. You don't have to lie to me," I tell her as I keep driving. "It's okay to be stressed out. It's a lot to plan. Taking your horse, packing up all the stuff, and getting there. It's overwhelming."

Skylar nods. "I know. I just feel like I shouldn't be overwhelmed by this."

"I understand," I promise her. "I really do, but it's okay."

Her phone buzzes, and I adjust myself. Of course her phone has to be on vibrate. She's still not getting it back. This is going to be an uncomfortable car ride.

"I think I'm just getting overwhelmed with everything," she tells me.

I squeeze her thigh to comfort her. Her car rings, and I roll my eyes as I see Ale's name pop up. I don't know how he hasn't given himself a heart attack yet. Skylar hits the answer button.

"Where are you?" Ale immediately asks.

"We're on the way to Braxton's," Skylar tells him.

"Has he been nice to you?" he asks.

"Yeah, he always is," Skylar promises. "Where are you?"

"I'm in Braxton's apartment," Ale chuckles.

"In my apartment?" I ask, shocked. "How'd you get in?"

"Celia gave me her key," Ale answers honestly.

"Sorry, Brax! We're all here, too!" Celia shouts from the background.

"Hi Skylar and Braxton!" Leo shouts.

"Hi, Vancey! Hi, Skylar!" Diego shouts next.

I growl. "You let nitwit into my house? I'm going to have to get it deep cleaned," I groan. "He better not take any of my stuff! I'll be checking his pockets when I get home."

I can't stand that guy.

"Oh, Vancey? If you wanted to cop a feel, all you had to do was ask," Diego's annoying voice rings through the phone.

I hate that guy. Good thing he's a halfway decent fútbol player.

"He just wanted to check on Skylar," Ale adds.

He obviously hates me. I reach to click the hang up button.

"You really don't like Diego, do you?" Skylar asks before I hang up on Ale.

"I hate that guy," I roll my eyes. "I don't know what it is about him, but he makes me irrationally angry."

Chapter Thirty-Three

SKYLAR

When we get to his place, he leads me through the elevator and hallway before we step up to his doorway. He hesitates to open it. "Is everything okay?" I ask.

"We could leave. Could drive far, far away and go live somewhere else," he tells me.

I laugh before shaking my head. "We can't, my brother is in there," I tell him before reaching around him and opening the door for him. "We could have our own fun, Ryder."

I smile at him as he just stares at me for a second. "Ryder?" he repeats.

"Yes," I say with a nod.

Doesn't he remember me calling him that before?

"I like that," he tells me. He sighs before letting me step in front of him. "I'm here for my inevitable torture," Braxton says dramatically to everyone.

His flat is gorgeous. It's wide open, and there's a wall of windows showing the city underneath us. "Wow..." I say aloud as I take everything in.

"Looks like pretty boy picked a good place to live," Diego taunts.

"I picked whatever I wanted to," Braxton huffs. "It apparently lied about the security. I was promised top notch security. No weirdos breaking into my home."

I shake my head and walk to the living room where everyone is sitting. "I have an open seat beside me, beautiful," Diego says with a wave.

"Absolutely not," Braxton says, sitting down in the open spot on the other couch beside Leo and Celia and yanking me down into his lap without another word. "Diego has cooties."

Leo chuckles. "What are you, five?"

"No," Braxton says. "I'm just trying to make Skylar laugh."

I smile, and I swear I've never seen Ale look so angry. "I want it known that I don't like any of this," he rolls his eyes and digs out his phone. "He's going to be served with the restraining order paperwork no later than tomorrow," Ale tells me. "So everything should be all set for the show next week. It's not a day where we have practice or a game. So we're good to go."

"We're all invited?" Diego asks.

"Why is he invited?" Braxton groans as he tightens his arms around me. "He shouldn't be invited."

"They asked me to go," Diego tells him and points to Leo and Celia.

Braxton growls. Celia just smirks at him. Oh, they're enjoying this.

I think he's one of the newer people, so I guess that makes sense why he'd ask. "Yeah, of course," Ale tells him. "I'll get everyone tickets."

"I'm so going. I want to see her win the show. She's so talented. I've seen so many of your shows. River was bred perfectly. Her confirmation, her temperament, seems great. You honestly couldn't have asked for a better partner," Diego compliments. I fidget to get more comfortable.

Who knew he knew so much about horses?

"It annoys me that he knows so much," Braxton mutters under his breath.

I want to laugh, but I don't. It's cute that he hates him that much.

I want to lean back, but I don't know how he'd feel if I did that. I'm just going to get a little more comfortable and stop moving around so much.

"Thanks... She's really the best horse I could've asked for," I lean back into Braxton.

I swear I hear him inhale when I do that. His arms go around my waist, and he tightens them. I could get used to this.

"So, are we traveling out of the city?" Diego asks, wanting to fill the void.

"Nope, Princess over here has a stadium that she rents out," Leo announces to the whole room.

I'm so glad I don't have to pack up and go to the United States anymore. I hate it there. Ale pulled me out of the race just in time.

"Leo, you're not supposed to be telling everyone that," I complain.

I knew it was a bad idea to tell him, he's a blabber mouth.

"Yeah, Leo," Braxton adds for backup.

"It's fine," Celia says, trying to shove it to the side like it's nothing.

"It's not fine. You can't tell people that, Diego," I tell him.

He puts his hands up in surrender. "I promise that I won't tell anyone," Diego crosses his heart. "Who's planning this little trip?"

"Me and my girlfriend," Ale says and everyone turns to stare at him.

Girlfriend? Ale has a girlfriend?

"Girlfriend?" we all say in unison.

"Yes, I have a girlfriend," Ale huffs. "She's real."

Braxton laughs. "Why do you feel the need to say she's real?" he asks.

"Because he doesn't date," Leo snickers. "So, of course he's getting defensive."

"He doesn't date?" Braxton repeats.

I don't remember a single time he's ever gone out on a date before.

"Nope. Doesn't date. He likes to have his one night stands though," Leo taunts.

I definitely didn't need to know that information. Good for him?

"I'm not defensive," Ale adds.

"When will I get to meet your girlfriend?" I ask, tilting my head slightly.

Is that who he's been spending his time with lately? I didn't know it was getting that serious. He's been spending so much time with her, and I've been spending most of my time with Braxton, so we haven't been able to catch up. I'm a little surprised.

"She's a model, so she had to travel for work. She'll be back in time for your show, though," Ale says before putting his phone down and looking up at me.

"Okay, that's cool. I'm excited to meet her," I tell him.

Braxton moves his head to see Ale better. "I think we're all excited to meet her. Just to make sure that she's real and all that," Braxton teases, which gets Leo laughing again.

"At least he's finally getting laid again," Celia adds.

"I'll agree to that. He's less crabby at work when he gets laid," Diego says.

Ale groans. "This is why I wasn't going to say anything," he complains.

"We're just busting your balls," Braxton laughs. "Don't take it too harshly."

"I'm sure she's great, especially since you picked her." I try to calm him down a little bit.

Ale smirks. "I can always count on you, Skye," he tells me. "What're we going to watch since we're stuck here?"

"Stuck here," Braxton rolls his eyes. "You could leave. I could protect Skylar all by myself."

"I will throw a pillow right at your head," Ale threatens.

"And risk hitting Sunshine?" Braxton gasps and shakes his head. "How dare you. What if you hurt her pretty face?"

I bite my bottom lip. If I laugh, it's only going to make Ale more annoyed with him.

"It's a pillow. She'd be fine. Why is she sitting in your lap anyway?" Ale asks, gripping one of the pillows near him in his hands.

"Because," Braxton starts. "I wanted her to. It's comfortable. Besides I don't want her sitting by nitwit over there. He'd try to touch her, and then I'd have to break every single one of his fingers."

Diego looks terrified. "You would break all of my fingers?"

Braxton nods. "Yup. Slowly, too. I know how to make it hurt," Braxton tells him.

"Okay guys, you don't have to get so violent," Celia says, trying to defuse the situation.

"Let em fight," Leo says. "Braxton would win."

Braxton grins before reaching over and giving Leo a high five. "I definitely would."

"Okay, someone play a movie before Diego gets his fingers broken," I say to everyone.

Braxton huffs and moves us so I have my legs over his and am able to sit down on the couch. I guess this is going to be interesting to watch how Ale reacts to us right now.

Would he be okay with us? I know I need to have a conversation with him soon...

Chapter Thirty-Four

BRAXTON

It's been a couple of days with everyone staying at my place. While I like the company, I'm going to be more than happy when they leave to go back to their own homes.

I'm used to everything being in order in my home. Everything clean. Everything in the way I want it to be. These couple of days have made me so stressed out. Everything is out of order. Laundry isn't done. And yesterday, I found Celia rearranging my kitchen.

I want everyone to leave. But if I do that, Skylar will go home. I don't want her to go home. So, I'm sucking it up. I'm dealing with it. Because she makes everything easier to deal with. I'm waiting impatiently for everyone to leave this morning and go about their lives.

I haven't heard anything for a while, so I get out of my bed and head into the hallway. There's soft music coming from my kitchen area. When I turn the corner, I see Skylar in my kitchen with pans all over the place.

"This one went here..." she mumbles to herself.

I grin. She's putting my kitchen back the way I had it?

"This one goes here.."

I lean against the doorway and just watch as she moves around my kitchen like she's lived here for years. Skylar gets up, and I finally notice what she's wearing. She's in one of my hoodies and I can't fight back the groan of approval.

Skylar turns around quickly, her cheeks a beautiful pink. "Good morning," she tells me with a smile. "I promise I wasn't moving around anything. I was just trying to put everything back now while everyone is gone."

Skylar turns around and scratches the side of her head. "I don't think I got everything right. You might need to check to make sure. I just know you've been so nice to us... And you didn't like Celia moving things around..."

I smile and walk up to her. "Thank you, Sunshine... This means a lot to me."

I want to kiss her. I want to turn her around and pull her to me. But I will settle for just being in this moment with her. "I don't like when things are out of order..."

"Me either..." She turns to look up at me. "You've been super nice to us. I'm sorry that they messed with the flow of things..."

I shake my head at her. I don't want her to feel bad. "There's no apologies needed, Sunshine," I promise her. "You didn't do anything wrong. I would let them mess my entire house up if it meant I got to spend more time with you."

Skylar blinks her pretty blue eyes at me. "Really?"

"Of course! Hey! Do you want to go to the dealership with me?" I blurt out.

Skylar laughs. "But we didn't eat breakfast yet."

"I will take you to breakfast. I want to make sure you eat," I tell her and turn to head back to my bedroom.

I came out in shorts, so I at least need a shirt on. "Ryder?" Skylar calls out to me.

"Huh?" I turn back.

"Aren't you going to fix this?" she asks.

Skylar's standing at the end of my hallway looking like the perfect angel she is. She belongs here with me. "No, Sunshine."

"Why?" Skylar asks.

I smile. "Because. You fixed my kitchen. I want you to be

comfortable here, too," I explain before turning back to my bedroom.

If this is how I get Skylar to be comfortable here, I'll do whatever it takes.

AFTER WE GOT DRESSED, we go to the dealership first. I pull up to park my rental car. "Funny enough, right over there is where I got this junk," I tell Skylar.

She looks to where I'm pointing. "If you call this car junk, why do you have it?" she asks me.

I laugh. "Convenice?" I offer before getting out of the car.

I'm not going to tell her that I wasn't planning on making Spain my home. I wasn't planning on getting attached to anyone because I planned on leaving as soon as I could.

I'm not going to tell her that she's the reason that I want to be here. That she's the only reason I have for wanting to settle down anywhere. She's the reason. She's the best reason.

I open Skylar's door for her and help her get out. I'm glad she decided to still wear my hoodie. It's the hottest thing I've ever seen.

"I don't see how that's convenient, but okay," Skylar tells me before laughing. "Everyone picks on you."

I shake my head. "It has great gas mileage?"

It's not the reason why I keep it. I don't care how much I spend on gas.

"Don't you make a lot of money?"

I grin. "You've got me there." I throw my arm over her shoulder as we walk through the Mercedes Benz lot.

We could always go somewhere else if I don't find anything. Or, at the very least, pick up something for now so I don't have to drive around a rental anymore.

"Hello," an employee dressed in a nice suit waves us over.

I stop and pull Skylar tightly into me. "Hey," I answer, and Skylar smiles at them.

"I'm Maxwell. Is there anything I can help you with today, or are you just looking?" he asks with a bright smile.

His eyes trail over to Skylar, and I growl low. If he's fighting for commission, I will happily go somewhere else. I don't like the way he's looking at Skylar.

"We're looking for a car for my husband," Skylar tells Maxwell, and it's like my heart stops for a second.

My Husband.

I'm screwed. I'm a goner. There's no way that's ever leaving my brain.

My Husband.

I reach down to readjust my jeans. I feel hot. Is it hot out here? This woman is going to kill me.

"Oh..." Maxwell said sadly. "Your husband. What are you looking for?" He turns to look at me again.

I smirk. "Something big for our growing family. What do you have? We've been looking at the Cadillac Escalade. That dealership is right next door. So, I think we're going to walk across the street..." I look down at Skylar. "Is that okay with you, Sunshine?"

Skylar smiles. "Whatever you want," she tells me. I groan.

She's going to kill me. She's trying to give me a heart attack. I'm not subtle this time with readjusting myself. I'm hard. I don't care if I make Maxwell uncomfortable.

"Actually, we just got in a trade-in, it's not the Cadillac Escalade. But it's a Range Rover SV Autobiography. I think it would be perfect for your growing family," Maxwell tries to brighten his attitude. "We would love your business."

I tilt my head and sigh dramatically. "Since we're already here, we might as well take a look at it," I tell him.

He nods excitedly.

"It's just right this way!" He's like an eager puppy.

Skylar intertwines our fingers together as she leads us away from Maxwell. "I think it's right here, it's... lavender?" she says before turning to look at Maxwell.

I look at the SUV. It's nice. I was more looking for a sports car, but this would do. I like it.

"Yeah, a dad brought in his daughter to trade it in for something else. We could change the color to whatever you wanted, though, if that will help the sale go through," Maxwell tells us.

"How much is it?" I ask, pulling Skylar along with me to look at the exterior of the car.

"Two hundred and eight thousand euros. But with the new paint, it would be a little more expensive, depending on what color you'd go with," Maxwell continues on. "You can get in it if you'd like. I can go get the keys."

I don't even have the chance to answer him before he's walking off. "Do you like the color?" I ask Skylar.

She's opening the back door to look into it. "Shouldn't you be asking yourself that?"

"Nope. I want your answer," I tell her.

"Of course I do. It's purple," she laughs like I should've known that. "It's shiny. I like it."

"Perfect. I'll keep it that color," I tell her. "I'm probably just going to buy this car and keep looking for another one."

We both climb into the back of the car. "I like these seats. It feels nice," I say and shift around. "I know I won't be back here often, but I think it's comfortable."

Skylar nods in agreement and when she shuts her door, we're completely alone. The tint is dark enough that no one will know we're back here.

She moves closer to me. "Do you like it back here?" I ask.

I'm nervous. I haven't been in the back seat of a car with a woman in a long time. Let alone a woman that looks like Skylar. A woman that I have a crush on? Never.

"I do. It's comfortable."

Skylar is right beside me when she turns to look at me. Her eyes seem brighter in this lighting. "Skye..." I breathe out.

"Braxton..." She leans closer to me.

Her perfume fills my nose, and I sigh. I would buy this car just because it smells like her in here now.

"You're the best thing to ever happen to me," I tell her.

I mean it. I've never been this happy in my entire life. Her smile lights up the dark cab. "Really?"

I lean closer to her, letting my forehead rest against hers. "I've never meant anything more in my entire life," I promise her.

Skylar looks up at me, and right when I think she might lean closer, the front driver door opens, and Maxwell peaks his head in. "There you guys are!"

I groan and look over at him. "I don't care how much you want for the car. I'll take it. I don't want the color changed, though," I tell him.

"I'll have it right up, Mr. Vance," he says and shuts the door.

I turn to look back at Skylar. "Where were we?" I ask.

Skylar laughs. "We're getting you a new car," she tells me before stepping out of the car.

I groan. I was so close to getting to kiss her...

Chapter Thirty-Five

SKYLAR

It feels like we've been at the dealership for hours. Braxton kept his hand somewhere on me at all times. I don't know why I called him my husband. We're not even dating. But just something about that guy staring at me made me uncomfortable.

"Is there anything else we can assist you with?" Maxwell asks with that same fake smile plastered on his face.

"Yeah. Return my rental for me," Braxton practically demands.

After Maxwell figured out who we were, his attitude changed a lot. He's giving into Braxton's every demand. It's kind of fun to watch, if you ask me. Braxton's good at negotiating.

"Anything to make this experience better for you." Maxwell bows his head, and it takes everything in me not to laugh.

Braxton has him waiting hand and foot on us.

"If that's all, here's your keys. I hope I made your experience good enough that you want to come back." Maxwell beams happily, probably partially happy that we're going to be leaving here.

Braxton snatches the keys from him and places his rental keys in his hand instead. "Thanks so much," Braxton tells him before we're up out of our seats and heading out of the door.

"We should've gotten food before we came." I rub my stomach dramatically.

"Oh, you're right. I didn't think that Maxwell guy would stop checking you out long enough for me to even buy the car," Braxton tells me with a roll of my eyes. "I hate that guy."

"It seems like you hate most guys."

"Most guys who stare at you?" he asks. I nod. "Definitely. I hate them all. I don't want anyone staring."

I laugh. He's so protective. Braxton opens my door for me and helps me get in before he's running to get in on his side.

"Where are we going for lunch?" I ask as I pull my phone out of my purse.

I felt it buzz a little while ago, and I know it must be Ale.

Ale: I'm on my way back to Braxton's flat.

Ale: Are you still there? I brought breakfast.

Ale: Hey? I looked everywhere here, and you're not here. Where are you?

Ale: I just want to make sure you're safe.

Ale: Just looked at your location. I didn't know you wanted to look at cars. We're all on our way.

I look over at Braxton. He must've read over my shoulder because he's groaning. "Just once I'd like to hang out with you without everyone else being around. Is that too much to ask for?" He sighs dramatically.

I shake my head. "It's probably my fault. I didn't answer him, and he got worried," I explain as three brightly colored cars pull up in front of us.

Leo revs his car before backing up. It's his signal to follow after him. The rest of the cars follow suit. "I'm sorry," I tell him.

Braxton shakes his head. "There's nothing to be sorry for beautiful. It's a good thing they worry about your safety," he tells me. "I guess we're all going to lunch together then. I don't want to sit by Diego, though."

I smile at him. "I know."

✍

AFTER WE PULL up to The Secret Garden, I just stare at it. "Wow... It's beautiful," Braxton tells me.

I nod and smile at him. This is one of my favorite restaurants. The plants and ivy hide it extremely well. If a person doesn't know where to look, they'd never know it's here. "It has the best food!"

"You wanna know something, though? Really quick before we go in?" he asks randomly.

I nod. "Yeah?"

"It's not as beautiful as you are," Braxton compliments me.

I don't know how to handle it when he compliments me. I feel my face heat up at his words.

"Thank you," I say.

Braxton quickly gets out of the car before heading to open my door. He's so attentive.

"So, Vancey! Got a purple car now, huh? Not even a sports car?" Diego sing-songs to Braxton as I get out of the Range Rover. "What? Too much horse power for you to handle?"

"Nah," Braxton answers. "I'm gonna special order a Mercedes-AMG GT Black Series. That's over seven hundred horsepower right there. Adding a few mods onto it? Easily over a thousand."

Ale, Leo, and Celia are all heading into the restaurant. I tug on Braxton's hand and pull him towards the door.

"You are not going to order that. Isn't that a million euros?" Diego asks as we walk towards the door.

"Yeah, but nothing I can't afford," Braxton taunts him. "It won't even make a dent in my bank account."

Diego rolls his eyes. "I hate you," he walks into the restaurant.

"We could leave," Braxton tells me.

I shake my head. "No, Ale wouldn't like that."

He pouts, giving me the cutest puppy dog eyes I've ever seen. I'm about to respond before the look on his face changes. His eyes harden, and he looks annoyed.

Before I know what's happening, Braxton shoves me behind him, and cameras start flashing.

"Mr. Vance! Is this your newest fling!"

"Mr. Vance! Does Alejandro Rodriguez know you're dating his sister!"

"Mr. Vance! How does it feel knowing you've taken Spain's most eligible bachelorette off the market?"

"Mr. Vance! Do you have anything to say?"

A thousand other questions are asked.

"No comment," he says over the shouting.

His arm goes around me, and he's pushing through the crowd to get us back towards the car.

"Ms. Rodriguez! Do you have anything you want to tell the people about your new relationship!" the paparazzi asks me now.

"We said no comment," Braxton snaps before opening up my door and helping me in quickly.

He shuts the door before anyone else can take a picture. This is going to be all over the internet within hours. Not days. It's probably already across the internet.

Braxton is in the driver's seat and peeling out of the parking lot without another word about the paparazzi.

With how fast he's driving, they won't have the chance to catch up with us. "Are you okay? Did any of them hurt you?" Braxton keeps looking over at me every chance he gets.

I shake my head and take his free hand in mine. "I'm okay... Thank you," I say softly. "We're both okay."

"Right. We're both okay," he repeats my words.

I can tell he doesn't want to talk. So, I just gently rub my thumb over his hand and let him drive us back to his flat. I'll let him talk about everything that happened when he's ready.

Chapter Thirty-Six

BRAXTON

It's been a week of everyone staying over at my place, and I'm glad to say that they all decided to finally leave. Skylar and I haven't talked about what happened with the paparazzi at the restaurant. Ale hasn't brought it up either.

It's almost like I'm waiting for the other shoe to drop. I don't care that people know she's mine. I just don't know how she feels about it. If it's something she's uncomfortable with, I'll gladly put out there that we were never together.

I want her to feel safe and comfortable with me. I'm over at Ale's today. Skylar has been preparing for her show later today, and I'm anxiously waiting for when I'm able to see her again.

I stare down at my phone. I feel like minutes are ticking by like hours. I feel my phone buzz, and without thinking, I answer it.

"Hey, Sunshine, miss me?" I grin, but I don't hear her voice.

I hear my worst nightmare. "Hey, son. Have you missed me? I've been thinking about coming to visit. Especially after your brother told me there's a pretty blonde that would remind me of your mother." My father chuckles evilly. I feel numb.

This is my worst fear come true. I've been reckless... I shouldn't have let myself get as close to Skylar as I have. I can't bring myself to reply to him. He sighs dramatically. I feel like I did before I left his house.

"You know I hate when you don't respond to me. I see you need me to remind you of how things work. Maybe I'll start with that pretty blonde," he tells me. That's when I snap out of things.

I'm not that helpless little kid anymore. I can stand up for myself and the people I love.

I'll burn him alive if he even goes near Skylar. I don't care where that puts me. I'll protect her until my last breath.

"I swear to whatever is up there, if you even come within five miles of her, I'll find you, and I'll make you regret ever stepping foot near me again. I'm not a teenager anymore, Carson. If you come near me, you'll pay," I threaten.

My heartbeat quickens, my vision blurs, but I refuse to pass out. I need to get to Skylar. I need to make sure she's okay. Crap. I need to tell Ale about what's going on. I look up from the wall and see Leo, Celia, and Ale all staring at me.

They know something's wrong. I swallow. I'm going to have to move again. I'm going to lose Skylar. I rub my chest. Why does that pain me more than everything else I've grown to like here?

Carson chuckles. "I guess we'll have to wait and see what happens, Braxton. I'll see you soon... Maybe sooner than you think," he tells me before he hangs up.

Ale doesn't say anything. I feel like the walls are closing in around me. "Ale... I... I can explain," I start, but he just shakes his head.

"I can take a wild guess," he says softly, like he's talking to a child. "Abusive father coming after you now that you've made a name for yourself?"

My mouth falls open. How did he figure that out so fast? Did Cee tell him? I look over at her, and she shakes her head no.

"How did you know?" I ask, shoving my phone into my pocket.

I'm heading to Skylar after this. I don't trust my father. I feel like something bad is going to happen deep in my gut.

Ale tilts his head just like Skylar does. "It's cuter when your sister does that," I blurt out before I can stop myself.

Ale chuckles. "Everything is cuter when she does it." He shakes his head. He places his hand on my shoulder. It takes everything in me not to shrink back. "My father has never been... the best. He didn't start off like that, but when Sklyar came into the picture, it's like something flipped in him. He got abusive. He didn't like that I was spending so much time at my aunt's house." Ale takes a deep breath. "I kind of got that same feeling from you when I first met you. Then, as I noticed your actions more, it got easier to see."

I don't know how to feel about this. I've never had someone point it out before. "I didn't think that he was going to come after me..."

"I know," he tells me. "We've got your back, though."

I look up at him, then Leo and Celia. They're all nodding in agreement. My phone buzzes, and I grab it. This time, I make sure to look at the caller before I answer. **My Sunshine** appears on the screen with a picture of her. There she is.

"Go, we'll meet you there," Leo tells me before handing me his car keys.

I don't answer. I just grab the keys and head to the door. I answer her call.

"Hey, Ryder." Her beautiful voice comes through my phone, and I swear she knows exactly what I need from her.

"Hey, Sunshine," I breathe out. It's like a weight has been lifted off of my chest. I need to see her. "Miss me, beautiful?" I ask.

She laughs.

"Of course I did," she tells me. I grin.

I get into Leo's car and start the engine. "I feel like it's been days since I've seen you." I'm being honest with her. "Do you need anything before I get to you?" When she's quiet, I know she's not paying attention. "Of course, Sunshine, I'm going to stop and get you something to eat and drink. Considering I can tell you haven't done either of those things since I saw you this morning," I tell her.

She snorts at my words.

"I have..." she starts. "Okay, fine, yes I would like something to eat. I kind of got distracted while running everything."

I smirk. I thought so. She's getting way easier for me to read. "I know you, Sunshine," I pull down the driveway slowly. "I'll be there as fast as I can."

"No racing for pinks," she tells me.

I chuckle. "If you say so Sunshine. I'll see you soon," I wait to hear her say goodbye before I end the call.

I'm so screwed when it comes to this woman. But I wouldn't have it any other way.

Chapter Thirty-Seven

SKYLAR

I look down at my tablet with my check list on it. She's groomed. Her tack is good. I made sure to grab everything. The farrier came out to check on her before we got her in the trailer, so her hoofs were checked. Her shoes were checked.

She already had her vet appointment to make sure she was good to be here today. I click the boxes to mark them as done. We've done our warm up...

I feel like I'm forgetting something. I look up at River, and she's just looking out of the window. I know the show is going to start soon. I hear commotion down the hall, so I open the stall door before peaking my head out.

"Skylar Rodriguez," Braxton growls. "My girlfriend. I want to see her. I should be on the cleared list."

I grin, this is going to be good. I place my tablet in my bag on the outside of the stall before I shut the door.

"Babe! Wait!" I call out, jogging down to where the security guards are holding him back.

The security guards turn to look at me. "This is my boyfriend. He's good to come back," I tell them. They nod.

"My apologies, Ms. Rodriguez," the one guard says before he moves aside to give Braxton room to walk through.

I can never remember their names. Braxton is staring at me like he doesn't know what to think of this. He called me his girl-friend first, so he opened himself up for it. I also called him my husband, and he didn't seem to have an issue with it at all.

So, here's to hoping that I didn't just cross a boundary, and he's okay with it.

"Come here, babe. I've missed you," I turn to him, and he's smiling so big at me.

He walks to me before wrapping his arms tightly around me. He yanks me into him, I laugh. "I would've come out here if you would've texted me, babe," I tell him.

He shakes his head. "I'm pretty sure that's my line," he huffs playfully before kissing my forehead. "But it's pretty hot when you call me your boyfriend. You should keep doing it."

I smile at him before pulling away and leading him towards River's stall. "So, you're a fan?" I ask, bumping my hip against his. "Who's your favorite racer? I could get you an autograph. Maybe even a picture with them."

I can't help myself. This is fun. When we get back to the stall, Braxton turns me around gently so my back is facing him. I feel his hands run through my hair gently before he starts to part it to braid it.

"My favorite racer?" he says. "My favorite racer is this short, beautiful, blonde woman that's way out of my league. She's my favorite person in the entire world, but I don't know if she knows that or not. I also don't know if she's single or not... The paparazzi said she captured the eye of the most eligible bachelor in Spain."

I bite my bottom lip. I don't know what I did to deserve him being so nice to me.

"I think if you play your cards right, she might just let you come over for dinner afterwards, but I don't know if her boyfriend would like that very much. He hates any guy who looks at his woman," I tell him as he finishes the braid and puts the hair rubber on.

Braxton wraps his arms around my waist and rests his chin on my shoulder. "I think that sounds like the perfect ending to today. Are you ready? My girls ready to go and win?"

I laugh. "You have so much faith in me," I shake my head. "We might lose."

"Don't talk like that," his voice is deeper than usual. "I don't want you to go into this thing thinking you're going to lose. You and River are going to do perfect. Just like you always do."

Before I have a chance to say anything, I hear the loudspeaker. "Next up, The Matrix's Home with his rider Marley Meadows!" She's right before I'm supposed to go.

Braxton reluctantly lets me go and moves to help me get River's tack on. "You're a winner. You're perfect at this," he tells me. "I don't want to hear any sort of argument from you."

I shake my head and grab the saddle pad. "No arguing," I agree. "The saddle is kind of heavy, so be careful. I'll buckle the straps after you put it on her."

Braxton nods, and we work together to quickly get her ready. He learned fast about tacking her up. The saddle probably weighs more than I do.

After we get her ready, Braxton grabs my helmet and places it on my head for me.

"You're amazing... You're talented. You've got this," he tells me again. "You need to believe in yourself, even if you don't. I'll always believe in you, no matter what."

I smile as he buckles my helmet. "You're right. We've got this in the bag. I have a handsome fútbol player to impress so he takes me out to dinner afterwards."

Braxton grins and grabs River's reins to lead her to where I'm supposed to wait for my turn to go.

"That's my girl," he praises. "I'll wait here with you for as long as I can, but I'll be with everyone else cheering you on. I'll meet you right back here when you're all done okay?" I nod. He leans down to kiss my forehead. "Don't be nervous, okay?" He helps me get onto River. "I believe in you."

"Thank you, Ryder," I smile when he squeezes my thigh.

"Anything for you, my sunshine," he winks. "What are you thinking for dinner?"

"Spaghetti and a movie?" I ask.

"I like it. Only if we get to have meatballs, too."

"That's the only way to have it!"

River snorts, almost like she's in agreement.

"You are my favorite part of every day," he tells me. River turns her head to look at him. "You too, River," he laughs. "I'd never forget about including you."

One of the people wave me up. It looks like it's time for Braxton to head up to his seat. "I'll be right here when you get done with your run," he tells me with a smile. "You're going to do amazing. I believe in you. I'm your biggest fan." He walks away from me.

"You have a few minutes left. We need to reset up the polls," the woman tells me. I nod in response.

I run my hand along River's neck. She snorts.. As long as I stay calm, she'll stay calm as well. I breathe in slowly.

"We've got this, River... We've got this," I tell her. She prances in place.

I watch as Braxton disappears into the crowd, I miss him. I know I'm going to see him here soon, but it feels like a piece of me is missing.

Chapter Thirty-Eight

BRAXTON

I push through the crowd. I'm not going to be late for Skylar's turn. I don't care if I have to run. Everyone is trying to either go to the bathroom or head back to their seats after getting something to eat or drink.

I don't know how these things work. I stop in my tracks as I look at one of my nightmares in the face.

"Braxton..." my big brother, Brody, says to me.

My first instinct when I see him is to punch him in the face. Honestly. But I know if I do that, I'm going to get arrested for assault. I'd miss out on the life I'm building here.

"Coming for me in public? That's a bold move. Even for you, Brody." I'm shaking.

My heartbeat starts to speed up, but I make sure to breathe. If this is going to be a fight, I need to make sure I don't pass out for it.

"It's not that. I promise. Just let me explain. Can we talk somewhere in private?" he asks. "Please. It's important."

I laugh. He's lost it if he thinks I owe him a single second of my life. Not after what he's done to me. Not after everything I've been through to get here.

"No." It's the only word I'm saying to him.

I force my legs to move me past where Brody is standing. With everyone walking around us, I know Brody isn't stupid enough to attack me here.

But after...

When I'm walking to my car... Or worse... Skylar is alone going back to the stall.

My stomach turns. If anything happens to her... I don't know if I could handle it. Just as I'm walking past Brody, he steps in front of me.

But he keeps his hands in the air in surrender. "You can pat me down if you want, but I promise you, I'm not here to hurt you or anyone you care about," he tells me.

I shake my head. He's acting like I have a reason to believe him. Brody hasn't done a single thing all of my life to give me an ounce of belief in him.

"Don't touch me," I snap at him.

I won't be able to control myself if he touches me.

"I won't. We can talk here if it'll make you more comfortable," Brody tells me.

I look at the clock on the wall. "You have two minutes." He won't take two minutes, and I'll have the other one to book it as fast as I can to the seats.

Skylar made sure to get us a private seating area. It will be cool. I'm excited.

"I knew you wouldn't answer any of my calls. I wanted to tell you that we're done. I'll keep dad away from you and the life you've made here," Brody tells me.

I shake my head. Did he just... say what I think he just said?

"What?" I ask before taking a step back.

This is a trap. I need to get out of here. I need to make sure Skylar is safe.

The thought of me potentially getting Skylar hurt or even worse... *killed.*

I might throw up.

"I'm going to tell dad to leave you alone. He'll listen to me.

You know he always does. This will be the last time you see or hear from me. You'll never hear from dad again. I give you my word," Brody tells me.

I can't tell if this is a joke or not. This all could be this massive elaborate plan to get me to let my guard down. I'm not stupid at all.

"What brought this all up?" I ask before looking at the time again. "One minute."

"I have a kid," he says with the faintest smile.

I don't think I've ever seen him smile in my life. This woman must have him by the balls.

"Her mother told me that I need to clear my life up, or I'll never be able to see her. So, that's what I'm doing. She knows that I've screwed up a lot where it comes to you. One of her conditions is I make sure you know that I'm done tormenting you. Dad's done tormenting you, and if he tries to keep at it when I tell him to stop. I'll personally get him thrown in jail for everything he's ever done," Brody explains.

I don't know how to feel. Part of me wants to believe him. The bigger part of me doesn't. I'm so used to always having my guard up because of them. I don't have time to think about it because the speakers crackle before the announcer says that Skylar is about to start.

"Bye, Brody," I tell him before heading past him.

"Goodbye forever, Braxton. You've done a good job at making a name for yourself," Brody says to me, but I barely hear him.

I'm full on sprinting away from him so I can be there before Skylar's run starts. I kind of feel that I'm leaving my past behind me as I run to my future.

Ale, Leo, Celia, and Skylar. They're my family now. Skylar is my future. I... I can actually move on now. I shake my head.

I don't have time to unpack this all right now. Skylar is racing. Skylar has my focus. I bust through the door to our VIP area and everyone turns to look at me. I run to the glass without another word.

"Please. Please tell me I didn't miss anything. I ran as fast as I could. Something happened..." I feel like the walls are closing in.

Why did Brody have to tell me all of this right now? I need Skylar. I'll feel better when I have her in my arms.

Celia's hand gently squeezes my thigh. "She's just about to go now. They had to fix a few of the jumps because of the last rider," Celia explains. "Are you okay? What happened?"

I shake my head. "It's Skylar's moment to shine," I tell her with a smile.

"Are you okay, Braxton?" Celia asks me again.

"I'll feel better after getting Skylar in my arms again."

I hope she takes it and doesn't say anything else. I can't talk about it in front of anyone here. I just can't.

Thankfully, Celia only nods, and we all turn back to watch Skylar.

Chapter Thirty-Nine

BRAXTON

River canters beautifully around the arena, my eyes trail to Skylar. She's breathtaking. She looks in her element, like she was made for this.

River moves effortlessly as she jumps over the poles. I feel like I'm going to have a panic attack when I see her go towards the taller ones. One looks like bricks. I believe in her, but being on this side of things? With someone you love out there?

I swallow. "She's good at this," Celia moves to sit right beside me. "She's going to be okay."

I nod. I can't bring myself to say anything. Skylar's body moves with River's movements. While I'm stressed out, I can't help but be amazed at how she's moving through the setup.

"She looks pretty great," Diego starts, and I ball my fists.

I don't need him talking near me right now. I don't respond to him. I know he's just wanting to get on my nerves.

"She's beautiful," he keeps saying. "Does anyone know if she's single?"

I turn to glare at him. "I'd appreciate it if you would shut your mouth," I tell him. "I'm not asking you to do it. I'm telling you to shut up."

Diego tilts his head at me. I just want to strangle him. "Did I hit pretty boys' nerves?" he taunts me.

I grip the ledge in front of me as I continue to watch Skylar. I breathe through my nose. *Count to ten. I don't need to deck my teammate.*

"Oh, since I didn't get on your nerves, I'll just ask her out afterwards then," Diego continues.

But I don't even care anymore, River is galloping towards the highest jump there. That thing is huge. "She can't jump that, can she!?" I say, looking over at Ale.

Ale is pressed against the glass. "She's going for it," Ale whispers. I snap my gaze back to the scene in front of me.

River lowers her hindquarters before she pushes off the ground and launches into the air. She tucks her front legs before her back legs follow after. My heart stops for a second as I watch her glide over the top pole just barely missing it.

Her front legs stretch forward, and she lands perfectly. The crowd goes wild.

"Holy crap," I say as I turn to look at Ale. "She just did that."

"She just jumped over the highest fence down there," Ale looks over as the door opens.

"Mr. Rodriguez, we need to get you and your whole group out of here now," the security officer from earlier.

I hate that guy.

"What's going on?" Ale asks.

I hear a gunshot, people start screaming, and I watch in horror as I see River rear and Skylar fall off of her. I take off running to the door. I thought my dad was joking. Could it be him?

I can't think about that right now. I need to go to Skylar. I need to get her out of here. I know the rest of the group must be following after me.

"I'm getting Skylar," I yell to them.

Nothing is going to stop me from going to save her.

Chapter Forty

SKYLAR

I groan as I feel my chest tighten. Pain radiates from where I fell on the ground. I need to get up. Someone brought a gun. I need to get River. She must be terrified.

I try to get up, but I can't. A wheeze escapes me before I'm able to cough. I notice people rushing towards River, and I force myself up. They'll just scare her. I try to get up again, but pain makes it almost impossible. I think I broke a rib.

"No! You can't!" I try to yell over the crowd.

But everyone is screaming, running, and making every last possible effort to be as loud as humanly possible. River rears, her front hooves pawing the air in front of her.

When her hooves land on the ground, I can see the fear in her eyes. That's when another gunshot gets fired, and before I know it, I'm tackled back to the ground.

The urge to throw up threatens to overwhelm me. I landed right on my hurt side again, and it did not feel good... At all.

"Let me go!" I scream.

It must've been someone from our security detail. "No!" Braxton shouts at me.

I stare up at him, he looks so angry. "Ryder?"

"Yeah, Sunshine." He's getting up and pulling me with him. "We have to get out of here."

"No." I shake my head. "No, I need to get River."

Braxton is pulling me towards the exit, but I'm dragging my feet. He growls, and before I know it. He throws me over his shoulder and is bolting through the crowd.

"No! No!" I yell. "River!"

I look up to see Ale running towards her as she rears. "She's scared! She needs me!"

"I need you to be safe," Braxton snaps at me.

I feel his arm wrap around me to keep me against his shoulder. I want to throw up. He runs with me like I weigh nothing. Before I know it, I'm in a car and buckled in.

I feel like my mind is spinning. Braxton gets into the driver seat and turns the car on. "Ryder?"

"Yeah, Sunshine?" His voice is deeper than usual. He's stressed. I reach out to him. He takes my hand and intertwines our fingers. "We're heading to the hospital."

"No, I don't want to go."

He just shakes his head. "I didn't ask. You need to get checked out." Braxton honks the horn before speeding up through the parking lot. "I know you don't like the hospital, but I'm not going to leave your side. Not once. I promise you. Ale and everyone else will be right behind us. They're going to make sure River is safe while I make sure you are."

I squeeze his hand. "I feel okay..."

"You could be seriously hurt and not feel it because of adrenaline," he explains.

The engine of the car roars as he speeds up. I'm surprised that we haven't gotten pulled over yet.

"Breathe for me please," I ask him.

I don't want him to pass out.

Braxton laughs before stopping at the hospital. He doesn't say anything before he shuts the car off and gets out. I go to open my door, but he's there. Unbuckling me and carrying me into the hospital before I even can take a single step.

"I'm breathing... It's time for you to get taken care of. I need to make sure you're okay." He doesn't look down at me as he walks through the doors to the hospital.

This is going to suck.

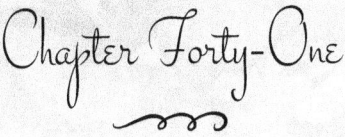

Chapter Forty-One

BRAXTON

I t doesn't take them long to get us into a room. She's looking at me like she wants to leave, but I want her checked out first. Any number of things could be wrong with her, and I'm not willing to risk it.

"Did you text Ale?" she asks.

I nod. "I told him the room number and everything. Leo's going to bring you something from my car for you to change into," I tell her.

I didn't think about grabbing something before, but she looks comfortable, at least for now.

Skylar reaches up to take her helmet off. I shake my head and get up.

"Let me," I tell her before unclipping it and gently taking it off. "Do you want me to take your braid out?" She shakes her head.

My phone buzzes so I pull it out to look at the text.

Ale: Don't even think about staying in the room.
Celia: You're being rude Alejandro.
Ale: Not rude. Just telling him how it is.
Leo: You just don't like that he likes your sister
Braxton: ;) Gotta keep him on his toes.

Leo: Atta boy Braxton!

Braxton: ;) She's MY Sunshine after all.

Ale: I hate you all. Especially you Vance.

Celia: Shut up. We're heading to the hospital now. Want us to pick up something to eat?

Leo: YES!

Celia: I didn't ask you.

Braxton: Totally up to you guys. I'm not planning on leaving her room though.

Ale: Ew.

I shake my head before pocketing my phone. "Ale?" Skylar asks.

"Yeah."

"He's not happy that you're here with me?"

I grin at her. "His pretty princess?" I tease. "I think he wants me as far away from you as humanly possible."

Skylar smiles at me. "I'm glad you're here, though," she tells me. "Do you want to lay with me?"

"Yeah, I will, Sunshine." I get back up from my chair and climb into her bed.

Skylar wastes no time in cuddling up next to me. She lays her head on my chest, and her warmth makes me feel better. It's like this is just what I needed to calm down. "I like this."

I chuckle. "I do too, Sunshine." I smile before placing my arm gently around her. "I'd like for you to stay awake, though. Just until after the doctors check you out."

"I know," she huffs. "This isn't the first time I've ever been in a hospital for this."

"Really?" I ask.

"Yeah. It hasn't happened a lot, but it has happened," she explains. "I've obviously walked out just fine from everything. I've never had something like this happen, though. What happened?"

"I..." I trail off.

I don't know. There's a lot of things it could be. This could've been part of the plan from my brother... I'll have to see what Ale says.

"I don't know, Sunshine. I knew you were in trouble and took off to make sure you were safe. I didn't stop to ask any questions." I draw soft circles on her arms. "I can find out, though."

"The security team hasn't gotten back to me yet. But I'm expecting a call in less than an hour," Ale says as he walks into the room before looking down at his phone. "River is safe. I'll be having her taken home shortly. The doctor said that they'll be in to run your tests so you can go home. Leo has your clothes."

"My clothes," I correct.

I shouldn't provoke him, but it's so much fun to do it. I like it when she wears my clothes.

"Don't start with me ,Vance," he growls at me.

I grin. "I can't help it. You look stressed out, and I thought you would enjoy a laugh," I tease him more.

Ale narrows his eyes at me. Leo and Celia slide into the room next. "He's been stressed on his phone since the security team took down the shooter."

"Killed?" Skylar asks.

"Yup," Leo nods. "I saw it with my own eyes. It was crazy. They had him surrounded. I think it was that guy who was obsessed with you. You don't have to worry about him anymore."

I stare at Leo. He just said that like it's nothing at all. I look down at Skylar. She seems lost in thought.

"Hey..." I squeeze her bicep gently to bring her attention back to me. "They probably had no choice. They wouldn't have done it for no reason."

Skylar nods. "Yeah... That makes sense. At least we won't have to worry about him anymore..."

"Right. I'll have to talk to the cops about everything. But I think it'll pretty much be over pretty soon, if not over today," Ale says with a shrug.

He fidgets in place like he doesn't know what to do with

himself. I'm about to ask about what's going on when the doctor comes into the room.

"Oh. We have a full house, don't we?" the doctor asks with a laugh.

"Yeah, she's loved by a lot," I answer before I reluctantly get off the bed. Skylar looks up at me with the prettiest puppy dog eyes I've ever seen. I take his hand in mine. "I'm right here Sunshine. I'm not going anywhere, I promise you."

Chapter Forty-Two

TWO MONTHS LATER
BRAXTON

I never thought I would say that I truly love Spain, but I love this place like no other. I've been spending a majority of my time with Skylar, and it's been heaven. She's so... perfect. Kind. Loving. Caring. Sweet. She's so helpful. I don't deserve her. I don't deserve any of it. She's giving. She helps me practice when I'm feeling anxious before a big game. The list of things I love about her is endless.

I've been sleeping over at her house every night since she called me scared. I can't stand the thought of her being afraid. I do feel better knowing that her stalker isn't something we have to worry about anymore.

Potentially even not having to worry about my brother and father. I'm still going to have to bring that up to Skylar. I just don't know how.

I can't sleep without her anymore. I just lay there awake. It's like my body craves her being near me. It's almost like I'm a lighter person when she's around me.

I rub my face. How did I even let myself get this close to someone I haven't even slept with?

I don't recognize the person I am right now, but I like the change. It's... different. Good.

I look over at the time and groan when I see it says midnight. Celia said that she wanted to spend time with Skylar without me. I roll my eyes. She just likes to see me in pain.

When I open my phone, I see that Skylar texted me to tell me that she made it home. Late, but she made it home safely and is going to try and get some sleep so she can train tomorrow.

I could go over there. I could just drive over there and climb in her bed. I've done it before. I could do it again.

But before I even have a chance to get up, I hear my front door open and shut. I grin. I know who it is. It's the only person I gave a key to. After Celia kept walking in on me naked, I took her key away from her.

When my door opens, I see Skylar standing there. I lean up and smile at her.

"Miss me, Sunshine?" I tease, even though I was about to do exactly what she did.

Skylar huffs before placing her phone, keys, and wallet on my dresser. "I can't sleep without you. So, I totally blame you for this. Also? I hate driving in the city. Especially at night. Why couldn't you have a house closer to me?" she asks me before shimming out of her shorts and getting on the bed.

I wasn't going to tell her, but I have a realtor looking for a house for me. Specifically because I know she hates driving at night and in the city. I thought it would be nice to have a space for just us.

I laugh before grabbing her and pulling her into me. "Want to know something funny?"

"Of course," she replies as I cover her up with my blanket.

"I was just about to get up and do the same thing. I figured you wouldn't have cared," I tell her, wrapping my arms around her and pulling her close to me.

"I wouldn't have cared. You've done it before." She places her palm on my chest. "I'll have to get up early tomorrow so I can head to the barn, so I might be gone before you get up."

Hm... That's perfect, actually. I'll be able to get her present to surprise her without having to worry about where she is.

"I have to go and workout, so we'll see each other. Your brother's having some sort of movie watching party tomorrow?" I ask. I know it's in my calendar.

"Yeah, but we could always just go there together," she offers, and my cheeks warm.

My heart skips a beat at the thought of being able to go anywhere with her. I need to get my head out of my butt and just ask her already.

"Well, I have to meet my building manager, and then I'll be heading to your place," I remind her. I'm sure she forgot. But that's okay. I'll be here to remind her of things she forgets as long as she'll let me. "It's time to go to sleep, beautiful," I kiss the top of her head. "We both have a lot to do tomorrow."

But she doesn't respond to me. Her soft snores fill the silence in my bedroom. I laugh softly. That's the cutest thing.

Chapter Forty-Three

SKYLAR

The next morning, I make sure to make Braxton and myself breakfast before I head out. He always texts me to make sure I'm eating, and drinking properly. These past two months have been... a lot of fun. We spend most of our free time together.

I wouldn't ask for anything different. He's so protective of me, so kind, caring. I never thought I'd find someone who cared so much about me. Other than my brother and Leo, of course.

I'm standing on a stool braiding River's mane. She did amazing today. We have a show coming up right after the charity gala. I like to make sure we're in tip top shape before any show we do.

Music softly plays from my speaker. I'm not worried by any means. The gate I have at the stable is the same one at my house, same security company, same everything.

That doesn't stop me from getting startled when I hear someone walking up behind me. I squeak before I feel strong arms catch me as I start to fall.

"Wow, beautiful. I thought I'd make you fall for me, but not this way," Braxton tells me with a wink.

"You startled me!" I laugh. He places me back on the stool next to River.

She's taller than me so to be able to perfectly groom her, I need to get on a stool.

Braxton grins at me before gently petting my horse. "Well, you are pretty perfect, River. Thanks for not kicking me for scaring your owner," he talks to River, causing her to snort in response.

I smile as I watch them interact together. He's so sweet to her. I laugh when he pulls out a carrot from his pocket.

"What?" he asks me. "I need to make her love me. She will never approve of me when I get you to admit you're helplessly in love with me." He winks, and I blush in response.

I do really like him... more than I think I've ever liked anyone else. I know I've never liked anyone as much as him. He makes me feel safe... centered. Calm.

He knows how to turn my mind off without even trying.

"You're adorable," I giggle.

"You're gorgeous."

"Did I lose track of time again?" I ask putting a rubber band at the end of River's braid. "I thought I had an alarm set or something."

Braxton laughs. "No, no. I would've called you if you were. I finished my workout, but I picked up something for you. It's outside if you want to come with me."

I scrunch my nose before looking back at River. "Uh... Yeah, of course. I just need to put River in the paddock out there, and then I'll be ready," I tell him, unhooking River from the cross ties before using her lead and taking her to the open paddock.

Braxton is right behind me the entire time, he's always so patient with me. I don't know what I did to deserve him. He shifts in place. I can almost feel his anxiety from here.

"Are you okay?" I ask, opening the gate and taking a few steps in.

I always make sure to take her halter off while she's in here.

There's no reason that she has to have it on. After she trots off, I close the gate and turn to Braxton.

"I'm great. I'm just excited and slightly worried that you're going to secretly hate what I have for you." He laughs, but holds his hand out to me anyway.

I take his hand, intertwining our fingers. I let him lead me to the front of the barn where a truck and a trailer sit. I tilt my head. Did he get a horse?

"Did you get a horse? Like you want to ride now?" I ask. That would be so cool!

He'd really understand why I love the peace so much then. Braxton grins at me before opening the door and stepping into the trailer. He undoes the beautiful black Stallion. I nearly gasp. He's gorgeous...

I think he's the exact one I was looking at.

"Is this The Midnight's Star?" I ask, the horse jumps off the end of the trailer, and I take a step back.

Braxton hands me the lead rope, and I stare in awe at the gorgeous horse in front of me.

Braxton nods. "Yes. I noticed you left your laptop on while I was over once... I saw he was up on your computer, so I reached out to the owner and asked to buy. He said yes, he's a big fan of yours. So, yeah. I know you've been stressed out about finding River a friend to be with... And I know you hate leaving on vacation knowing she's here alone. So, I thought since we're leaving for Italy tomorrow, that it would help. And I know I'm already talking a lot, but I had him quarantined at a private stable, so he can go right in with River.

"I also wasn't sure if you wanted a Stallion or a mare... So, I got you both," Braxton says, before climbing back into the trailer and walking to the back. He takes out a beautiful white and black mare.

I'm speechless. No one has ever given me this much thought... No one has ever listened to me this much before. I'm staring at Braxton, and all I can think about is kissing him.

"Do you hate them? I can take them back. Actually, I'm not sure if you can do that. But I can sell them, and you can pick out another horse, or you can tell me I'm being too much," he's rambling. I want him to know how much I appreciate him.

I still hold onto Midnight's lead, but I wrap my arms around him and hug him tightly. "This means more to me than you could ever know..." I whisper to him. He takes a second before hugging me back.

"I just wanted you to be happy," he tells me before kissing the top of my head.

I smile up at him. "I'm so happy... This will make it much easier for me to leave tomorrow. I'll just have to send my stable hand a message that two horses are going to be added to their schedule. I'm sure it's not going to be a big deal," I tell him. I'm so excited.

I know the horses can feel it because they start to get antsy with me. I breathe out. Okay, I need to relax. I need to relax. I can't have them accidentally getting hurt or anything.

Braxton holds the mare while I walk with Midnight to the paddock beside Rivers. I'll stay here for a while with them, just to make sure everything is okay.

"This means so much to me... You have no idea." I try to explain how happy I am, but he just smiles at me.

"I didn't want you to have to worry about River while we're gone... I know we're not going to be gone for a long time, but I just wanted to make it easier for you," Braxton tells me. His cheeks tint a cute pink color.

I want to tease him, but I don't want to actually hurt his feelings.

"It really has..." I open the gate to the other paddock before taking off each of their halters and letting them run.

I'll be calling my vet after Braxton leaves just so she can come out and check them out. They look okay. I'm sure the private stable had them checked out. Braxton doesn't look like the type of guy to be into horses, and I like to cover all of my bases.

"Are you going to stay here with me before the party?" I ask, sparing him a glance.

Braxton sighs sadly. "No. I really want to, but I have to return the truck and trailer, and then I need to head to my flat to see my building manager before heading to your house." He frowns. "I hate being an adult."

I laugh, turning to give him another hug. "Well, I understand. I have a few things to do here before I can head to my house anyway. We'll probably get there right around the same time." I do my best to assure him.

He gives me a soft smile before hugging me back. "You're too good at making me feel better." He kisses the top of my head. "I'll miss you."

"I'll miss you," I tell him as he reluctantly lets me go and turns to walk away.

I bite my bottom lip before turning back to my horses. I know everyone hates him; Ale doesn't want him near me.

But I can't help it.

I wake up happy in his arms. I don't see that changing... Ever.

Chapter Forty-Four

BRAXTON

After I return the truck and trailer, I speed back to my flat. I don't want to be late to Skye's house. The team has already started to haze me about how much time I spend with her. I think Ale is one wrong inappropriate joke away from killing me in my sleep.

But I also know that he would never risk Skylar crying, even slightly. I smirk. I would commit murder if she cried, but that's beside the point. When I go to pull into my parking spot at my flat, I slam on my brakes when I see a tiny white and black ball of fur run across the spot.

Am I seeing things?

I think I'm seeing things.

I creep up into the spot slowly, just in case. I don't want to run anything over. When I'm pulled in enough, I park and turn off my car. I open the door. Immediately, I hear the tiniest little meow I've ever heard.

I shut my door gently, not wanting to scare the little thing. I squat down, seeing the prettiest green eyes. I click at the kitten.

"Come here..." I say, holding out my hand to her.

I will sit here all day if I have to. Skylar will love her. The kitten meows at me again, and I smile when she waddles over to me. I let her sniff my finger. She rubs against me. She's so soft.

I pick her up, frowning when I feel her ribs. I'll have to take her to the vet to make sure she's okay before giving her to Skylar.

Hm... I wonder if I can get it done by tomorrow. I shake my head. I need to focus. I hold the kitten against my chest as I walk to the elevator that will take me to my flat. I press my thumbprint against the scanner and wait for it to turn green before the elevator starts to move up to my floor.

All I have to do is see why the building manager keeps leaving notes on my door. Then, I need to see if I can get an appointment with a vet today and place a delivery order for some cat stuff. Seems pretty doable.

I laugh. That seems like a stretch, but one thing's for sure. I'm not leaving this cat here alone while we go to Italy. Ale and Skylar own a private jet, so it won't be a hassle to bring her.

When the elevator stops, I head to my door. I roll my eyes when I see another note. I unlock my door and take a step inside. I text Celia quickly, asking her to go to the store and get me a few things for the kitten.

Celia: You're such a simp for her. I'm here for it. I'll get you whatever and set stuff up while you get everything else done. Need me to take the kitten to the vet? I know someone who could get me in today. P.S. You put too much on your plate, Kthanksbye.

I laugh when I read it. She has a point. I do put way too much on my plate, but it's alright. I have everything handled. I leave the kitten in my bedroom, tucking her into my blanket before heading out of my flat. I rub my face. I just want to be near Skylar. She makes me... better. She makes me a better person.

I take the elevator down to the first floor before heading to the build manager's office. I knock on the door before opening it and walking in.

"Hey. It's Braxton Vance. You left sticky notes on my door to come and see you," I tell him. He looks up at me and nods.

"Yeah, I tried texting you, but I'm sure you changed your number. I wanted to talk to you about your rent," he explains, motioning to the seat in front of his desk.

I sit down, placing my hands on my lap. "I've been sending you rent for my place. I thought we were doing a month to month lease."

"Oh, yeah, that's not what I wanted to talk to you about. The building was purchased recently. The new owner said that you don't have to pay for rent anymore." He leans back in his chair. "Whoever you've got in your corner is a pretty great one."

I smirk at the thought. I know who bought the building. There's no one else who would do something like this for me. There's no one else that would even care enough.

"She's amazing." I sigh at the thought of her.

I look down at my phone. I should leave here. Get the kitten checked out before I head to Ale's house. I narrow my eyes at him.

"She's mine. Taken. Don't even think about it," I growl before standing up.

He smirks at me before nodding. "I wouldn't want to anger Mr. Vance," he teases, and I roll my eyes.

"Is that it?" I ask, tilting my head as I head to the door.

"Yeah, that was it." He waves me out.

That girl is truly one of a kind. I don't know what I did to deserve her, but there's one thing I know for sure...

I don't care what I have to do.

I'm going to make her mine.

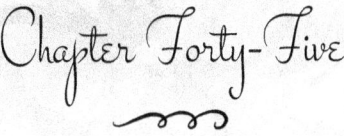

Chapter Forty-Five

SKYLAR

I rub my hands on my thighs. I'm sure everything is going to be just fine. I look at myself in the mirror. I know Braxton's favorite color is red. The bikini compliments my skin tone. My belly button ring sparkles underneath the light.

"Everything will be just fine," I remind myself out loud.

He'll love this. I know he will. I don't know why I'm so nervous. I look out the window. It's almost time for everyone to be here. Celia had to leave for something. She wouldn't say.

I walk downstairs. Everyone is outside. Leo, Ale, and Diego are talking in a circle. I wait a minute before opening the back door and heading out.

"I think I ne..." Diego trails off as his eyes move to me. "Wow."

"Wow?" Leo asks, before he smirks at me. "Wow, look at little Skye all grown up."

I blush, fidgeting in place. "It's nothing, honestly." I try to brush it off, but I know Leo knows...

Leo and Celia always know. I don't know how, but they do. Leo grins, but doesn't say anything.

"You look amazing, Skylar. Red really is your color," Diego compliments me.

It takes everything in me to not laugh. He wouldn't be saying that if he knew that I specifically bought this for Braxton. But I'm not going to say that. He'll know.

"Where's Cee?" I ask, brushing my hair off of my shoulder.

Leo shrugs. "She didn't tell me anything, but that's my wife. She can do whatever she wants."

Diego chuckles. "You don't care as long as she does you at the end of the night."

Ale gags. "Stop. There's little ears!" he whines, covering my ears.

I look up at him. He's just being protective. I know that. I smile before taking his hands off of my ears. "It's okay. I can go inside and wait for Cee," I offer, even though I know he's going to say no.

"No. Absolutely not. I'm not staying out here without you," he tells me.

I knew that was coming.

"Cee is here anyway, and wow... You look fine." Celia grins at me. "I just got a text from Braxton. He's on his way."

I smile at that before looking down at my phone. I see I missed a text from Braxton.

Ryder: Could I just plan everything I need to do around your schedule?

Ryder: Not being with you sucks.

Ryder: I was just told by someone passing by that I look grumpy. And then I was asked if it was because you dumped me.

Ryder: Now I am grumpy thinking about you potentially leaving me.

Ryder: :(Don't leave me baby. Please?

Ryder: I miss you. I wish I would've just taken you with me. It would have made all of this a lot more fun. I got you a tea, though. So, I'll be there soon. I can't wait to see you, Sunshine.

Skylar: I would never leave you Ryder <3 You're one of the best things to ever happen to me.

"You got a text, too?" Celia teases, bumping her hip against mine.

I nod. "He typically does text me to update me throughout the day," I tell her before scrolling through our conversation.

"Looks like someone is in l-o-v-e." Celia giggles as I set my phone down beside my chair.

"I am not," I tell her, but I look away from her.

I don't know what my feelings towards Braxton are, but they're definitely there. He's... he's quickly become my favorite person to be around.

"You are such a terrible liar." Celia laughs before waving Diego over to us. "Di! Tell Skye how beautiful she is!"

"Gladly!" Diego grins, walking over to us.

Oh I don't think this is going to be a good thing. "You look..." He pauses, looking me up and down slowly.

I wish I didn't even put this on now. Him looking at me like that makes me feel weird. I want to put one of Braxton's shirts on to cover myself.

"Gorgeous... Maybe a gold one would look even better on you. With a D on it." He winks at me, and I want to shrink back.

That's gross. I'm sure my face is showing how I'm feeling because Celia is laughing.

The back door opens, so I turn around and smile when I see Braxton in a pair of shorts and a hoodie. His mouth falls open as his eyes slowly take in my whole body.

I knew he'd love this. It's so easy to get him going. I bite my bottom lip. He's still standing there and not saying anything.

Maybe this was a bad idea.

Chapter Forty-Six

BRAXTON

Is it possible to have a heart attack because of someone in a bikini? I think I might have died and gone to heaven. Look at her...

The bikini hugging her curves...

The deep red color...

My favorite color. That's my color.

I need to sit down.

My vision blurs slightly, but when I see Skylar smiling at me, my heart calms. I smile, placing the drink down on the table closest to me.

"Hey, Sunshine." I smile, rushing over to hug her and spin her around.

Her giggle is like music to my ears. She wraps her arms around me, before I place her down on her feet. "Hey, Ryder."

"Well, that was a special hello," Celia says as Leo walks up to her.

"I really think it was," Leo agrees with her.

Of course he does. He would agree with her if she said that the sky was purple.

"Sexy bikini. Bet you'd look better without it," Diego flirts.

I think I see red. I tighten my hold on Skylar as I glare at him. If he so much as touches her, I think I'm going to lose it on him. Before she has a chance to respond, I make sure I do.

"Such white teeth. Bet you'd look better without them," I snap in response.

Leo spits out his drink, laughing uncontrollably. "Oooohhh, someone has struck a nerve with Powertrain Vance. Look out, Diego. He might break your kneecaps on the field." Leo laughs, smiling at Cee.

I roll my eyes. "I won't break his kneecaps right now, but if he touches her, I might."

Skylar laughs in my arms. "He was just messing around. It's fine, really." She tries to calm me down.

I sigh. I place a kiss on her head before letting her go. I don't know how someone so beautiful can't see when someone is flirting with her.

"I know," I tell her with a smile. "I just don't like it when other people flirt with my girl." I wink, her cheeks warm instantly.

That is the type of reaction I love to see.

"Would you look at that...," Leo says with a smirk.

I grin, throwing my arm over Skylar's shoulder. "I have to mark my claim in any way I can, right?"

Skylar leans into me, and I grin. I'm glad she's feeling more comfortable with me doing this.

"Would you look at that? Someone likes to flirt with me even though my brother is standing right over there... With his new girlfriend, apparently?" Skylar says, tilting her head as we all turn to look at Ale hugging a red headed woman.

Hm... Good for him. That must be why he disappears every week... At least once a night. Not like I'm complaining. He gets in less of a mood when I come downstairs with Skylar in the mornings when he's there.

He can't say anything. I grin.

"Good for him. He deserves to finally get laid." I look at Leo, who's grinning like he knows something.

Skylar makes a disgusted face. "I really don't want to listen to you guys talking about my brother getting laid." She gags at the thought. "That's gross."

I laugh, but before I can say anything more, she grabs my hand and leads me to the hot tub. I follow after her, stepping in behind her after taking off my hoodie. Before she picks a spot, I pull her into my lap so we can talk face to face.

"I have a surprise for you back at my place...," I tell her. I'm so excited to give her the kitten. "And speaking of my place, did you buy the building?"

Skylar smiles at me. "Why do you want to know?"

"Well... I would love to tell you thank you. It means the world to me that you would do something like that for me," I tell her, gently placing my hands on her hips.

Should I tell her now that I was planning on buying a house because I knew she hated having to drive in the city? Or should I keep it a secret?

"Well, you mean the world to me. I wanted you to not have to worry about it... I thought it would be nice for you to not have to worry about that," she tells me with the brightest smile on her face.

I'm so screwed when it comes to her. I reach up and gently brush a piece of her hair behind her ear. "You are the greatest gift in my entire life."

Skylar leans into my touch with a smile. "You know... I would say the same thing about you. You make me feel less... all over the place."

I grin. "Good. I'm glad. It's not hard to keep you on track," I tell her, my eyes drifting to Ale practically speed walking over to us.

I don't move Skylar, though. Ale doesn't scare me. He wouldn't yell at me in front of her.

"Can I speak with you for a minute?" Ale asks, never taking his eyes off of me.

He seems stressed... Panicked almost. I don't think this is about me.

"If you're going to be mean to him..." Skylar pouts, and I can't help but laugh.

She knows exactly how to get his feelings going. Ale smiles at Skylar.

"No, not this time. It's just about some team stuff. He'll be back. I promise." Ale turns and walks away. I frown as I reluctantly place her on the seat beside me.

"I'll be back soon," I promise her before I hop out of the hot tub and follow after Ale.

When I turn the corner of the house, Leo, Celia, and Ale are all waiting there for me.

"I'm not going to get shanked, am I?" I ask, somewhat joking.

I eye them all. I don't know about being in this situation. I stay away from them just in case I have to run.

"No, we're not going to shank you. What's wrong with you?" Celia snaps, grabbing my arm and pulling me closer to them.

"What's going on?" I ask, turning my focus to Ale.

"There's something going on at the gate. I..." He gags, before scrunching his nose just like Skylar does.

I smile. "It's cuter when Skylar does that nose scrunch thing," I tell him.

Ale breathes deeply. "I want to break your nose," he growls at me. "Focus. Focus. I need you to take Skylar to your place for the night. You can take one of my cars. Not hers. When I know more information, I'll text you and let you know."

Oh... I guess that's not really leaving me an option. But if she's not safe...

"Okay, that's fine. I think she was planning to come home with me anyway." I grin, winking at Ale.

He looks like he's turning red. "Leave."

I laugh before turning back to Skylar. "Oh, Sunshine! The King of the castle wants to have some alone time with his girlfriend. So, it looks like I get to take the Princess back to my place."

Skylar is already sunbathing out of the hot tub. I will never get this image of her out of my head. It's the hottest thing I've ever seen.

Skylar stands up, and I force myself to look at her face. *Breathe, Vance. Breathe.* I can't be getting hard right now. I think Ale would actually castrate me.

Maybe he still will if the problem at the gate ends up being my dad or brother.

"Ale's okay with that?" she asks me, and I smirk.

"You don't have to ask him to do anything," Celia chimes in.

"Well..." Skylar laughs, rubbing the back of her neck. "Yeah... I know that. But... It's like second nature. I've done it for so long."

She's looking to be the youngest gold medalist in the Olympics for show jumping. She's going to be turning twenty years old here in a few months. Why does she still ask her big brother for permission to do something?

"We know, Sunshine, it's okay. He cares deeply about you." I place my hand on the small of her back. "But yeah, he's chill with it. So, let's go." I give her my hoodie after grabbing it from a table and help her put it on.

The hoodie covers her body all the way down to the middle of her thighs. "Beautiful." I kiss the top of her head before leading her into the house and to the garage.

I don't know what's going on, but if it's something that has Ale turning to me for help, it's better to get her away from this place.

Skylar doesn't question me as I lead her to Ale's SUV and open the passenger door for her. "He said I should try this out. The people mover is what he calls it, right?" I ask her, causing her to nod.

I quickly get into the driver's side. It's spacious, but I want a sports car.

"We'll stop for some takeout, and then head to my place. I can't wait to give you your surprise," I tell her before starting the car and backing down the driveway.

Skylar smiles at me. "I forgot my wallet."

"Pfft, it's not like you need that anyway." I playfully roll my eyes.

Chapter Forty-Seven

SKYLAR

When we got back to Braxton's flat, I'm cold. I want to change, but I don't have anything here to change into.

"Are you cold?" he asks me, shutting the door behind us.

I shake my head no, but I know he knows I'm lying. Braxton hums at me as he places the food on the table.

"Do you want to retry that answer?" He grins, crossing his arms as he looks at me.

I smile, biting my lip. "No?"

Braxton smirks, placing his hands on my hips and pulling me closer to him. "You are cold, Sunshine. Do you want to take a warm shower before I show you your gift?"

My gift? I tilt my head and scrunch my nose.

"I have no idea what you're talking about," I tell him with a soft smile.

Braxton's smile is bright and beautiful. My heart warms. I want to keep seeing that for the rest of my life.

"I got you something. I think that you'll love it," he tells me before walking away from me.

I'm not sure if I'm supposed to follow after, but I do it anyway. Braxton opens the door to his bedroom, and I watch as this tiny, little black and white ball of fur runs out.

"Oh my gosh," I say, squatting down as the kitten runs to my feet. "She's so adorable!"

Braxton turns around to watch me as I gently pet the kitten. Is this the present?

"Do you love her?" he asks, squatting down in front of me.

"Of course I do! She's so small, adorable, and so perfect," I tell him as I pick the little kitten up.

Her fur is so soft. She's already purring as I hold her against my chest. Braxton's smiling at me. I keep looking between him and the kitten. "What's her name?"

"Well. She's yours... I thought you would want to name her. I got her checked out by the vet. She has a clean bill of health. I wanted to make sure she was okay before giving her to you," he explains before sitting on the floor in front of me.

I smile up at him, copying him so I can be more comfortable. "What if we named her together?" I ask, looking up at him.

He's quiet for a moment, and I'm instantly worried that he thinks that's weird. Maybe I pushed him too far..

Braxton's face lights up, finally. "Of course. I would love to. What are you thinking about for a name?"

Hm... I pick the kitten up and bring her to eye level. "I'm not sure." I turn her to Braxton so he can look at her. "What are you thinking?"

"I like the name Saint. She's so sweet. Very much like a Saint," he offers with a slight shrug.

"I love that name!" I tell him, moving so I'm sitting in his lap instead of on the floor.

I place Saint in my lap. She immediately curls up into a ball. "You even got her a purple collar." I grin at him. He's become one of the only people who knows me this much.

"Of course I did," he tells me, wrapping his arms around me and holding me. "She needed to match my favorite girl."

My cheeks warm at his compliment. He's so quick with them. I snuggle back into him. He's warm. He's my favorite place. He leans his head against mine.

"What do you think about taking a warm shower? I'll get the food set out and a movie pulled up for us. That sound good?" he asks me.

I nod. "What am I going to wear?" I ask, unless he's been shopping for me, and I never knew about it, I have nothing to wear here.

"I'll get you one of my hoodies," he tells me.

I reluctantly stand up. He reaches up and places his hands on the back of my thighs. I laugh as I turn my head back and look at him.

"Yes?" I ask.

"Your skin is just so soft," he tells me before standing up.

He presses his strong body to mine, and I smile at the closeness. I don't know what I'm going to do with myself when he finds someone else.

"I love it. I love everything about you," he tells me.

His voice is commanding, leaving no room for questioning him. "Thank you... That means so much to me. I love everything about you.".

It's the truth. I wouldn't lie about that.

"You don't have to say that, Sunshine." His smile falls for a second before it's back again. He takes a step away from me so I can get in the shower.

"I would never lie to you, Ryder... You are perfect to me. The best person I know."

His smile brightens the room. "You are the greatest thing to ever happen to me. I hope you know that," he tells me before walking back towards the kitchen. "Now, be a good girl and get in the shower for me. I'll have everything ready for us."

I nod before heading into his room and into his connected bathroom. I fidget as I look around at his bathroom. There's things of mine here... The exact brand that I use. She-Alpha. Roses and Vanilla... Is this all for me?

Or for someone else?

Chapter Forty-Eight

BRAXTON

The next morning, Skylar and I arrive at the hangar where the private jet sits. A group of people are walking around fueling the jet and getting it ready for take off. I look over at Skylar. All she's doing is petting Saint.

Saint falls asleep curled up in Skylar's lap.

"On a scale from one to ten, how mad do you think that Ale's going to be about me wearing your hoodie?" she asks me.

I grin at her. "Oh. At you? Zero. At me? One thousand." I smirk at the thought. "But he has no room to question it. He's the one who asked me to take you home, so I did exactly what he asked. Actually?" I tilt my head. Would he be mad? I think she's worn my clothes in front of him before. He's never said anything. "Maybe he won't say anything. You've worn my clothes in front of him before, I believe. I don't think he'll be mad," I tell her. "If he is, I'll deal with it."

Skylar nods. "I guess you have a point there. I like your hoodie."

"I like when you wear my hoodie. Make all the other morons out there leave you alone," I tell her without an ounce of remorse.

I hope that Diego sees her in my hoodie and leaves her alone. She's mine. He's getting on my last nerve with being near her. I need to just get him laid so he moves along. I think the next time he tries to touch her, I might just break his wrist.

He could still play with a broken wrist. I shake my head at the thought. I'm not going to get violent with him, no matter how much I want to.

Skylar pulls my hoodie up and over her nose. "It smells like your cologne. Did you just wear this?"

I haven't. I dosed that thing in my cologne before I gave it to her this morning. I'm going to tell her.

"Nope. Not recently. I dosed it in my cologne, though, before I gave it to you," I explain with a big smile. Skylar looks at me like I'm joking. "I'm serious," I tell her, crossing my arms.

She laughs. "Why?"

"Because one, you like my cologne. Two, this is probably one of the bigger reasons, but so Diego smells me on you and stops looking at you. I mean if he'd stop breathing in your direction, I'd like that to." I grin. I can smell my cologne from over here.

Oh, Ale, is going to hate having to smell me in here. It's just another pro.

Skylar giggles. "I like that you're so protective of me. I don't really think that Diego really means anything he says. I think he's just trying to be nice," she assures me.

I groan, leaning my head against the headrest. "No. I think he means everything he says, and that makes me want to give him a black eye. You're too gorgeous and sweet to see that people do mean it when they flirt with you."

Skylar blinks at me, and I can't help but smile. I know for a fact I mean it when I flirt with her. Diego definitely means it when he does. Thankfully, she doesn't like going anywhere alone, so she always invites me.

If I could get her to wear my jersey with my last name and my number on it when she goes out alone. That would be hot. I like that idea.

No. Nope. Can't go there. I'll be hard the entire plane ride, and it'll be the longest hour and a half of my life. Diego better not be on this plane.

"Well... I only like it when you flirt with me," she tells me before going to open the door and get out.

I'm quick to grab her hand. "First, no opening up your own door. Second, you really can't just say that and then try and leave."

Skylar grins at me, before kissing me on the tip of my nose. My face heats up, and I'm left stunned and staring at her. How can someone be so... perfect? There is no other way of describing her.

Perfect.

I'm in love with her. I just need to tell her.

"Every good chapter has a cliffhanger," she tells me with a smile big enough to show her dimples.

I grin, moving my hand to brush a piece of her hair behind her ear. I gently cup her face, before moving mine closer to hers. I look between her eyes and her lips.

"Every good story ends happily ever after," I whisper against her lips. "You're my happily ever after," I tell her, before getting out of the car.

I take a steady breath before jogging over to her side and opening up her door for her. She holds Saint to her chest while I help her out of the car.

"You know just how to fluster me." She blushes with a soft smile.

"I'm just telling you the truth, baby girl," I remind her, placing my hand on her back.

"Mr. and Mrs. Vance, may I help you with your bags? I believe the rest of your group will be arriving shortly," a guy says as he walks up to us.

"The bags are in the trunk," I tell him before unlocking the car for him.

Skylar doesn't correct him, and that makes me happy. I wrap my arm around her and hold her to me. "Want to get on the plane and wait for everyone? I thought I saw them coming down the road."

Skylar nods. I let her walk up the stairs first before I follow right after her. We'll get the best seats, at least. Skylar moves to take a seat where there's a blanket on the chair. It's white with purple clouds all over it. Her name is on it in cursive lettering.

"Ale treats you well," I tell her, taking the seat next to her.

I don't like that she's sitting in the aisle seat, but the plane is big enough where we don't have to be sitting next to each other if we don't want to.

"Ale... has always gotten me anything and everything I've always wanted or needed. No matter what he had to do," she tells me as we watch everyone else climb onto the jet.

"You two had a crazy life to get to the point you are now, so I don't blame him." I tell her. My eyes fall right back to her.

Diego moves to sit on the opposite side of Skylar. I growl, before pulling up the arm rests between us and pulling her legs on top of mine. I hate that guy. I absolutely hate that guy.

Diego laughs. "Call your dog off, Skylar. I'm not doing anything."

"Woof," I say, earning a laugh out of Skylar.

I grin at her, that was the best reaction I could've gotten from her.

Celia and Leo sit in front of us, and I try my best to not groan. I say we don't have to sit all together. But of course they won't leave us alone.

"Di, want to sit over here with us?" Celia asks. Leo nods in agreement.

"Cee can sit in my lap," Leo offers.

"Nope," I say.

I grab Skylar, holding her to me as I stand up. We're going to go and sit on the couch, then. Or the bedroom. Anywhere but by stupid Diego.

"You really don't like Diego, huh?" Skylar asks me.

"Nope, I hate his guts." I roll my eyes. I'm not going to lie to her.

I decide to sit down on the couch, but I pull her legs into my lap again. If Diego comes closer to us again, the next step is the bedroom, and I don't care what Ale has to say about it.

Chapter Forty-Nine

BRAXTON

Diego keeps looking over at Skylar, and I swear I feel my blood boiling every single time he does it. Skylar looks up at me.

"Are you okay?" she asks.

"Yeah, of course. Do you want to go to the bedroom on the plane? It would be more comfortable," I ask before tilting my head to the side.

She looks at me for a second before nodding. I don't waste a second. I stand up and pick her up. Everyone seems lost in their own conversations, so we're able to go into the bedroom without anyone saying anything to us.

When we get there, I close the door and head to the bed. I already feel better being alone with her. We sit down on the mattress, and I sigh.

"Are you okay?" she asks me.

"I am now." I wink.

She smiles at me. "Do you want to watch a movie? Or talk?"

I lay back on the bed as she sits up beside me. I turn to look at her. "Maybe I can tell you about my dad.

Skylar stares at me like I've lost my mind. But I haven't. I know that I can trust her. I feel comfortable with her. She won't tell anyone.

"You want to tell me about your dad?"

I nod. "Yeah... I haven't seen him or my brother in a while. I don't have a relationship with any of my family, honestly," I trail off for a second before shaking my head. "He mostly favored my brother. I don't think he wanted to have another child. But obviously, I'm here."

"And you're amazing," she interrupts.

I chuckle. "Thanks Sunshine," I tell her. "My mom died shortly after I was born. I think that kind of set him off. Things got worse after that... He wouldn't buy food for me. He'd hurt me. He'd lock me in a room and leave for days..."

I close my eyes. My heart starts to ache as I speak this outloud. I know I'm safe to tell her all of this. I'm a grown adult. I know nothing is going to happen to me, but it still hurts having to put it all out there for someone to hear.

I feel her hand over my heart. I open my eyes to look at her. "You're okay..." She speaks softly to me. "You don't have to continue if you don't want to."

I shake my head. "It... it feels good to finally tell someone about my side of the story," I explain. "It's just... He always threatened that no matter where I went, no matter how far I traveled, when I was the most happy, he'd come and take it away from me. Just like I took his happiness away from him when my mom died."

"How did your mom die? If you don't mind me asking?" she asks in the sweetest way possible.

"My mom was taking me to the hospital. I was super sick, and she wanted to make sure I was okay," I breathe through my nose. "I don't remember much about how it happened. But one second I was in the back of the car. The next I was in the hospital getting told my mom died."

"That's not your fault," she tells me and shakes her head. "Your dad has no right to blame you for that."

I nod. "It took me a while... but I know that." I watch as Skylar lays down beside me.

"You're amazing in every way Ryder..." she tells me before cuddling right up next to me. "We'll take care of it together if your dad ever comes for you. You're a part of this family now, too."

I smile at her words. I've never been a part of a family before... It feels different... But I like it.

"Speaking of my dad, though... There's something that I did want to talk to you about," I blurt out.

We're already talking about that whole mess so why not bring everything up in the meantime?

"Yeah?" Skylar asks, rubbing her thumb over the top of my hand.

"The day of your event... right after I was done talking with you and went to my seat, my brother, Brody, stopped me and started talking with me." I swallow thickly.

It still feels weird to think about. I don't have to look over my shoulder twenty-four-seven.

"And what did he have to say?" Skylar asks before squeezing my hand gently.

"He said that they're going to leave me alone. That I won't have to worry about them anymore." I look into her pretty blue eyes that I want to spend the rest of my life staring into.

"You're joking..."

"No. I'm actually not. That's what I thought at first, too." I nearly laugh. "But no... He said that he has a kid now, and the kid's mother said that he needs to fix his life. Or she'll never let him around her kid."

"I mean, I don't blame her for making him do that,ut that's good, right? How are you feeling about it?" She asks.

I wrap my arms around her and pull her closer to me. "I don't know... It feels weird. It feels different. I'm so used to having to worry about my dad or brother coming for me. They always found me whenever I got comfortable and ruined it for me. But when I moved to Spain, I changed my last name. It seemed to work for a while..." I shake my head.

"You protected yourself. Now you don't have to anymore," she tells me and leans her head against my chest. "Do you think that they're going to come back around?"

"Brody seemed genuinely worried when he brought up never getting to be around his kid... So honestly? I have no idea... They haven't messaged, called, or shown up anywhere. So so far so good?"

"Well keep our eyes out." Skylar looks up at me. "I won't let anything happen to you."

I chuckle before kissing her forehead. "I think that's my line," I tease.

It feels like a weight has been lifted off my chest being able to tell her that. She's the only one I've ever felt comfortable with opening up to...

Chapter Fifty

SKYLAR

The plane ride was quick. We ended up staying in the bedroom for most of the ride. It was peaceful actually. We ended up just watching a movie and talking. We went out near the end and I could tell Ale wasn't happy.

Braxton was attentive to me, nothing more than that. It's what he's always done since I met him. It's the end of the day now. By the time we got to our house in Italy and got everything put away and settled, no one wanted to go out and do anything.

So, that's how we ended up here. Sitting around the campfire. I'm in the hammock chair. Leo had Braxton sit beside him and Celia, and Braxton just keeps looking at me.

I feel horrible. He looks so sad being away from me. I can't help but smile, and wave slightly at him. He pouts before waving back at me. Ale is sitting beside me with his girlfriend, Rosalynn. I guess that's who he's been spending most of his time with lately.

"Who wants to play truth or dare?" Celia asks.

"I'll play if I get to sit by Skye!" Braxton says, perking up at the thought.

I giggle. He's too cute.

"No," Ale says, shaking his head.

"Babe." Rosalynn rolls her eyes at him.

Everyone else agrees reluctantly. "Okay! Diego, do you want to go first?" Celia asks.

Braxton audibly groans, and I try my best to hide my laugh. I know exactly why Braxton hates him so much. It's something I didn't realize until now. He doesn't like anyone who comes near me. Well... any man, I should say.

"Of course. Braxton, truth or dare?" Diego asks. I keep my attention on Braxton.

"Truth," Braxton says without hesitation.

I give Diego a split second of my attention, just long enough to see his evil smirk.

"When's the last time you had sex? You've been pretty crabby towards me lately," Diego asks.

Braxton takes a second to think. "Uh..." He pauses again. "Do you want the exact date? Or just a roundabout?"

"Roundabout is fine," Diego says.

"Like, a couple of months. Give or take some days. I could figure out the exact date later," Braxton answers. "My turn to ask someone?"

A couple of months? Isn't that around the time we met?

"Yeah, it's your turn." Celia nods in response.

"You can't ask Skylar to come and sit by you," Ale says.

Braxton groans. "I hate you. Kidding, of course," he says with a wink. "Okay, Ale. Truth or dare?"

"Dare," Ale answers.

"I dare you to give me your blessing to be with Skylar," Braxton says. We all snap our attention to Ale.

"What do I have to do if I deny a dare?" Ale asks, looking at Celia.

"Take off a piece of clothing," Celia says with a giggle.

Ale nods, before pulling off his hoodie and giving it to Rosalynn. She holds it in her lap.

"Truth or dare, Celia?" Ale asks, and I regret not taking my kindle out here.

I wonder if Braxton would go get it for me.

"Uh... Let's go truth." Celia shrugs.

"Um," Ale thinks for a second. "When did you know Leo was the one for you?"

Celia grins. "After he gave me the best orgasm of my life, the first day I met him."

"You can say that again," Leo says before pulling Celia onto his lap. "That was the best decision of my entire life."

They're the cutest couple that I know.

"Skye? Truth or dare?" Celia asks me.

I shake my head. "Uh. Dare?" I offer, not knowing what to say.

"Oh, I like this version of Skye!" Leo grins, and I just know they have something cooking up between them.

"Pick someone's lap to sit in for the rest of the game," Celia tells me.

I nod, getting up out of my seat. I know who I'm going to. I wouldn't want to be anywhere else. I start walking over to him, but before I can even sit down, he's grabbing at me and yanking me into his lap.

I laugh as I fall into his lap perfectly. "Someone's impatient."

"When it comes to thinking about you sitting in another dude's lap? Yeah, I am," Braxton huffs, wrapping his arms tightly around me.

I smile. "I wouldn't have gone anywhere else," I promise him.

Ale looks like he's about to say something, but Rosalynn is quick to lean over and whisper something in his ear. I look at Braxton, but he doesn't say anything. He just shrugs in response.

"Okay... Leo, truth or dare?" I ask, leaning closer to Braxton.

He tightens his arms around me. I feel good at this moment. Safe. Protected. Nothing can happen to me here.

"Dare, my little niecey. Show me what you've got," Leo tells me, with all the confidence in the world.

I grin. "I dare you to have Celia go braless tomorrow."

Celia bursts out laughing.

"Over my actual dead body would I let any other person see

my wife's nipples through her shirt," Leo grumbles, slipping off his shoes and socks. "Good one, niecey. Good one."

Braxton's laughing at Leo's face. Leo can be such a sore loser.

The game continues on from there, but I don't pay any mind to it. I just hear Braxton's heartbeat, feel his warmth, smell his scent.

And before I know it, I feel my eyes closing against my will.

Chapter Fifty-One

BRAXTON

After Skylar fell asleep last night, I brought her to her bedroom and climbed into bed with her. Ale huffed, pouting that he wasn't the one taking care of Skye.

But Rosalynn quickly changed his mind. I think this is going to be good, not just for Ale, but Skylar, too.

Today we decided that we're picking up rental cars for those who don't have cars here. So, everyone besides Ale and Skylar.

Skylar shivers, rubbing her bar arms. "I didn't think it was going to be this cold out," she tells me, shifting closer to me.

I shrug off my jacket before slipping it around her. "The wind picked up pretty quick. Do you want to leave? I'll tell everyone that we'll meet them there."

Her little button nose is getting red. I wrap my arms around her.

"You want to ride with me?" she asks me like it's the most surprising thing to her.

"Of course I do. There's no one else I would rather be with," I promise her. She smiles at me.

"Should we see if anyone else wants to ride with us?" she asks.

I shake my head. "No, absolutely not. Diego is getting his own rental. Leo and Celia are riding with Ale and Rosalynn. Dipstick can drive by himself or ride with Ale," I tell her.

She cares so much about everyone else. I don't. I only care about her.

"Dipstick." Skylar laughs, shifting her weight from one foot to the next.

"Yeah. Dipstick," I repeat with a nod. "It's a play of his name."

Skylar giggles, shoving her hands in my pockets. "We could at least go sit in my car," she offers before turning and heading towards it. "I didn't think it was going to be this long."

"Yeah, getting rentals can sometimes take hours. I'm sorry. I should've told you." I frown, opening her door for her and getting in on the driver's side.

"Why are you sorry?" she asks. I turn on the car and crank the heat for her.

"Huh?" I tilt my head.

Did I say sorry?

"You said, 'I'm sorry I should've told you'. So, why are you sorry? Ale typically deals with the car stuff for me, so I just never knew," she explains to me.

I'm so happy that she has someone who would do absolutely anything for her like that. I can just see in the way Ale looks at her that she's his whole world.

"Now you have me, too. Car stuff is boring. But yeah, I didn't think about telling you that rental stuff, so that's why I said I was sorry," I tell her, I look over at her as she grabs my arm and bites it.

I laugh. "Did you just bite me?"

"Yeah." She grins brightly at me.

"Why?" I laugh again. She's the light of my life.

"I just thought about it, and I decided to do it." She shrugs at me.

I lean over and kiss her cheek. "I love it. Keep doing that," I tell her. "I like seeing how your brain works."

Suddenly, there was a knock on the door. I'm quick to push

the lock button so no one tries to get in. I roll the window down, and tilt my head at Diego.

"I was just coming to ask Skye if she wanted to ride with me." Diego says.

I shake my head. "No. If she leaves me, I'll be lonely. Then, who would stop me from punching you when you speak?" I ask, smirking at him.

Skylar snorts beside me, but is quick to try and cover it with a cough.

"I mean, I didn't ask you. I was asking Skylar," Diego sighs, and moves his head to look over at Skylar.

She smiles politely. "No thanks, Diego. I want to ride with Braxton. Because he's right. Who's going to stop him from punching you when you make him mad? Which is every time you look my way," she says with a wink.

I smirk. I feel like the dog who caught the bone. I rev her Durango, causing him to nod and walk away to his rental.

"That's my girl!" I tell her. "Thanks for telling him no."

"This is the only place I want to be," she tells me with so much love in her eyes that I feel my heart skip a beat. "And that's never going to change."

She doesn't know how much she means to me... I need to figure out how to tell her and show her how much I need her in my life.

Chapter Fifty-Two

SKYLAR

We went to the mall because the last time we went to the mall, it was just so amazing. This time, we have to pick out dresses and suits for the upcoming charity ball that the team throws every year. I'm fidgeting. I'm not sure what I'm going to pick out.

I thought we were all going as a group, but Celia has Leo. Ale has Rosalynn now. And I have Braxton, I think. Unless he has a date to go with. But he hasn't said anything about a date or anything.

"So, Skye, what color are you going to go with? Do you have a date?" Diego asks me, walking beside me.

I shake my head. When did he show up? Have I been ignoring him?

"Oh... I'm not sure what color. Probably a shade of purple, and no. I don't have a date. I just kind of thought we were going as a group again? That's what we've done the past few years." I shrug, I look around, trying to find Braxton.

He's talking to Ale and Leo. They're walking together in a small little group. That's weird... Ale goes from hating Braxton to loving him?

"I'm hungry," I randomly say out loud.

I haven't been listening to a single thing that Diego has been saying, and I feel awful about it.

"Okay, I'll take you to the food court, and we can meet up with everyone after?" he offers.

I shake my head. "Oh no, that's completely fine. I can wait. B's gonna take me after the fittings and stuff," I tell him. I didn't ask.

But I know if I asked him, he would drop everything for me.

"Are you and Braxton together?" Diego asks. "I don't want to keep flirting with you if you're taken. Celia and Leo said that you were single."

I laugh at his words. I knew that Diego flirting with me was something they set up.

"No. We're not dating. We're just friends... He's my best friend." I keep my eyes in front of me.

I don't feel comfortable with Diego yet... I don't really know why. I don't like how he's looking at me either. I wish I had my earbuds with me. This is starting to get to be too much.

Almost as if he sensed it, Braxton breaks away from the conversation and comes right over to me. He wraps his arm around my shoulder, pulling me into him.

"Are you doing okay?" Braxton asks, glaring at Diego. "Did he do something to you?"

Diego scoffs. "I would never hurt her."

"He didn't do anything to me. It's just starting to get to be... a little much," I try to explain.

But hearing it come out? It makes no sense. How am I supposed to tell him that the lights, the people walking around us talking, the squeaking of shoes, and all of the music coming out of stores is making my body feel like there's too much going on at once.

I'm so overstimulated right now, it's not funny, and I just don't want to be here. Even though I know I need to. I need to get fitted and pick something out for the party so I'm not stressed when it comes closer.

"Makes perfect sense," he tells me before digging into his pockets. "Want to listen to music with me? Or I downloaded some audiobooks for you if you would prefer that?" he asks, taking out his wireless earbuds.

We stop for a moment, but instead of him handing me one of the earbuds, he places it in my right ear, and then places the other one in his left. "I read that giving you something else to focus on helps with the overstimulation."

We start walking again. I can't believe he's been looking things up for me... He's trying to learn things to help with my ADHD?

"I don't know what I did to deserve you," I blurt out.

Braxton smiles, before pressing a kiss to my forehead. "You were born, sweetness. That's all it took," he tells me before pressing play on the album.

A soft instrumental plays, and I don't know if it's Braxton being near me or the music, but my body starts to calm down. I shift a little closer to him as we walk.

"Thank you... This helps a lot," I tell him.

It helps a lot more than I thought it would. I should probably start bringing my headphones everywhere.

"That's what I'm here for, beautiful. Do you want me to pick the color of your dress? Would that help take away some stress from you?" he asks me, making sure to keep me close so no one else can touch me.

"Yes, please. That would help a lot. I don't go to parties a lot... Let alone super fancy ones like this. I mean, I go every year to this one. But every year I worry about not picking out the right thing. Celia ends up picking it out. And Ale ends up getting mad because he thinks whatever Cee picks out is wildly inappropriate for me." I laugh at the thought. He always demands that I change.

It turns into a whole thing, but I always end up wearing whatever Celia picks out.

"You look amazing in whatever you pick out, beautiful. You could do no wrong. But I'll be happy to pick something out for you. It would be my pleasure." He winks down at me, and I smile before looking away to hide my blush.

Maybe I'll get lucky, and he won't bring a date to the party. He'll spend all of his time with me, and I won't have to worry about anything.

"Maybe after we're done with picking out everything, we can go get some pretzels? Maybe a strawberry milkshake? That sounds amazing." He groans at the thought.

"You and I think a lot alike. I was thinking the same thing, too." I smile up at him. We end up right behind everyone else again.

But no one turns back to look at us. It's like they didn't even notice we were gone in the first place.

"I guess you're rubbing off on me. Or I'm finally learning how to take care of you the way you deserve," he tells me, reluctantly letting my shoulder go.

I want to frown at the loss of his touch, but he's quick to grab my hand and intertwine our fingers together. He knows exactly what I need, even without me saying it.

I squeeze his hand, my silent way of telling him thank you.

He looks back at me, and winks. "I've got you," he mouths to me.

Chapter Fifty-Three

BRAXTON

As we walk through the store together, I don't let her hand go. I don't care how annoyed Ale looks right now. She doesn't want to be here, but I know she'll feel better if we get the outfit picked out today.

"Skye, want to come with me? We can go look at the dresses while the guys look for their suits," Celia offers. Skylar squeezes my hand gently.

"We'll go look together," I say, tilting my head at Skylar. "Sound like a good idea?"

Skylar smiles at me, and I want to kiss her. How is she so perfect?

"Why shouldn't we just let the girls go start looking while we pick out our stuff?" Ale grumbles. "You don't have to spend every single second with her."

I grin. I shouldn't get this much joy out of making him uncomfortable. "Because I'll happily get my suit from Spain at some place if I don't pick it out today. Besides, I'll be able to pick mine out super fast after we pick out Skye's."

Because I'm going to match hers. Whether that means I wear purple or not.

"Why are you acting like you're together, Vance? Unless you haven't been telling us something?" Diego asks.

Is it illegal to break someone's jaw? Because I want to do that right now. I move towards him.

"What? Are you jealous or something, Diego?" I ask him.

I hate everything about this guy.

"Jealous of what? Nothing? I could take Skylar away from you in an instant if I wanted," Diego presses.

I feel my body vibrate with anger at his words. "Take Skylar away from me?" I growl and ball my fist. "If we weren't in public, I would've broken that jaw of yours already."

"Come on already and do it. You talk all this game, but you never ever act on it," Diego taunts me.

I can tell he wants to get a rise out of me. That's all he wants. But if that means I get to finally punch him in the face, I might just give it to him.

I feel Skylar's hand creep up the back of my shirt, and I stop. I'm not going to fight someone in front of her. I don't have to explain myself to him.

"He knows I get nervous in different environments like this. So he's just trying to be helpful. You don't have to be so rude to him." Skylar almost glares at Diego, holding onto my arm now.

It's like my body knows she's the one I've always needed to calm me down.

I grin. Everyone is staring at Skylar like she's grown two heads. "That's my girl," I tell her, putting my arm around her shoulder.

I lead us towards where the ball gowns are. "You're perfect. That was amazing. Thank you."

Skylar bumps her hip up against mine. "I was getting a bit tired of hearing him complain and almost whine to you. I don't want to spend time with him. I just want to spend time with you."

The way she's looking at me while she says it, I swallow thickly. I need to make her mine before I lose her to someone else.

"Oh, Sunshine, you don't know how much that means to me.

I feel the same way. I only came on this vacation to be with you," I tell her before winking. She blushes almost immediately.

We start walking through the random dresses that they have out. I want to see her in red again... I need that in my life.

"Your whole outfit is my choice?" I ask her, peeking down at her for a second.

The rest of the group wandered off by themselves, finally giving us more alone time.

"Whatever you want," she tells me with a confident nod.

Perfect. This will be incredible.

My eyes land on the perfect dress. I know she'll look amazing. I could even send a picture of it to my stylist in Spain if I wanted to.

Chapter Fifty-Four

SKYLAR

It doesn't take long for Braxton to find what he calls the most perfect dress for me. It looks like it's going to be my size, so I grab Cee so she can help me tie the dress in the back. I'm looking in the mirror in the dressing room.

The ruby-red formal dress is stunning. It goes all the way to the floor, but has a pretty high slit up my one leg. There's sequins on the corset, but the rest of it's plain.

I'll need to get a bag to hold my inhaler and phone. But it's gorgeous.

"Are you going to come out?" Celia asks before knocking on the door. "I want to see you!"

I laugh before opening up the door, and she stumbles backwards. "My goodness, Skylar. Look at you. You're beautiful. I mean you always are, but wow. This? This is a whole other level."

I bite my bottom lip. I nervously brush my hair behind my ear. "Do you think he'll like it?" I ask, because that's what I care about.

I want Braxton to love it... I want him to tell me how beautiful he thinks I am.

"If he doesn't love it, I'll take him to the eye doctor because there would obviously be something wrong with his vision," Celia says with a laugh.

I hear a cup drop to the ground, and I turn to look at Braxton. "Wow...," he breathes out. His eyes drag over my body slowly.

I'm still barefoot. He was supposed to be looking at shoes for me, so I nervously rub my bare foot against the cool ground.

"You're... Wow," he says, unable to complete his thought. "Wow. Doesn't she look... Wow..."

Celia looks over at Braxton. "It looks like he might need your inhaler because I don't think he's breathing," Celia teases.

"She just looks... Wow," Braxton says again as his eyes go from my bare feet all the way to the top of my head.

Slowly. Almost like he wants to memorize every single inch of me.

I giggle before heading over to him. "Want to try and finish a sentence for me?" I tease him.

He chuckles. It's that deep throaty chuckle that I love so much. "You just look so stunning that I couldn't think properly. I still can't. You're... you're just... wow... You're the most beautiful woman I've ever laid eyes on." He drops to his knees. I didn't even notice the shoes he has in his hand.

I lift one foot at a time, so he can slip the heel on my foot and buckle it for me. "How did you know my shoe size?"

"I know more about you than you think, sweetness." He winks at me, before he stands up again. "You look amazing... What do you think, Cee?"

"I think that my opinion here doesn't matter." Celia grins. "I think she wants you to tell her how amazing she looks."

I blush at her honesty... I probably should've been the one that told him that. But in my defense, I already thought he knew.

"You are the most stunning woman I've ever laid eyes on. How do you feel in the dress? We can pick something else out. I know it's more seductive than what you usually wear," he explains, looking down at my body again. "We could even get a little diamond thing to go around your thigh."

"Careful there, Brax. You might turn yourself on," Celia teases, and I laugh.

"Jokes on you, Cee. It doesn't take much for Skye to turn me on," he shoots back, and I don't know what to say.

"I didn't know I turn you on," I say, tilting my head at him.

Braxton smiles, before placing a kiss on my forehead. "You do. Of course you do." He spins me around, before dipping me. His face is close enough where I can't look anywhere but into his gorgeous, green eyes. "You are what I call the favorite parts of my days. The first and last thought I have. You are what I look forward to seeing," he almost whispers to me as he slowly raises me back to my feet.

I'm flustered. I don't know how to respond to him. Well, I do know how to respond to him.

But I don't know how to say it.

I want him to know that he's my favorite, too... That he hasn't left my mind since the day I saw him. I don't know what I would do without him. He's the calm to my chaos. He's one of the only people I know that will keep me on track; who sees me for more than what everyone else does.

"What do you say we change out of that and go pick out the accessories? And then head out of here? I think I heard the guys talking about wanting to stop by somewhere for dinner before they head out to the bar," Braxton tells me, and I nod.

Celia is grinning wildly at us. "Gosh. I can't wait for you two to finally make this thing that's been going on official. You two are like a match made in heaven."

I giggle, turning to look back at Braxton. "Well, I'm just waiting for this one to get his head out of his butt and realize how much he's hopelessly in love with me." I flip my hair with a wink at him before I head back into the dressing room.

Braxton starts laughing, and then I hear him start talking to Celia.

"I'm going to marry that girl one day... I really am," he says, and I swear I feel my heart stop for a second.

He wants to marry me?

He actually wants to marry me?

Chapter Fifty-Five

BRAXTON

After we finished up at the store, I paid for both me and Skylar's stuff. Skylar tried to tell me that she could pay for it, but I refused. She doesn't have to pay for anything while I'm around.

Ale nearly had a heart attack after I told him I paid for her stuff. He would've had a fight on his hands if he was up at the register with us and tried to pay for it himself.

Skylar takes a sip of the milkshake that we got to share. "I would've bought the milkshake. You already spent so much money on me today."

I shake my head before parking in the garage at the house. "I would give you anything you asked for, no matter what it was. Also, sweetness." I look over at her, making sure she's focusing on me. "I'm paying for you to get your nails done before the ball, gala, whatever it is, too." Skylar goes to open her mouth, but I'm quick to press a finger under her chin and shut it. "Nope. No arguing with me about this. I want to take care of you. Just let me take care of you, please?"

Skylar swallows, but nods anyway.

"Good girl. Want to go inside?"

She nods again, and I smile.

I get out of the car before opening her door for her. "I like that everything you own is purple. It's cute. It makes it easy knowing what belongs to you."

Skylar laughs before leading me into the house. "Yeah... that's with everything. River's stuff. My stuff. It's been that way ever since I can remember. Are you going to go to the bar with them?" she asks me.

I shake my head. "Nah, I want to stay here with you. We can watch *Lady and The Tramp* or something," I offer. I walk right behind her as we head into the living room. "Going out to the bar seriously sounds awful."

"Are you sure? I don't want you to miss out on anything," she explains, sitting on the love seat.

I sit right beside her before pulling her legs on top of mine. "But hear me out here. What if I go, right? And I miss out on all the fun we would have here. I would be so sad. I would also miss you. Who would keep me from knocking the dipstick out?" I wonder out loud.

She laughs and smiles at me. "Well... you have such an excellent point. We wouldn't want you getting arrested, would we?" she asks me, and I nod quickly.

"I wouldn't make it in jail, at all. I wouldn't be able to be with you all day, and I would end up getting life." I groan at the thought. She lays down before I lay down on top of her. "That sounds like torture."

Skylar laughs, before running a hand through my hair. "It really does. I don't know what I would do without you."

I smile at her words, watching as everyone is getting ready to leave.

"Are you coming out with us, Vance?" Diego asks.

"No, I'm staying with Skye," I tell him.

"You don't want to go out?" Leo asks, confusion written all over his face.

"No, I don't want to go out. I want to stay here, right here, with Skylar. We're going to watch a movie," I tell him, making sure I leave no room for discussion.

There's so many reasons why I don't want to go; why I'm staying here with Skylar. One, I just don't want random women hitting on me. I don't want any part of that. Two, Skylar hates being alone. Especially in Italy. She gets worried. Three, Skylar hates going out.

This isn't the first time I've said no to going out. It's not going to be the last either. I would pick Skylar each and every single time with no hesitation.

Chapter Fifty-Six

SKYLAR

The next morning, I hear commotion around me. I blink a few times, before I feel hands grab at me. "I'm just taking her to put her in her bed," Ale whispers to someone.

I don't know who.

Braxton groans underneath me before he tightens his hold on me and pulls me back into him. "Mine," he growls, shoving his face in my hair. "Don't touch. Mine."

"She's not yours," Ale tells him. I don't know if he knows that I'm awake or not.

"Mine," he says again.

I don't think he's fully awake.

"My Sunshine. My girl. My wife. Mine," he repeats.

I giggle as I'm crushed against Braxton. "Shh... We're sleeping. Ale doesn't need to know that we're awake," he tells me, and I can't help the snort that slips free.

Ale is probably boiling angry right now, and I can just imagine his face. It's not like we're doing anything bad. We're just sleeping.

Braxton groans dramatically. "You really couldn't have given us five more minutes?" he whines, before taking the pillow and throwing it at Ale's head.

"No. You're lucky that I let you sleep with her anyway," Ale huffs.

"Newsflash," Braxton says, "I sleep with her every night."

I laugh. "Okay, okay, okay... Let's not start this now, okay?"

"Every night?" Ale asks me.

"Yup," I answer with a grin.

"I need a shot. Vodka. Whiskey. I don't care what. I have too much of a headache to deal with this right now." Ale rubs his temple and walks away.

"Had to tell him every night?" I ask Braxton.

He smiles at me.

"I have to stake my claim somehow, right?" he asks, "Besides, I don't know how he hasn't figured it out yet." He glares playfully when I sit up away from him. "I was comfortable."

"Well, it's a good thing that I'll need you to sleep tonight, huh?" I ask, causing him to hug me after he sits up as well.

"You are the best part of my days. I want you to know that," he tells me, with a kiss on my forehead.

"And you are the best part of my days and my nights," I repeat to him.

His cheeks turn pink at the compliment, and I just want to take a picture. I want to remember this moment forever. Before Braxton says anything to me, we hear a loud engine outside.

"Who's that?" I ask, getting up to go check.

Braxton grabs my hand and quickly pulls me behind him. "Absolutely not. What if it's someone that wants to hurt you? Or break into the house?" he questions.

I nod. "I didn't think about it. I'm sorry," I tell him.

Braxton walks into the garage and sees everyone standing there. "Who's here?" Braxton speaks up, causing everyone to look over at him.

I peek around Braxton to see who it is, and what that loud engine is from.

"It's just me, Vance. Did you miss me?" Diego sing-songs, before getting off of his motorcycle.

I don't know anything about motorcycles, but this one is black.

"Nope. I didn't even realize you were gone. You rented a motorcycle for the trip?" Braxton asks. I step away from his back since we know it's okay.

"Nope. I bought it." Diego slaps the seat before putting his helmet on it.

Braxton and I walk up to the group. Leo and Ale move so we can get through.

"He's going to get it shipped home before we leave. Are you going to take a ride, Brax?" Leo asks, and I'm worried he's going to say yes.

Motorcycles are dangerous. He could die if he gets into an accident. Or at the very least, get extremely hurt. I don't want him to say yes.

"I'm not going to, that's for sure. Motorcycles are death traps. If any of you ask my sister to get on there, I might actually kill you. Bury you in the backyard so no one finds you," Ale tells everyone.

I smile. "I would've said no anyway. I don't want to get hurt." I rub my elbow, before Braxton takes my hand.

I honestly don't know what I would do without him.

"Come on, Vance. Want to take a spin? Or are you chicken?" Diego taunts him.

I look up at Braxton and wonder if he's going to actually take the helmet and get on. He's been quiet for too long, and I want to answer for him.

"No. No, he's not," I say. Everyone turns to look at me.

"I'm pretty sure he can answer for himself, Skylar," Diego tells me, and I feel Braxton stiffen next to me.

"She can answer for me if she wants," he practically growls at him. "But..."

I let go of his hand, and shake my head. If he wants to kill himself on that bike, I can't stop him. My hands start to shake, and I feel like my chest is closing in on itself. I don't want him to die, or get hurt. I don't know what I would do with myself if he did.

I head to go back inside, not wanting any further part of this.

"Sunshineeeee," Braxton calls out after me, but I don't stop. "Baby girl, please." He runs after me. I hear his footsteps behind me.

I'm in the kitchen by the time he grabs my arm and spins me to him. He crushes me to his chest, and I force myself to inhale. I smell his cologne, inhaling the deep smell of vanilla.

"I'm not going on that death trap. You said no, so that means no. I would never do anything to make you upset," Braxton tells me, gently running a hand through my hair.

I wrap my arms tightly around him. "I don't want you to get hurt... I don't want you to die. I need you to be okay." I sniffle, refusing to let him go.

Braxton picks me up, wrapping my legs around his waist. "I'm not going to die. I'm not going to get hurt. I mean... I might get hurt on the field, but you knew what I meant. I'm not getting on that motorcycle. I promise you. I give you my word that I will never get on that thing, or any motorcycle," he promises me, only pulling me away enough to look me in the face. "Do you believe me?" he asks, and I nod. "Be good for me and use your words."

"Yes. I believe you. I'm sorry for panicking..." I trail off, not wanting to finish that thought. Braxton leans down and bites my arms. I look at him. "What was that for?"

"You taste delicious, first off. But I don't like it when you apologize for something that is completely out of your control," Braxton tells me.

There's a slight glare, and I can't help but smile. He's trying to be so serious right now, and he's so adorable. Braxton grins at me before wiping my tears.

"There's my girl. Are you feeling better?" he asks me.

"Yeah," I say, before laying my head back on his chest. "I just want to lay here with you for a little. Is that okay?"

He wraps his arms tighter around me, making sure I only feel his strength. "Anything you want, Sunshine. No matter what I have to do."

Chapter Fifty-Seven

BRAXTON

The night of the charity event rolls around, and I'm anxious. It was decided that the girls would get ready together. While the guys got ready and went to see if they needed any help setting up the charity event. I hate this. I don't like not being near Skylar.

It's supposed to start any minute, and they're not here yet. I keep checking my phone but neither one of them has messaged me. They have a driver, so either one of them could.

"Dude," Leo says, like I'm annoying him.

"What?" I snap at him.

I'm not in the mood to deal with his crap. Leo laughs like I just said the funniest thing.

"Skylar really keeps that awful mood of yours away." Leo taunts me.

"I'm done for. I really am," I tell him with a shake of my head. "It's like just being around her makes me happy."

Leo smirks. "That's what happens when you are in love with someone."

I could punch him. I really could. No one would even bat a single eye at me punching him. My phone buzzes. I'm quick to look at it.

Sunshine: I'm here. <3 We're waiting in line. So if you want to come out to meet us I think Celia is texting Leo too. Or you can tell him if you're near him. I have a small surprise for you. I think you'll love it.

Braxton: :) A surprise? Yay! I always love what you're wearing. No matter what it is. As long as you're happy that's all I want. I miss you Sunshine :(Leo's being mean to me

Sunshine: What's he doing?

Braxton: Teasing me about you. Can I punch him?

Sunshine: No. Don't punch him. Come out to the car to get me

Braxton: Your wish is my command

I pocket my phone and follow Leo outside where the red carpet is. The lights from the cameras keep flashing almost nonstop. If I could change one thing, it would be that. The flashes give me a raging headache.

I walk out of the building and down the red carpet just as their Escalade pulls up. It's a red one, so I knew that it was them. When the car stops, I open the door, and Celia gets out first. She's in a pink, skin tight dress. I don't know much more than that because Skylar steps out next.

I thought she looked amazing the first time I saw her in it. No. This? This blows it completely out of the water. Her hair is down with the slightest curl towards the end. Her lips are a deep red. It's taking everything in me not to grab her and kiss her. She's breathtaking.

"Wow..." I breathe out, stuck staring at how beautiful Skylar is.

Her bright blue eyes look up to mine, and she smiles. "I'm glad you like it Ryder..."

"I love everything about you," I say honestly.

Even if she wasn't wearing blush, her cheeks would be pink now. She links her arm with mine so we can walk into the event. I smile down at her. I'm glad I'm here with her. There's no place I'd rather be.

Reporters are shouting out question after question. But I don't stop until we're in the building and in our group of friends. We'll make an announcement together when we're ready. Everyone seems to be paired off beside Diego. Skylar and I are matching. Leo and Celia are matching. Ale and his girlfriend.

Diego keeps looking at Skylar, and I might punch him. I growl before wrapping my arms around Skylar. "I will lick her. I will. Don't even try me. Mine," I snap at him. Everyone turns to look at me. "What? I don't like him. I don't like him staring at her," I huff. Skylar just wiggles further into me. "What's the saying?" I ask Skylar. "If I lick it, it's mine?"

Skylar laughs. "I have makeup on. I don't think you'll like the taste of that. But I have something else that will give you a mark," she tells me before turning around in my arms.

Skylar takes a step away from me. "It's right here," she motions to the slit up her thigh, and I finally see it.

It's a chain wrapped around her thigh with red diamonds spelling out the word Braxton. My head spins. I'm going to pass out. I'm staring at her perfectly tan, muscular thigh with my name plastered across it.

"Do you like it?" Skylar's soft voice finally filters into my mind.

"Do I like it?" I repeat her words. "Sunshine. I LOVE IT!"

I wrap my arms around her and spin her. "That's the best surprise you've ever given me. Thank you. Thank you. Thank you. Thank you," I repeat the words over and over again.

"I was a little worried it wasn't going to get here in time. But I just wanted you to see that you're the only person I want to be with," Skylar tells me with a shy smile.

I kiss her forehead again. "You are my entire world. Nothing will ever change that." I can't explain to her in words how much she means to me.

"I have one more surprise for you after the event back at the house. Maybe we can leave early?"

I chuckle. "You don't have to tell me twice." I intertwine our fingers together and lead her into the ball room. "Just tell me before you want to leave, and I'll come up with an excuse."

"You will?" she asks.

"I would do anything for you. But yes. Of course. It'll be super easy. Everyone knows that I hate these things, so I'll just say I'm done for the day, and no one will even try to argue with me. If they try, I'll threaten to punch Diego. That always works," I tell her honestly.

She laughs. "What will it take for you to like Diego?" She giggles.

"Nothing. I'm always going to hate him being around you. Maybe if he ever gets married. Maybe I will hate him a little less. But ever fully not hating him?" I think about it for a second. "Never. I'll always hate him."

Skylar smiles and pulls me closer to her. "I'm yours. Till the end of time. I promise you," she tells me.

My heart skips a beat, and I smile at her. "That's the promise that I want to hear," I tell her before leaning down.

I want to kiss her. I want to feel her lips against mine. I want to show her that I love her more than life itself. But right before I can kiss her, Dipstick Diego comes right up.

"Where's the drinks guys!? I'm THIRSTY!" Diego smacks me on the back.

I groan. "This is exactly why I hate him," I explain to Skylar.

She just shakes her head. "I think he might just be lonely," Skylar tells me. "He doesn't have a girlfriend."

Diego gasps, but I can't tell if he's truly hurt or just being dramatic."That's my girl!" I laugh and wrap my arm around Skylar again. "Starting to tease back. I'm here for it."

Chapter Fifty-Eight

SKYLAR

We've been dancing and talking with friends for hours. We're just finally sitting down when Braxton groans dramatically beside me.

"Can we leave yet?" he asks before laying his head on my shoulder.

I smile and look at him. "Don't you want to eat before we go?" I ask. "I didn't bring a car."

"No. I'll just pick us up food on the way home," Braxton tells me. "I brought my car."

"You mean your lavender colored Range Rover." Diego snickers at the mention.

"No. My lavender colored Range Rover that smells like Skylar. And that's something you will never get to experience. But I do mean Skylar's purple Durango. Because I can drive a car that's purple," Braxton shoots back with a grin.

"Are you guys leaving already?" Rosalynn asks as she and Ale walk up to the table.

"Yeah, probably. I think we've talked to enough people," I tell her with a soft smile.

"Want me to order you something for dinner at home? I have

to be here for a while longer, or else I'd leave with you," Ale explains.

Braxton shakes his head and gets up from his seat. "Nah, I've got it. We're going to get something on the way home," he adds. "I've got it all taken care of." Braxton pulls out my chair for me, and I stand up.

I make sure to give Ale a hug, and he squeezes me tight. "I love you so much," he tells me.

"I love you so much," I repeat to him. "Have fun talking with all the big wigs here."

Ale rolls his eyes. "I hate having to do this." He shakes his head. "But goodnight. I'll see you in the morning."

Braxton is eager to wrap his arm around my waist as soon as Ale lets me go. He holds me tight and leads me through the ballroom back towards the exit.

"I was so bored there," Braxton says to me. "But you look so beautiful. I'm happy that we came tonight."

"I'm happy we came tonight, too. It was a lot of fun," I tell him with a smile. "What are we going to have for dinner?"

"I already placed an order from The Secret Garden. It should be delivered by time we get home," Braxton tells me before opening my door for me.

I laugh. So he's been wanting to leave for a while but just didn't tell me. I thought he was going to make a scene.

His car smells like the perfect mix of our scents. I like it. When he gets in, he leans over to kiss my cheek. "Thank you..."

"What for?" I ask, tilting my head slightly as he turns on the car to leave.

Braxton backs out of the spot before pulling away. "For being the only person in the entire world that cares about me."

It hurts my soul that he's been so alone. But I'm glad that I can be here for him now. I won't let him be alone again.

"You're welcome!" I tell him with a grin. "It's my great joy being the only person in the entire world that cares about you."

Braxton chuckles but doesn't say anything else as he drives out of the city.

⁂

AFTER OUR SHORT drive back to my place, Braxton pulls up my driveway. "OH!" I randomly shout.

Braxton looks over to me. "What?" he asks.

"Your surprise. It's over here!" I get out of the car quickly, and Braxton follows right after me.

"You're not supposed to open your own doors," Braxton complains.

I laugh. "That's not important right now!" I tell him before going to stand in front of the garage door. "Stand right here and close your eyes!"

It took me the longest time to find this car. But I finally found the Mclaren Speedtail in the perfect shade of red. I'm nervous. I hope he loves it.

Braxton stands in the spot I showed him. "Perfect," I tell him before reaching into my purse and grabbing my phone. I quickly find the app and click open on the garage door I want. The garage door opens behind me, and I turn to look to make sure the light is on.

The car looks perfect. The only thing it's missing is the bow.

My heels click against the blacktop as I move to stand beside him.

"When can I open, Sunshine?" Braxton asks me.

I look at him. He's perfect... And gorgeous... And wonderful... I like it when he's dressed in a suit.

"Gorgeous, you can stare all you want at me. But when can I open my eyes?"

I blush. I can't help but stare. He's stunning.

"I can't help but stare," I huff. "But you can open your eyes."

Braxton opens his emerald green eyes and his mouth drops

open. "You did not," he says before looking between me and the car.

I smile and nod. "I definitely did! Do you love it?"

"Sunshine..." He's so in awe of the Mclaren in front of him.

The car sits beneath the bright LED lights of the garage. The bright red almost gleams like hot metal as it stretches long and low across the floor. Even though it's just sitting there, it looks like it's ready to speed out of here.

I don't know much about sports cars, but Leo said that this was one of the top rated ones to get.

"This is my dream car... In my dream color... You found it?" He's walking slowly around the car like he's too scared to even touch it.

"I did... I did just for you," I tell him softly.

Getting to see him be so in love with it is worth all the time I put into finding the car.

Braxton looks up at me, his eyes watering. He walks over to me and wraps his arms tightly around me before shoving his face in my hair. "Thank you..." he mumbles. "Thank you... This is the best present I've ever been given."

I smile and hug him as tight as I can. "You're welcome... I'm so happy that you love it."

"Love it? Are you kidding? This is perfect!" he says excitedly. "This is my biggest dream come true. Besides meeting you, of course."

"Do you want to give it a spin?" I ask.

He's practically bouncing in place. "No. We need to eat dinner," he tells me.

I shake my head. "Drive your pretty new car first," I tell him and walk over to the passenger side. "It'll get me out of these heels."

Braxton opens the door for me and sighs. "This is so beautiful..." he says when he looks inside. "I'm so excited."

I smile at the look on his face. This is what he deserves.

After we get into the car, Braxton reaches over for my legs. I tilt my head before he slowly unbuckles my heels. "I know they're uncomfortable... But I couldn't stop staring at you the entire night. You're beautiful... The most breathtaking woman I've ever laid eyes on."

"You are the perfect match for me," I tell him with a smile. "I couldn't and still can't believe that you went to the gala with me... I had the hottest man in the room."

Braxton kisses the top of my right foot and then my left. "You will always have the hottest man in the room. I promise you that."

He starts the car and groans at the sound of the engine. Without wasting another second, he speeds out of the garage.

Chapter Fifty-Nine

BRAXTON

Two weeks... It's been two weeks since we came to Italy. Ale has started to calm down with me being near Skylar. She's been more open to holding my hand and being really affectionate in front of everyone. Diego has stopped coming near her, so I take that as a win.

I never knew how heavy the thought of my dad coming for me randomly was. It feels like my past is finally where it belongs. It feels like I can finally move on with my life with Skylar, now that I know that she's going to be safe being with me.

I sip some of my water, as I listen to everyone else around me talk. It's weird. I'm so used to having Skylar here with me that I feel awkward when she's not.

But she had to take an urgent call about River, and I'm just out here waiting for her. I shift my legs, making my seat swing.

"What are you so antsy for?" Diego asks me, causing me to turn and look at him.

"I'm not antsy. I'm bored. There's a difference," I tell him with a shrug.

Maybe I am antsy. I don't like not being with her... I crave her being around me. Not in a sexual way like I'm used to, but just her presence. Her presence makes me feel at home.

"Because Skye's on the phone?" Diego keeps at it. It's like he gets a thrill out of annoying me.

Yes.

"No." I glare at him.

"You're a liar." He laughs. "So when are you going to ask her to be your girlfriend officially?"

I turn to look at him. I could answer him. But at the same time, it's really none of his business. She's mine... She knows it. I know it. Everyone else knows it. It doesn't matter. But I know deep down...

I'm not going to stop until I make her mine. What I told Cee the other week is true. I'm going to marry her. When I think about my future, I think about being with her. I think about the family we'll have. The children...

I swallow hard. The children. I never thought I'd ever have that. I never thought I was good enough for that...

"I'm in no rush. She's mine. Everyone knows that." I turn to look at him. "If you think about asking her out, I swear."

Diego shakes his head. "Nope. Not gonna do that. I don't need you to actually kill me. I was just curious. She looks at you like you've hung the moon, and you look at her like nothing else will ever matter to you. You need to ask her out; make her yours officially. Or someone else might come up and steal her from you."

I nod. "I'd kill someone before they do that," I tell him.

He laughs like I'm joking. Just so he continues to think I'm joking, I laugh along with him.

But when I hear the back door open and Skylar walk out as she's wiping her eyes, I'm up and jogging to her before she can even make it out to the group.

Once I get to her, I wrap my arms tightly around her. "What's going on, Sunshine?" I ask, refusing to let her go even when everyone else walks up to us.

"River got injured. Badly. I don't think she'll be able to race again," She sniffles, clinging to me like her life depends on it.

My heart stutters, but I close my eyes. *Not now. Not now. It's about Skylar right now.*

"What happened?" Ale asks, frowning at her.

This must be killing him.

Skylar shakes her head. "They don't know. Honestly anything could have happened in the pasture. But they noticed that she was barely putting any weight on her one leg, so they called the vet out and had her get examined. The vet believes that it's a superficial digital flexor tendon injury," she babbles out. I feel her body shaking in mine.

"Didn't Braxton just buy you a new horse?" Celia asks. Ale snaps his head in my direction.

I don't know if that's going to help right now.

"Yeah, Midnight. He has training," I explain, looking down at Skylar. "He's not as trained as River is, but at least some. We're heading back home tomorrow, so you can immediately start working on your routine with him instead. There's nothing you can do about it today, unless you want to go home today."

"No, we're all heading home tomorrow morning. That way, she can sleep, and then get a fresh start tomorrow," Ale tells us all, raising his voice so that people know there's no room for discussion.

Skylar isn't saying anything. I know she won't. She'll do whatever Ale says.

"If she wants to go home tonight, we're going home tonight. If you don't want your sister on a regular plane, I'll rent a private plane tonight," I tell him.

I don't let Skylar go. I'll fight Ale on this. I don't care. Ale's quiet for a moment as he just stares at me. I don't break eye contact. I'm serious when it comes to Skylar.

"I think staying is better. I want to be there with River, but I know she's getting taken care of. She'll be back at the stable by time we get home tomorrow. She's at the vet right now," she explains before rubbing the bridge of her nose.

I rub her back before leading her to the fire in the living room.

I think she needs to take a minute to just breathe.. I take her to the couch before sitting her down and sitting right next to her.

"Okay. We can handle all of that tomorrow. Or at least most of it tomorrow before and after practice," I tell her. She nods.

"I'll make some phone calls tonight so it will be easier on you tomorrow, Skye," Ale tells her.

Skylar just stares at the fire, lost in thought. "Everything is going to be just fine," I try to tell her.

"I know... I just. I don't know. I just have worked so hard to get to where I am now. I wanted to be the youngest gold medalist." She frowns slightly. I wrap my arm around her shoulder and pull her into me.

"Nothing is stopping you from doing that still. We have time to practice and get you ready to show again. You still have time to get ready for the Olympics," I promise her.

I'll do whatever it takes to get her on track to getting her medal. She's so talented. She deserves for all of her dreams to come true.

Chapter Sixty

SKYLAR

The next day goes too fast. We got home. Braxton immediately drove me to my stable. My car was already waiting for me there. I knew the vet was going to be on her way over to talk with me about our options, so I told Braxton to head back home and drop our luggage off.

River did injure her tendon... A strained superficial digital flexor tendon. It's going to end her show career.

I rub my temple as I sit at a red light. Driving in town is awful. The lights take forever to turn. Everything is going to be fine. I'll start training with Midnight and make sure we're prepared. If I don't win this year, there's always next.

I made sure to text Braxton when I was on my way to pick him up. So, I'm sure he's waiting at the stadium for me. He never keeps me waiting. He's always early for me.

I can see the stadium from where I am. He seems so close, but so far away.

I feel my mind spinning. Is he going to keep doing this for a while? Him being protective of me? Possessive? Not wanting anyone else to even step near me? But not officially dating me? I want everyone to know that he's mine. I want to be able to go out with him and hold his hand without worrying about the paparazzi posting some sort of lie about us.

But it's not a lie. It's not. We're practically together, just not officially. And with the charity event coming up, where we're all going together, I just want him to ask me to go with him.

Or maybe I could just ask him... Get the stress out of the way and ask him to be mine...

Chapter Sixty-One

BRAXTON

I rub my palms against my jeans, I know it's only been a couple of hours since I got to see Skylar, but it feels like it's been too long. Time feels slow right now. I see her Range Rover at the light that's outside of the stadium parking lot.

I could run to her. I'd probably beat the light, and then I'd finally be with her again.

"You're practically vibrating," Diego tells me.

I groan. "I miss my girl." I glare at him. "So, yes, I see her car. Yes, I'm excited to see her again. You can just leave me alone."

Diego laughs, tossing his keys in the air before catching them. "You are so in love with her."

I'm quiet... I don't think that needs a response, does it? I know I'm in love with her.

I've never been in love with anyone... I've never had someone love me either. Skylar's the first person to ever put me first. She's the only one who has ever cared enough about me to make sure I'm okay.

I look up to see if her car moves, and I'm thankful it is. I need her to make my brain stop. I need her to calm me down. I just need her to be with me.

I feel like time slows down. My heart stops as I watch a truck speed across the intersection and ram into Skylar's car. I take off running, running like my life depends on it because... in some ways... it does.

That's my life right there, and I need to make sure she's okay.

Chapter Sixty-Two

SKYLAR

My vision spins. I hold tightly to the steering wheel as my car spins in a complete circle. I need to get out of here... I struggle to find the door handle. When I do, I pull on it, and my door swings open. I try to get out, but my seat belt stops me.

Tears stream down my face. I just want out of this car. I need to get out of this car. My hands are shaking. I feel trapped.

"Skylar!?" Braxton's yelling my name.

I try harder to get the seat belt undone.

"Skylar!" Braxton yells. "Get your hands off me! That's my wife! That's my wife in that car, and I need to make sure she's okay!"

"Ryder," I cry out. I just want him to hold me.

I want him to tell me that everything's going to be okay. Before I have the chance to try and unbuckle the seat belt again, Braxton is there. He's quick to click the button and pull me into his arms. He's touching me everywhere.

"Are you okay? What hurts? Are you okay?" He spits out question after question. "The ambulance is on its way. I think I hear it coming."

I cling to his arms. "Don't let me go... please," I cry, hiding my face in his chest.

The lights and the sounds are killing my head.

"Sunshine... You're bleeding," Braxton tells me, but I don't want to move.

He leans down, just enough to pick me up in his arms and carry me. "I'm not going to put you down," he promises me, and I just nod to him. "I don't know what happened. I was at the stadium over there waiting for her when I saw what happened. I'm assuming the light turned to a green arrow, so she was turning when the other car came speeding across and hit her," Braxton's talking to who I assume is the paramedics, but all I can hear is his strong heartbeat.

His warmth.

His arms...

My eyes start to close, and I slip into the darkness.

Chapter Sixty-Three

BRAXTON

I sit beside Skylar just watching her chest rise and fall. I can't move. When they come in here to check on her, I don't move. I need to be right here. She hates hospitals. She hates doctors. She would be so upset if I left her alone here.

Her forehead didn't need stitches, just a bandaid. She looks so peaceful. My knee is bouncing. My heart aches. I'm not going to feel okay until I see her blue eyes.

Her beautiful, blue eyes.

I look down at her hand at the diamond ring I placed on her ring finger so they would think we were actually married. Who would do this to her? I didn't see anyone in the other truck. It was completely empty.

I flinch when I feel someone grab my shoulder. "Brax, go home. I'll stay with her," Celia whispers to me.

I shake my head. "No. Absolutely not. I'm not leaving her. She doesn't like being alone. I can't leave her. Don't make me leave her, Cee." I shake my head again, before climbing into bed with her.

I'm careful. I don't want to hurt her. I'm not sure how much pain she's in. Almost immediately, Skylar snuggles right into me, and Celia helps cover the both of us up. Ale had gone home to get her blanket since they said they wanted to keep her overnight for observation.

But in his fashion, he wasted no time in getting back here.

Celia looks over at Ale sleeping on the couch before looking back at me.

"You really love her, don't you?" Celia asks me.

I can't look at her. I can't drag my eyes away from Skylar. I close my eyes and nod.

"I love her more than I ever thought possible... It scares me. It terrifies me. I've never cared about someone as much as I care about her. What if I screw it up? What if I upset her? What if I break her heart? What if I'm not good enough for her? She deserves so much... She deserves more than me," I explain, my heart beating too fast.

I can tell. It's my cue to calm down, but I can't. When I saw that accident happen, even from that far away, my heart stopped. It was like the whole world stopped until I could get to her.

"Brax..." Celia chides like she's my mother. "The change I've seen in you in the last few months has been... incredible. You don't go out anymore. You don't go to parties. You haven't been caught with any woman since you've met Skylar. You go hang out with her every chance you get. And lastly. When's the last time you've had sex?"

My cheeks warm at her question. I'm not ashamed to say I like sex. But I just know that Skylar's never been in a relationship before... I don't want to push her into doing something that she's not ready for. She's more important to me.

"Skylar's never..." I start before Celia cuts me off.

"I know Skylar's a virgin. I was asking when the last time you had sex was," Celia presses, and I groan.

"Not since before I met Skye," I tell her. "There. Are you happy with my answer? It grosses me out thinking about someone other than her touching me. When I go to bed, I dream about her. When I wake up, I'm happy because she's asleep in my arms. My car, my house, my clothes. Everything smells like her, and I like it.

I'm building a house near her brother because I want her to be happy. Nothing compares to how I feel about her. She's my whole world. I love her. I'm in love with her, and that's never going to change. No matter if she chooses to be with me or not." I'm rambling at this point.

But everything I said is true. She's the air I need to breathe. She's my world. I don't know what I would do without her, and here I am... struggling to get the courage to just ask her out. I know she'll say yes. I know she will.

But the more insecure part of me worries that she's going to say no. The part of me that believes every word my father beat into me. The part that I've spent years trying to quiet.

That part is holding me back from doing it. But I know I need to because what Diego said is true. Someone else could come and take her from me.

"Have you told her about everything that your father did to you? About how you got your heart condition?" Celia asks, and I laugh.

"Yeah... Actually, I forgot to tell you that my brother and father are going to leave me alone apparently," I tell Celia.

She was there through the worst of my father abusing me. We ended up moving, and I lost touch with her.

"Your brother and father are going to leave you alone?" she repeats.

"Yeah. Brody came up to me when we were at one of Skylar's races. Went on this whole long rant about how he has a child now. The child's mother said he needed to fix his life or she'd never let him see their kid," I tell her.

It still feels weird to say out loud. I still can't believe it. I really can't. I want to be everything for her. No matter how that makes me feel.

"I... I think that's what's been holding me back. The fear of my dad coming in at any moment and killing her. At taking the one thing in my life away that's been going right. But I did tell her everything. It was nice to get it off my chest," I explain.

It might not make sense... but it makes sense to me.

"There's a lot of things that Skylar is amazing at. Listening? Making someone feel better after they trauma dump on her? Those are things she's always been amazing at. She knows what people need and knows how to give it to them," Celia tells me with a wink.

I shake my head. "That's probably not happening any time soon," I explain. "She has the lead in that. I make no complaints." I look over to where Ale is sleeping. "He still hates me."

"He doesn't hate you per se..." Celia trails off for a moment. "He hates the thought of her growing up. He hates the thought of her going through another heartbreak. He doesn't hate you, but he hates the thought of what you, and I'm not saying that you would do anything to hurt her, but he hates the thought of what you could do to her. He's been her rock through a lot... Through her parents abandoning her. Through his parents abandoning both of them. Their aunt dying... A lot. Just a lot. He hates when she cries. He hates when she gets hurt. He wants her to stay the happy woman she is," Celia tries to explain.

I nod as I listen. "I don't know what to do to make him see that I hate that, too... Her tears are what I hate most in this world. I want her to be happy; to be taken care of. She's the thing that means the most to me." I shake my head at the thought.

I'm good enough for her. I am. I don't need to put it inside of my head that I'm not. I'll be everything for her, no matter what it takes.

"Just... keep doing what you've been doing. Keep taking care of her. Keep dropping everything to be there for her. Just like today... You ran to her when she was hurt. You dropped everything. You fought to be by her side. Just keep doing that. Keep loving her. Keep being her everything. And maybe think about actually asking her to be your girlfriend. It's been long enough," Celia tells me before laughing.

"If I thought she would've said yes, I would've asked her the first day I met her. But I just... I don't know. I wanted to show her that I could be better. Ale had it in her head that I was some player... I wanted her to trust me. To know that I was more than that," I tell her.

I smile to myself, before pressing a gentle kiss to the top of Skylar's head.

"She knows that. She's known that. She loves you just as much as you love her." Celia shakes her head. "You just can't see it because you're blind to everyone around you that loves you."

"Well..." I can't say I'm perfect. "Hey. Speaking of that, what's with the dipstick trying to flirt and touch Skylar?"

"Dipstick?" Celia asks.

"Diego." I glare.

Celia grins. "You can't tell me that you're not the most possessive person I know. You fit right in.. Diego knows how to push your buttons; to push you into making a decision or letting Skylar go."

I stare at her. I don't know how to respond to her. I don't know what to say.

But one thing I do know for sure.

My decision is made.

It was made a long time ago. I just never wanted to admit it to myself.

Skylar is mine.

I won't ever let her go.

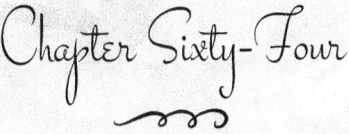

Chapter Sixty-Four

SKYLAR

The next morning, I wake up, and my whole room is packed. Braxton's holding me. Ale's sleeping in the chair right next to my bed. Leo and Celia are sleeping on the couch in the room. I look through the window and see Diego and Rosalynn there.

I'm curious if they've been here the whole night, too. I start to move. I want to get up. I want to leave.

"No." Braxton tightens his hold on me, keeping me against him.

"No?" I ask. I want to look up at his face, but I can't.

"No. No leaving me. Just no," he tells me before I feel his nose press against the top of my head. "I'm coming with you."

"To the bathroom?" I ask, but I can't deny him.

He sounds so sad, so stressed out and worried. I will never tell him no.

"Yup!" he tells me before getting up with me in his arms.

I look at him, looping my arms around the back of my neck. "I could walk," I whisper to him.

Braxton just shakes his head. "Nope."

He opens the door effortlessly, before gently setting me down on my feet. "I'm really okay," I try to tell him, but he just shuts and locks the door.

"What's your pain level?" he asks me, ignoring the fact that I said I was okay.

I pause for a second, my head hurts but nothing I can't manage. "Eh, my head kind of hurts, but nothing like yesterday. I feel sore. But really, I feel okay," I tell him as I pull my pants down.

Braxton sits up on the sink like we've done this a thousand times. I smile at him before sitting down. "You're really serious about this, huh?"

"Oh, deadly, baby girl. Deadly serious when it comes to you," he tells me with a wink.

"And what about when I need to shower?" I ask, grinning at him.

Braxton looks lost in thought for a second. "Dang," he says. "You got me there. I don't want to make you uncomfortable."

"I don't think you could ever make me uncomfortable," I tell him with a soft smile.

He's always been so incredibly nice to me. I don't think he could ever do anything like that to me.

"I don't want you to ever feel that way. So, if that is crossing a line, then I won't do that. I just... the last time that happened... you..." He trails off before shaking his head. "You know what happened. I can't do it. I can't do it."

I frown. He's so worried about me. My heart skips a beat. I've never had someone care so deeply about me that wasn't Ale, Leo, or Celia. I just want to hug him, but I think that might hurt. I want him to know that I'm okay. I'm completely fine. Slightly sore, but I'm okay.

"I know. I'd let you do whatever you want to me," I tell him with a wink.

"Baby. You can't say it like that," he groans before rubbing a hand down his face.

I laugh before I shake my head. I try to get up, but wince. My entire back tightens in pain, and it takes everything in me to not cry out. Braxton's quick to get to me, gently placing his hands under my armpits and helping me stand up.

I want to cry. I didn't think this was going to hurt this bad.

"Getting thrown into wood poles hurts less." I try to make Braxton laugh. Laughter makes everything hurt less.

"What?" he asks me, helping me pull my pants up when I'm done.

"When I was younger, and just starting out for show jumping, I fell... A lot. It was probably embarrassing. I was so awful," I explain.

He's quick to pick me up in his arms again. "You were not awful. You were learning. There's a big difference, baby." He shakes his head, before heading out of the bathroom and back into my room.

Everyone is awake now.

"How are you feeling?" Ale asks, sitting up as soon as Braxton lays me back down.

"I'm okay. Can I go home today?" I ask him, tilting my head slightly. "I'm just sore, that's all. But that will go away."

Ale looks to Celia, who stands up. "I'll go see. Rosalynn and Diego were outside waiting to hear about how you were doing. I'm glad you're okay, Skye." She walks out of the room with Leo right on her heels.

"How's my car?" I ask, looking at Ale.

He laughs, before shaking his head. "It's totalled. I'll be getting you a new car. And after I get you settled in at home, I'm going to head to get your car cleaned out." I frown, but before I can get any further, Ale's taking a hold of my hand. "I know you loved your car... I'll get you a new one just like that one if you want. It's completely your choice," he tells me with a soft smile.

Braxton climbs into bed beside me and gently pulls me back into him. "That sounds great..." I tell Ale, leaning my head back against Braxton's chest.

"They haven't found the guy who ran into you yet, so until they do, I want you to go back to having a security detail. Especially when you travel on shows," Ale explains. "Just as a precaution. Just in case. I know it could be a complete accident. But why would the person run?"

Chapter Sixty-Five

BRAXTON

"Do you think it was an accident?" I question, staring at Ale.

"I'd just rather be safe than sorry ya know?" Ale tells me with a shrug. "They think it's an accident. Mason is dead. So, he obviously isn't the one who did it."

"We mean..." Skylar starts off. "I travel a lot for racing. Well, he means, I should say, I win a lot of the races I go to. People don't like it. So, they could try and take me out before a race. I typically travel around with a security detail anyway when I'm not with Ale. Or well... you now, too."

I blink a few times. I need to calm myself down before I yell. "And you didn't think to tell me? About any of that? I know about the stalker. But is this something that happens all the time?"

"It never came up," Skylar explains. "And no, it doesn't happen all the time. That would definitely suck. I've had that car for as long as I've been driving."

It never came up? It never came up.

I inhale deeply. This isn't her fault. I'm blaming Ale.

"It's something I've been dealing with," Ale tells me, and I want to punch him.

He's looking at me like he's the only one who cares about her, and that's just not true anymore.

I'm here now, and that's not going to change just because he doesn't like me. I glare at him.

"And you just thought to not tell me because...?" I question. I'm actually curious about his answer.

"Because she's my sister. She's my responsibility. I know how to protect her. You didn't have to know until right now," he explains with a cocky smirk on his face.

I might actually punch him.

"I'm going to go and talk with your doctor, and then call up the security team again," Ale tells her before standing up and pressing a kiss to her forehead.

She closes her eyes, a soft smile crossing her beautiful face. "I'm sorry for not telling you."

"You don't need to apologize to me... I just want you safe. That's all, sweetness." I hold her against me and close my eyes. "I just want you to be safe. That's the most important thing to me."

Chapter Sixty-Six

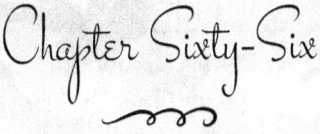

SKYLAR

I rub the side of my face, but then I feel Braxton's arm slip around me, and I'm pulled into his side.

"Are you getting a headache again?" he asks me. His voice is nothing more than a whisper.

"No, I just want out of this car," I tell him with a frown.

I rest my head against his shoulder. It feels weird being driven around again by the security team. It reminds me of when Ale first got on the team and things got so crazy for us.

I've never been in a car accident before. Now having been in one, I don't remember anything that happened. Well... other than Braxton yelling for me. Calling me his wife in front of everyone. My cheeks warm at the memory. He was so worried... I think a part of him still is.

His hand rubs at my arm, and I groan slightly. "We'll be home soon. The team will stay around patrolling, but since I'll be staying with you, I told them they don't have to be in the house," he tells me, and I nod.

"That makes sense. How is Ale taking care of everything?" I ask. He left right before I did, and he looked like he wanted to punch something.

"He's... stressed. Irritated. He's mostly just worried about you. He wants you to be safe. So do I. That's why I don't want to leave your side, even when you have the team, too." His hand moves down to my hip.

I'm glad we're in a Suburban. It's spacious back here. I don't feel crowded. We just have a driver in this one, but there's another Suburban in front of us and behind us.

"I do want to talk to you about something, though..." Braxton trails off, looking out of the window.

I look up at him. We're in the back, so we have privacy.

"What's wrong?" I ask, placing my hand on his chest.

His heartbeat gives me comfort... Ever since he told me about his heart, I'm worried that it's going to stop randomly.

"Well, nothing is wrong. But I wanted you to know that while we were in Italy... Ale and Leo pulled me aside one day, and they wanted to give me a plot of land by them. It's big, just like theirs. So, I'd have more than enough privacy. But... I'm meeting with a contractor tomorrow to tell them what I want for a house... I was wondering..." He breathes out. He just looks so stressed.

I can't help but smile brighter. He's so cute.

"You don't have to be worried about me being upset. What are you wondering?" I ask.

He brings his free hand to mine and intertwines our fingers. "Well..., I was just wondering if you would help me design the house. I want you to be comfortable there, too, and I'm sure that you'll feel better knowing that Ale is just right next door to us. I'm not sure if we're going to be right next to Leo and Celia or Ale's house." He's babbling, but I can't get over the part where he says 'we're'.

'We're'. Like I'm going to be moving in with him. I mean, I practically live with him already.

"You can tell me no," Braxton tells me.

"What? Why?" I shake my head. Did he say something after that? I wasn't listening! "If you said something after 'I'm not sure if we're going to be right next to Leo and Celia or Ale's house',

I'm going to need you to repeat yourself because I most certainly zoned out."

Braxton grins down at me. "I didn't say anything, but I know you were getting lost in that beautiful mind of yours, and I just wanted you to know that you can tell me no. You can say that I'm asking for too much. I won't be upset. The choice is yours." He kisses the top of my head gently.

I lean into him, smiling to myself. He's so thoughtful.

"Yes. Yes I want to help you with coming up with a plan for our house," I tell him. I can't bring myself to look up at him.

Braxton laughs, keeping his hold gentle on me. "That's perfect, sweetness. You are the best thing to ever happen to me."

We roll through the gates to our house, and I look up more. I have so many questions about this... Will it be by everyone? Or did they give him a spot on the other side? I guess Ale really is coming around to the thought of Braxton.

"I've given him little choice, Sunshine... I'm not going anywhere. Ever. He needs to just realize that," Braxton tells me, and I quickly turn to look at him.

"Did I just say that out loud?" My cheeks are turning pink, I can tell.

"Yes, yes you did. It's adorable. I don't know. They said they were going to have someone come out this week and tape off the plot they want me to have. So, I guess we'll know then," Braxton tells me, before gently brushing a piece of my hair behind my ear. "Don't be ashamed. I like when you tell me what's going on in that mind of yours."

When we park in the garage, Braxton gets out first before helping me out. He's quick to shoot the driver a glare before leading me into the house.

Saint immediately runs to us, meowing loudly. Braxton smiles before reaching down and picking her up. "Well, hello to you, too, little miss. We've missed you, too," Braxton tells her softly.

I think I like where this is taking us... I'm hoping it keeps going the way I want it to.

Chapter Sixty-Seven

BRAXTON

It's been one long week. Between my practices and Skylar's training, I haven't gotten to spend any time with Skylar. My mood has been paying the price for that.

She said she would drive to my place, but she hates driving, and definitely hates driving in the city. So no, I'm not going to make her come to me. I feel like paying the construction people more to build this house in a smaller time frame. I can't stand not being with her.

I'm bent over lacing my cleats as I wait rather impatiently for my beautiful blonde to come into the locker room. Cee might have her seated already, but every inch of me is hoping that's not true. I rub a hand down my face.

I'm tired. I'm cranky. I want Skylar. I want to see her. I want to hug her. I want to just be around her again. I feel like I haven't seen her in years. I've gotten so used to getting to see her everyday. Is this how it would be if she was with someone else? I wouldn't be able to steal all of her time?

I shake my head. I need to get this out of my head. The faster we win this game, the faster I'll be able to be back with Skylar.

"Have you seen all of the headlines about Braxton and that whore?" Max's annoying voice fills the silence.

I grind my teeth.

I won't survive in jail.

If I hate a week without Skylar, I'd never make it in jail.

"Saying they're married. Saying how she somehow managed to tie down the most eligible bachelor." Max laughs like it's some hilarious joke.

"Careful," Diego warns. "He doesn't like when people talk about her."

I grin. At least dipstick is learning something.

"Oh, please. I don't believe it. Out of all of the people he could be with, why would he choose to be with a prude? A pathetic homebody who doesn't like spending time with anyone?" Max seethes .

I see red.

I'm out of the seat in what feels like the blink of an eye. But before I can get to him, I feel hands and arms pulling at my arms and neck. Leo is taller than me, but no one is going to stop me from standing up for Skylar.

"What does this dude bench?" Leo groans, struggling to hold me back. "Ale! I need help! Get over here!"

"Don't you ever, and I mean ever speak of her again!" I growl.

Ale grabs one of my arms, and he grunts. "I need him to stop working out. Calm down, Vance!"

Max smirks at me, and I lunge forward. Diego's getting up next to join the other two people holding me back.

"What're you going to do about it?" Max asks.

The guys behind me groan, struggling to hold me back. My vision blurs. I feel my heart hammering against my ribs. I want to kill him. I want him to die.

No one gets to talk about Skylar like that.

I don't even want him looking at her.

He doesn't even deserve to breathe the same air as her.

"If you so much as mutter her name, I will shove my cleat so far down your throat that you'll feel me in your intestines until the day you die a slow miserable death. Cause I promise you, if you so much as breathe wrong around her, I will spend the rest of my life making sure that you are miserable! That will be my life's mission until the day you die, and then I'll dance on your pathetic gravestone!" I'm yelling, but I don't care. "You don't deserve to even know her." My muscles are tense.

I need to calm down.

"Do you understand me?" I spit in his face.

Max looks so pale, and I grin evilly. No one is going to talk about her like that. Never again.

"I said, do you understand me?" He just nods his head quickly, and stumbles away from me. "I'm good," I tell the guys that are holding me. But they don't let me go. I take a deep breath. "I'm not going to kill him," I promise the teammates around me.

"Are you sure?" Leo asks, hesitating to let me go.

Ale's quiet, and immediately I'm thinking that he's going to kill me. I overstepped. I should've told him about what was being said and let him deal with it. He's the captain after all.

"Wow..." Ale whispers, and I don't respond.

I don't have anything to say to him.

"You're in love with my sister..." He trails off, and I swallow.

I've been battling with admitting those feelings for a long time... I've never felt love before. I never knew that this is what love felt like. Skylar is like waking up to fresh air.

I don't feel so alone anymore.

I would protect Skylar with every inch of my being until the day that I die. She's mine. I love her.

I freeze.

Wow.

Did I just say that?

The world in front of me starts to spin, and I panic. I can't pass out. Not in front of them.

I shake my head, and shove Leo off of me. I can't think about this right now. I have a game to win.

A girl to see...

I have my girl to see.

She's waiting in those stands for me... And I know I need to play my best.

Chapter Sixty-Eight

SKYLAR

Celia and I are sitting up close to the field with the other fútbol players' wives and girlfriends. I rub my arms slightly. Everytime I go to a game, I typically wear a jersey with Rodriguez on the back of it.

Today... I swallow thickly.

Today, I'm in Braxton's jersey. Vance is plastered on the back of it. It's one that I took from his house the last time I was over.

I could almost groan at the thought. It's been a week since I've been able to see him. Everyday our schedules, in some way, clash. It ended up just not working out with seeing each other, and my sleep and mood has paid the price for it.

I don't like being away from him. He just has this way of keeping my mind from spiraling out of control. I can actually get my list of to-dos done with no problem anymore.

It's like since he's come into my life, everything... fell into place. My mind doesn't feel so cluttered anymore. I feel less crazy.

And then this week everything spiraled all out of control. I can't wait to sleep again. I didn't realize how much I relied on him until he wasn't there for me anymore. I rub my face slightly.

What if he moves on from me? What if he gets tired of me? I don't know what I'm going to do.

I rub my arms. Celia is grinning at me like she wants to say something.

"Okay... Say it. I'm wearing B's jersey. They aren't sold anywhere else, so it's obvious that I've been staying with him. Tell me I'm crazy for doing this because he hasn't officially asked me to be his girlfriend. Tell me I've lost my mind because everyone thinks we're secretly married already because of the car accident. Tell me that I need to distance myself because he likes to be with anyone, and I'm not as special as he makes me feel."

My mind is spinning. My heart is beating too fast. I need to calm down. I don't like being away from him. He's the only one who can make it stop. I rub my temple.

"Skylar..." Celia frowns. "You know he doesn't feel that way. He loves everything about you."

"My eyeball hurts," I tell her, forcing a smile. "But I'm fine. I really am fine. I promise. I'm just spiraling slightly. I haven't slept very well. But that's not anyone's fault, honestly."

"That's not what I was saying. You're amazing. You're really, really amazing. You're beautiful, wonderful, all around a perfect woman. When are you going to start seeing that? When are you going to start seeing that you've changed Braxton a lot since you came into his life? When are you going to see that that man looks at you like you are the sun, the moon, and the stars?" she asks me, crossing her arms and tilting her head at me.

I look down at my legs. I've been anxious a lot, but at this moment? I don't think I've ever been more anxious. Realistically? I can see the differences. He doesn't party. He spends all of his free time with me. He texts me throughout the day when he's not with me to make sure I'm okay.

But the bigger part of me... I can't see that it's because of me. I think it could just be because he wanted to change. Why would it be because of me? We're not dating. We're not anything besides friends.

I shake my head when I see Celia waving her hand in front of my face. "Earth to Mrs. Vance," she tells me. "Get out of your head. You are the reason he wants to be better. He's told me. He wants to be with you. But he wants to be good enough for you. He wants to be better for you. So, that Ale won't want to kill him when he looks at you. He wants you, Skye. He could have anyone, but he wants you."

I smile at her. She's right. I know she's right. Why can't I understand that?

"Wait...," I say, scrunching my eyebrows.

"What?" Cee replies.

"Did you just call me Mrs. Vance?"

Celia starts laughing before she shakes her head at me. "It took you a minute to respond to that," she tells me with a grin.

I look out to the field. I can't look at her when I say this.

"Do you think he meant it when he said he wanted to marry me?" I ask, even though I don't know if I actually want to know the answer or not.

Celia is quiet for a moment, and I immediately hate that I even brought it up.

"I have known Braxton for an extremely long time... I knew him in high school while he was in the town I lived in. With his anger issues, outbursts, and him all around acting like he doesn't care about anyone but himself, I knew he deserved more. That he needed someone to show him that the sun is shining on the other side. I think before he met you, he would've never gotten married. But when he's with you?

"When he looks like you, when he talks about you... Even when he's not with you, he's constantly thinking of you. Looking and buying things you would like. Heck. He's even building a house because he knows you hate driving and especially hate driving in the city," Celia rambles out to me.

I turn to look at her. What is she trying to tell me?

"What I'm trying to tell you is I honestly don't think that he has ever meant anything more than him saying that he wants to marry you. I think you just need to give him some more time... Or I can push him a bit more."

I bite my bottom lip. "You don't have to push him... Really. I don't want to upset him at all."

Cee snorts. "I'm telling you, he's already upset, but I also know that he needs a push. And I promise to you that I can be that push that he needs."

I don't know if I want to know about what she's going to do to him. But I also know that if she wants to do something, nothing and no one is going to stop her from doing it.

So, I guess I can just sit here and hope that she doesn't push him completely away from me.

Because a week sucked without him.

I don't think I could manage a lifetime without him...

Chapter Sixty-Nine

BRAXTON

After the game, all I'm thinking about is getting to Skylar. Holding her. Keeping her. Going home with her. Just getting away from everyone that I can't stand. I'm quick with my shower. I should be tired after running.

But I'm not.

I'm excited. I feel like my body is vibrating with this need to see Skye again. I've missed her more than I've missed anything before.

"Hello. Earth to Vance." I hear my name getting shouted, and it forces me out of my daydream.

I shake my head before pulling on my hoodie. "What?" I snap, and I don't even care about it.

"Dang. Down boy," Diego laughs. "We were wanting to know if you wanted to go out with us."

I laugh. I actually laugh. "No. Absolutely not. I'm going home with Skye, and that's the only thing that I want to do."

Diego smirks. "Okay. That's fine."

I wasn't asking. I don't have to ask anyone. She's mine.

I dig my phone out of my pocket. Her present should be at the house by the time we get there. Or I'm at least hoping. After I put my phone back in my pocket, I make sure I have everything I need. My phone. My wallet. My keys.

I'm good to go. I open the door, and jog out. She's supposed to meet me at my car. She has a key, so she can unlock it if she beats me there. If there were less people, I would be running to my car instead.

The paparazzi is in full force. I ball my fists. I sometimes hate being a famous fútbol player. I'm forced to slow down to a walk to get through the crowd.

"Mr. Vance! Is it true what everyone is saying?"

"Mr. Vance, have you been married to Skylar all this time?"

"Why haven't you spoken up about your relationship?"

"Are you ashamed of being with your wife?"

I swallow. I take a deep breath in. I can't punch anyone. I can't kill anyone. This sucks. My girl is waiting for me. She's so close, I can practically feel her. I roll my shoulders and push through the crowd.

"No comment," I say, trying to ignore the rest of them.

They don't deserve my time. They don't deserve to even get to talk about her. They move out of my way, so I'm able to pick up speed and walk faster.

I see a blonde head, and I smile. I knew she'd head straight to my car. I look both ways before running the rest of the way. I startle her when I grab her around her waist, spinning her in a circle as I hold her to me. She laughs when I put her down on her feet.

"Well, isn't that just a fancy greeting," she teases me with the brightest smile on her beautiful face.

I'm so in love with her.

I don't know how to tell her.

"Well, of course. I haven't seen you in so long. I've missed you," I tell her with a kiss to her forehead.

The smell of roses and vanilla fills my nose, and it takes everything in me not to shove my nose in her hair. I feel her nose against my chest before her soft inhale.

"You smell good. You smell like me," she tells me before smiling up at me.

"You smell good. I like being able to smell you even when you're not with me," I tell her.

I lean over, opening up the passenger door before helping her in. I know our whole little greeting will be plastered over the internet, but I don't care. I don't care who sees how much I need this girl in my life.

I look at the paparazzi and smirk. This is so going on the news. I go to the other side and get in on the driver's side.

"Are you hungry?" I ask, looking her body over.

She's been eating more lately. I like seeing it, but I know she tends to forget about herself, and this last week has sucked completely.

"Have you been eating regularly?" I ask next. I feel like she's taking way too much time to answer.

Skylar smiles at me. Her lips are darker. I tilt my head. Is she wearing light makeup? I think she is.

"You haven't slept either, huh?" I ask again. "I don't like when you don't talk to me."

"Well? If you would stop talking for one second, I might be able to get a word in." She laughs.

I grin. She's getting better at that.

"That was a good one, beautiful. Slick." I laugh along with her. "Okay, I'll stop talking so you can finally answer me."

"Well, I am hungry. But I ordered our food, so we can just pick it up on the way home. I have been eating regularly. Because if I don't eat, I feel like I'm starving. You know, it's really inconvenient when I'm training, and then I'm starving randomly," she teases me.

I grin. "Keep going," I tell her, pulling out my phone and sending her money for our food she ordered.

"I haven't slept super great, but it's okay. You were busy, so I'm not, like, upset, or anything. We can go home and watch a movie and nap together. That sounds amazing, doesn't it?" she asks me, buckling herself into her seat.

I smile at her, buckling up next and turning in my seat. She's truly one of a kind, and I don't know what I did to deserve her in my life.

"That sounds like the best date I've ever heard. Food. Snacks. Cuddles. What's better than that?" I ask.

The truth is, any time spent with her is the best time I've ever had. She is the best part of my life, and I don't know how to prove that to her.

"I have a present for you. I think it should be there when we get home. If not when we get home, later tonight or tomorrow morning," I tell her.

I know she doesn't like surprises, so I try my best to tell her ahead of time.

"You got me something?" she asks.

"Yes? Why is that so surprising?" I ask her, scrunching my eyebrows. I get her things all of the time.

"Not surprising. Just... I don't think I deserve all of the things you get me," she tells me, like it's the most regular thing to say.

Ale gets her everything she wants. If she even looks at it for too long, he gets it for her. So, why would she think she doesn't deserve it when I get things for her?

That's going to have to be something we talk about another day. I just got her back in my arms, and I don't want to upset her.

"You deserve all of it, and so much more. I've had this one getting made for a few months now, so I'm extremely excited for you to see it," I explain.

I'm nervous and excited. She could hate it. Ale could be mad that I bought this for her, but at the end of the day, I want Skylar to love it. I don't care about anything or anyone else.

Chapter Seventy

SKYLAR

I rub my hands against my thighs. He has a present for me? What could he have gotten me? He already got me more than enough. He shows that he cares about me. He's so attentive.

I don't think I could ever need anything else. He's so obvious with his actions. He loves me.

Wow...

Does he actually love me? Or am I just imagining that? I look over at him. He's so focused on driving. His hand's on my left thigh. His grip isn't tight, but he's holding me enough that his hand won't slip or move anywhere.

I want to ask him how he feels about me, but I'm nervous about his answer. What if he says he just thinks of me as his best friend? What if he doesn't think of me as more than that?

I shake my head. I don't want to spiral. I won't let myself. He's been nothing but nice to me. Why shouldn't I trust him? There's no reason. He's given me no reason to not trust him.

"Are you doing okay, baby girl?" he asks me, drawing me out of my thoughts.

He had to slow down because it started raining, but I trust him. He won't let anything bad happen to me.

"Yes. I'm just tired... That's all," I tell him.

I'm not lying. I'm exhausted. I don't want to tell him that I'm worried that he doesn't love me. Because I know I love him, and I don't think I can handle it if he doesn't love me back.

"Well, we're almost home. We can wait to see your gift 'til tomorrow if you want?" Braxton offers.

I shake my head. "No, I want to see whatever you got me," I tell him.

It's the truth. I know he puts a lot of thought into what he gets for me. So, I know it's going to be amazing.

When he pulls up to the gates, they automatically open for him. I can't help but smile. I love how he hates talking to everyone but me. Braxton winks at me before he slowly pulls to my house where I see a dark purple Dodge Durango sitting outside of the garage.

Braxton's quiet when I look at him. Did he buy this for me? Or did Ale buy it for me, and he was just in on it?

"Holy crap," I'm stunned.

How is this real? I didn't get in that car accident that long ago. Is this new? I have way too many questions.

"Is that a 'holy crap, I love it'? Or 'holy crap you've overstepped and you should've let my brother buy this for me'?" he asks me before laughing uncomfortably.

I turn to look at him again. Why would I not love this? How could I not love this?

"I love this! It's so beautiful!" I tell him. When he parks, I don't wait until he opens my door.

I'm out and heading over to where it sits. I'm in love... It's gorgeous. The dark, matte purple matches my last car. But this one... I smile when I see 'Property of Braxton Vance' in delicate hand writing across the side of the car in bright red.

I laugh as he leans up against the car and smiles at me. "What? I can't have people thinking that they can just come talk to my woman, now can I?" he teases me, causing me to blush.

I love how he's so possessive of me.

"I love it," I tell him, heading around the back of the car where 'Vance' is in place of 'Dodge' on the trunk. "Really?"

Braxton's smiling so big at me. "Yes. Because that way, if I'm not with you, people know that you're mine. No one will mess with you."

I don't say anything as I move to the driver's side. When I open the door, I gasp.

Everything inside is completely customized to match the outside. It's beautiful. It's perfect. Everything is purple and black. There's purple ambient lighting. I sit in the seat before looking at the rearview mirror. There's a hanging keychain. I lean closer and look at the picture frame.

It's us in Italy. I'm holding the water that we shared while we were holding our bag. We're in front of the waterfall we hiked to see.

I flip the frame over and read what it says.

'Drive Safe. I love you- B'

Braxton is shielding me from the rain. I turn to look at him. "B...?" I ask. I can't think of anything else to say.

His hair is falling in his face, but the seriousness in his gaze makes my heart skip a beat. I step out of the car so I can shut the door.

"Ryder?" I ask again, wanting to know what's going through that beautiful mind of his.

He walks closer to me, backing me against the side of the Durango. Braxton's way taller than me. So, he's perfectly shielding my face from the rain.

"There is nothing in this world... that I love more than I love you," his voice is barely a whisper.

Braxton keeps looking between my eyes and lips. I swallow. Does he really mean that?

"I know where your mind is going. That I don't mean it. That I don't want you. But, Skylar. Look at me," he tells me, and when I don't immediately listen, he gently lifts my chin to bring my eyes back to him. "That's my good girl," he praises. "I have never loved anyone in the entire world more than I love you. You're every-thing to me. I can't imagine my life without you."

I smile up at him. I believe him. I believe him with my whole heart. I wrap my arms around his neck as he steps closer to me. I feel his body press to mine, and I'm warm again. The rain doesn't feel so cold anymore.

"I love you..." I tell him. "I love you more than I ever thought was possible. I just... I didn't think that you would feel the same about me because -"

Braxton growls. "Be careful how you finish that sentence."

I laugh, wanting to just brush it off. "Because there's no reason for you to not love me. I'm so great," I offer, dipping my hands into the back of his wet shirt so I can feel his skin.

Braxton smiles, leaning his forehead against mine. "Tell me to stop..."

"What if I don't want you to?" I whisper. I feel his hands slowly slide down my torso to my hips.

He grabs me and pulls me closer to him. "I won't be able to let you go."

I lean up slightly, before biting his lower lip. "I don't want you to let me go."

Before he responds to me again, he leans down and kisses me. His left hand moves up to the back of my head, tilting my head so he can kiss me deeper. I swear that time stops.

All I feel is his soft lips against mine, the warmth of his tongue as he licks across the seam of my lips. I open my mouth before he immediately slips his tongue in. I moan softly. A shiver wracks through my body.

Braxton stops, pulling away quickly. "What? What's wrong?" I'm quick to ask. He glares slightly before leaning down and biting the tip of my nose. I laugh before covering my nose. "What was that for?"

"That was the best kiss of my entire life. Nothing is wrong besides you being cold. We're both soaking wet. We should go inside," he tells me, leaving no room for discussion.

Braxton turns us around before walking into the house. I rub my arms, trying my best to not shiver again.

"Do you want a warm shower? I can get it started for you," he offers, leading me to my bedroom.

"For us?" I ask, my cheeks heating at my offer.

"I think it's official. I've died and gone to heaven," Braxton tells me before kissing the top of my head. "Whatever you want, my love."

I bite my bottom lip, smiling to myself. I know I should be nervous, since he'll see me naked and everything, but I'm not. I know I'm safe with him. He would never do something that would make me uncomfortable.

My whole body feels like it's lit alive. I don't think I've ever been happier than at this moment. Ale will be happy... He has to be... Right...?

Chapter Seventy-One

BRAXTON

After Skylar and I ate, I'm not entirely sure what happened. Once I felt her weight in my arms, I think I fell asleep. This morning was fast... We woke up. While Skylar got ready for the day, I made us breakfast. I got lost in my thoughts.

I wanted so badly for Skylar to love the car, I didn't think about actually saying the words that I wanted her to be my girlfriend; that I wanted to be with her. Sure. Everyone already thinks we're married. It must've slipped my mind.

But here I am... sitting in the stands waiting alongside everyone else for Skylar's turn in the arena. These jumps are huge. The other riders don't seem to have as great of a bond with their horses as Skylar does with Midnight.

"What's going on with you?" Celia asks, sliding up beside me.

I shake my head. I missed the opportunity to finally make Skylar officially mine. I lost track of what I wanted so badly to happen because I kissed her and it slipped my mind.

I rub my face. "I kissed Skylar."

"You WHAT?" Celia nearly shrieks, and I quickly shush her.

"Lower your voice. We haven't told Ale yet... I... I forgot to ask her to be my girlfriend, and today things were moving so fast.

I didn't get the chance to talk to her about it this morning." I'm stressing myself out for no reason.

She loves me. I know she does. I just don't want anyone taking her away from me.

"Well, Brax. The whole world already thinks you guys are married. So is the official title really important right now?" she asks me, and I glare at her.

"Yes. It is. I want her. I need her. She's mine. I would rather die than have someone take my wife away from me," I snap at her before standing up.

It's Skylar's turn. I take out my phone, wanting to take a few pictures of them together.

"Does one of those jumps look too big?" I ask, turning to look at Ale.

He's on the edge of his seat, but he's not saying anything.

"Ale." I say again, but I can't look at him.

I need to stay focused on Skylar. She's jumping over everything flawlessly. The sound of Midnight galloping sounds like my heart beat.

The group around me starts to mumble to each other. "Everyone shut your mouths," I snap at them. Thankfully everyone listens.

Skylar is galloping towards the tallest jump in the arena. I feel Celia's hand on my arm, but I can't say anything. None of the other riders jumped this. They all ran around it, but she's going straight for it.

"Breathe, Braxton. She's got this. She wouldn't try to jump it if she didn't think they could do it," Celia tells me.

But I don't respond.

I can't.

I need her to make this. Because if she falls and gets severely hurt, I don't know what I'm going to do. I make sure to take a few photos before Midnight jumps come up.

My heart stops while they're in the air, and then his hooves hit the ground without bumping a single pole.

The crowd erupts in cheers, and I'm yelling. "That's my wife! That's my girl! Did you all see that!" I'm looking around at everyone who's clapping for her.

Ale's staring right at me, and I want to shrink back. But I won't. I don't want him to think I'm weak. Or I'm not serious about Skylar. I've never been more serious about anything in my entire life. I love her. I want the whole world to know that I love her.

Ale walks closer to me before placing a hand on my shoulder. I look him right in the eyes, and refuse to look away.

"If so much as one single tear drops off of her face. or you hurt a single hair on her body, I will know. I will give you a slow, extremely painful death. Do you understand?" Ale tells me.

I nod. "I would kill myself if that ever happened. She's the best thing to ever happen to me. I want her to be happy... That's what matters to me," I tell him before looking back to where Skylar is heading with Midnight.

"We'll all make our way towards her," Celia says when Ale lets me go. "Go get your girl."

I don't say anything, I just jog off in the direction she went. I'm asking her to be mine. I don't care if it's weird, but I need to know her answer.

I need to know her answer like the need to breathe.

Chapter Seventy-Two

SKYLAR

My heart is still racing as I lead Midnight to his turnout. He snorts at me, but I smile in return. He did so amazing. I was worried that we wouldn't be able to get that last jump, but we were perfect. Everything was great.

We didn't hit a single pole, and I think we did pretty great with time, too. I know my security team is following closely behind me, so I know nothing's going to happen to me.

"That's my wife," Braxton huffs, I'm assuming to one of the guards.

I laugh before handing Midnight's reins to my stable hand so that he can get taken care of.

"There's my husband," I smile as I see him run towards me.

I laugh as he leans down, grabs me around the waist, and spins me. "You did so amazing! I'm so insanely proud of you. You looked amazing out there with Midnight! That last jump made my heart stop, though. I'm not going to lie to you about that, but you are perfect. You were perfect out there!" he tells me, but doesn't put me down.

Braxton carries me to Midnight's stall. I wrap my arms around the back of his neck. "I can walk."

"I never said you can't. I just want to hold you," he tells me with a kiss on my cheek. "While I'm holding you... I want to know something."

"What's that?" I tilt my head.

Braxton places me down on my feet before helping me unclip my helmet. "I want to know if you would do me the absolute honor of being my girlfriend?"

I snort. I'm so happy. "You want to downgrade me from the wife title? How dare you."

Braxton grins, pulling me into him again. "I don't want to downgrade you to a girlfriend title. I want you to be my wife. But you deserve to be wooed. To go on actual dates. Then for me to propose to you. I promise you that I'm going to propose to you someday, but today, I just want to be able to know that you're actually my girlfriend. That I can rest easy knowing that you're mine." His hands drop to my butt and pull me as tight to him as possible.

I grin, before standing on my tippy toes and kissing the tip of his nose. "I thought I was always yours."

"You have been. Since the moment I laid eyes on you. I just need it to be official. For my own peace of mind," he tells me before kissing the top of my head.

I smile and close my eyes. "It gives me peace of mind, too... It also helps that everyone thinks we're already married. So, I know everyone will know you're mine." I wink at him, and he grins.

"Who knew my shy little Sunshine could get so possessive of me?" he teases. "I love how confident you've gotten."

I slip my hands into the back pockets of his jeans. "Someone really wise told me once that I shouldn't be ashamed of what I want. So, I'm trying to be better about it."

"Good. You deserve everything and so much more, Sunshine," he tells me before we turn as we hear everyone come towards us.

"Well, look at you, Ms. Show Jumping Champion!" Leo nearly shouts.

"Looks like your winning streak is still going strong." Celia winks at me.

Ale looks like he has tears in his eyes. I'm quick to run over and give him a hug. "I'm so proud of you, Princess... You're incredible. It looks like you're still on track to being the youngest show jumping Olympian."

I smile as he wraps his arms around me tightly. "I hope so!"

I feel high on adrenaline still. I know it'll crash, and we have to go start getting ready for the charity event. I wonder if I could sneak in a nap beforehand. I won't be able to stay awake if not.

Braxton's hands are in his pockets. I know he's waiting for me to come back over to him. I'm slow to let Ale go. I don't want to let him go if he's going to start crying.

"My little girl is all grown up. Someone pinch me," Ale says with the most loving smile. Leo's quick to reach over and pinch him. "AH! I didn't actually mean that! What's wrong with you?"

We all start laughing at Ale's high pitch yell from Leo pinching him. "You said to have someone pinch you!" Leo complains.

Rosalynn shakes her head. "They're children, I swear. We're all so proud of you, Skye. You were amazing out there. They'll be announcing the winners here soon. Are we going to head home after that and get ready for the event tonight?"

Everyone else is nodding yes. I rub the back of my neck awkwardly. I know we all need to be there, but I'm going to need to take a short nap, at least.

Braxton groans dramatically. "You know what sounds even better?"

He makes grabby hands towards me, so I walk to him. He's quick to pull me back against him again. "What's that, baby?"

"Baby?" the group says at the same time, and I grin.

"Oh yeah. I put my big boy pants on and finally asked Skylar to be my girlfriend, and she said yes." Braxton looks so proud, and it's the cutest thing I've seen all day. "A nap, that sounds so amazing!" Braxton nods excitedly. "Just imagine. It would be nice. I'm tired. We can arrive later than them. I won't complain."

I smile at him, leaning my entire weight on his body. "If you need a nap that badly, I don't mind us arriving later," I tell him with a smile.

"Great! So let's go get your award, and then we'll go get a nap!" Braxton's excitement rolls through me, and I shiver.

He wraps his arm around my shoulder and leads me back towards the event. I hate being around the big crowd, but somehow, with him right beside me...

... I feel like I can handle it.

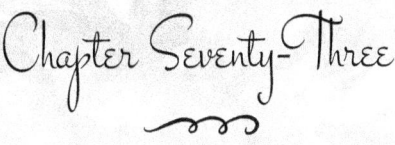

Chapter Seventy-Three

BRAXTON

After we got Skylar's award and came home, it didn't take long for her to fall asleep in my arms. I remember her telling me that she gets really tired after her shows, but I also know that she'd go along with whatever everyone else wanted.

I quickly pull out my phone when I feel it buzz..

Leo: I'll have everything ready for you when you get here. Are you sure this is what you want?

I glare at the screen when I read his message. I'm so glad that this is the last event of the season. I hate these things.

Me: I know what I want. I know what to do to make her happy. Stop asking me if I'm sure I've never been more sure about anything in my entire life So just get things ready for me okay?

I hit send. Almost as soon as it sends, I see Leo reads my message. He sends a quick reply.

Leo: Down boy I was just wanting to make sure. This is going to be the story of the century I'm happy for you man

I shove my phone into my pocket. I don't need to message him back. I'll see him soon enough, and I know he'll tell Celia. She'll make sure he's doing everything for me.

So, here we are. She's getting ready in her closet, and I'm waiting in her bedroom. I rub my face. This will be our official first outing as a couple, and I'm worried about how the team's going to react.

Ale seems to be okay with me being with her. Leo and Celia are, of course, so excited. But I'm going to lose it on Diego if he so much as -

My brain stops.

I think my heart stops.

My eyes connect with Skylar's, and I'm done for.

There's no one else I would rather be with for the rest of my life. I'm hers.

"Wow..." I tell her, standing from my seat so I can walk closer to her.

She's nervous. I can tell. But she's gorgeous. We paired everything perfectly together, and I can't wait to walk into that event with her on my arm.

Everyone will see, and it'll be clear that the rumors going around on the internet are true. She's my woman, and I'd rather die than have that change.

"Ryder?" Her voice draws me out of my thoughts.

I shake my head before I look back up at her face. I smile as I walk closer to you. "I'm sorry, Sunshine. But wow..." I say, taking her body in again. She's gorgeous. "I'm speechless."

"You're speechless, but you picked out everything I'm wearing?" she asks me.

I grin. "Well, yes. We picked out everything you're wearing. But it looks so much better with it all being together. You're the most beautiful woman I've ever laid eyes on. I hope you know that." I kiss her forehead gently.

Skylar's cheeks turn pink as she looks down at her feet. "Thank you..." she nearly whispers. "Are you ready to head to the event now?"

I nod, taking her hand and leading her to the door. I squeeze her hand as she follows me outside. My car is already started and is warming up for her. The stars are out in full swing. I spin Skylar before dipping her.

She gasps, but I don't drop her. I lean toward her. I want to make sure she can't look away when I say this.

"You are the light of my life. The light of my world. I promise you, I won't stop showing you how much I love you."

She smiles up at me, before giving me a quick kiss. "I trust you... More than anyone else in my entire life."

I bring her back to her feet, before leading her the rest of the way to where my car is sitting.

I make sure she's settled in her seat before getting in myself. I know what I have to do to prove to her that I'm all in.

And I know the perfect way to do it...

Chapter Seventy-Four

SKYLAR

B raxton kept his hand on my thigh the entire drive to the event. I'm nervous. I don't like big parties like this... I don't like a lot of people around me. Especially not twice in one day.

"We will leave as soon as you want to leave, okay?" he assures me again.

I nod before smiling at him. "Yes. I know you'll know when I'm ready to go." Somehow he always knows what I'm feeling before I do.

"I know you're nervous, but I promise everything's going to be okay," he tells me again.

I grin at him. "Are you getting nervous, baby? Do you not want everyone to see us together?" I tease. I want to lighten the mood.

"It would be my greatest wish come true if everyone saw us together. I want the world to know that I'm dating Ms. Skylar Rodriguez." He winks at me.

Braxton pulls to a stop in front of the red carpet. He doesn't say anything. He just gets out, straightens his suit jacket, and heads over to my side. I guess he's more used to this type of stuff than I am.

He opens my door for me before holding out his hand. I unbuckle my seatbelt before taking his hand and stepping out.

Immediately, the cameras flash. Thousands of pictures are taken of us. I feel Braxton's arm slip around my waist, and I instantly feel much better. We give them a pose. before walking up the steps to the building.

"Mr. and Mrs. Vance, when did you guys get married?"

"Mr. Vance! When did you know that you wanted to marry Skylar?"

"Mr. Vance! How's it feel being married to the most eligible bachelorette?"

Braxton grins, before stopping and looking at the reporter. "I knew I wanted to marry my wife the moment I laid eyes on her. And how does it feel being married to her? Like heaven," he tells them before placing his hand on the small of my back and leading me back to the building.

"You didn't have to tell them that..." I tell him, biting on my lower lip.

I probably need to stop doing that. I don't want to ruin my makeup.

"I didn't have to. I wanted to. I want everyone to know that you're mine."

The doors are opened for us before we're ushered into the party. The music is soft. The conversations among everyone are almost maddening. I don't know how long I'm going to be able to be here.

"Remember, sweetness," Braxton whispers in my ear. "I'll take the blame for wanting to leave early."

I smile before leaning into him. "Well, aren't you my knight in shining armor."

"That's right. Just call me Prince Charming, baby girl," he tells me, leading me to where everyone is standing in a group.

"Well, would you look at that? They're actually on time," Leo tells the group. "I thought they would've taken this time t-"

"Don't you finish that sentence. Because I will kill him and not think twice," Ale growls. Rosalynn moves closer to him and rubs his arm.

"Calm down. It's okay," Rosalynn says with a bright smile. "Do you feel better after your nap?" she asks me.

I nod quietly. I don't know her very well. I want to. I just don't know how to talk to her.

"Yeah. I always need a little reset after a big show," I say before looking back at Braxton.

He seems lost in thought, and I don't know if that's a good thing or a bad thing. Braxton tilts his head before looking down at me. "Yeah, sweetness?"

"I didn't say anything. Are you feeling okay?" I ask, turning around in his hold to be able to look at him.

Braxton nods, kissing the tip of my nose before looking at Leo. I turn to look at him, too, and they're apparently having some mental conversation because Braxton lets me go.

"I'll be right back, my love," he tells me before turning around and heading into the crowd.

"What is he doing?" I ask Leo.

Leo shrugs. "I don't know. I mean, I know. But I'm not telling you."

I look at everyone slowly, but no one answers me. So, everyone knows except for me?

Why am I the only one not in the loop about everything? I rub my bare arms, suddenly feeling cold and like I shouldn't be here.

Chapter Seventy-Five

BRAXTON

I quickly move through the crowd wanting to get back to Skylar as fast as I possibly can. She hates being in crowds, and I just left her. I shake my head. She's not alone. She's with Ale. She's going to be just fine.

I just need to do this. I want to do this. I want to show Skylar that I'm all in.

I look at Milo, one of the team's many employees. "Everything is all set up, Mr. Vance! Is there anything else I can do for you?" he asks me, shoving his glasses back up his nose.

"Nope. That's all that I needed. Thanks for helping me out at the last minute," I tell him before taking the microphone from his hand and walking up the stage.

The spotlight moves to me, and I tap on the microphone to make sure it's on. "Is this thing on?" I ask into it, and everyone turns to look at me.

I immediately see Skylar. Her eyes are locked right on mine. "Ah, so this thing is on. Okay, great. Well, hello, everyone. Thanks for coming tonight. I'm Braxton Vance. I'm sure most of you already know who I am.

"Just like I'm sure most of you know my reputation. When I was accepted onto the team, I had this image. I thought that that's all that I could ever be. But then I met this amazing, beautiful, kind, and perfect woman. She looked at me like I could do no wrong.

"I fell hard that day. But I thought that I wasn't good enough for her. I thought because of my past actions that she deserved someone else. But she woke up everyday showing me what true love is, and what true love feels like." I swallow as tears sting my eyes.

"I don't deserve her. But I won't stop showing her that I love her." The entire crowd is silent. I take a step off of the stage to head towards Skylar.

"Something's happened... The media got word of me calling this amazing woman my wife, which, she is in all terms of the word. She loves me. She cares about me. She's my entire world..." I continue on, coming to stand in front of Skylar.

The spotlight comes to stop on us.

"She's the reason why I wake up in the morning. She's the reason why I'm happy everyday. She's my everything... I want her to know that I'm all in. That this is what I want. That this relationship that we're in is what I need. The only thing I want, the only relationship I've ever wanted in my entire life. I'm all in... For the rest of my life, baby girl... I'm all in..." I tell her, giving the microphone to Celia.

Skylar's silently crying in front of me. I bring her into my arms and hold her to my chest.

"I love you..." she whispers to me. "I love you. Thank you for that... I didn't know that I needed it."

I grin, pulling her away just enough so I can look down at her face. "I know what you need... I'll always know what you need. For the rest of our lives."

"For the rest of our lives," she repeats to me.

Epilogue

S o much has happened since Braxton told the world about his love for me. We got engaged a couple months after that. Our wedding didn't take place for another two years. We wanted time to plan, and then we had Brooklyn, so we didn't feel the need to rush.

Braxton and I have a family business together. We do a lot of charity work. It ranges from helping foster children, helping businesses with loans, building homeless shelters. I could keep going on and on about everything we've been doing together.

Our son, Ryker, had to stay home from school today since he was sick. Braxton should be on his way home soon.

They share the same birthday. They were born in the same hospital. just minutes apart. It's really such a unique story. They've been inseparable since birth.

When I hear screaming, I'm up and out of my seat to see what's going on. Brooklyn and Aiden should be home by now from school. But they shouldn't be screaming.

I open the door to the garage before heading out to see. Aiden is on the ground. My heart stops as I see Brooklyn over a masked man's shoulder screaming and kicking as she tries to get free.

"I love you, Ace! I love you!" she yells as they throw her into the car and speed off.

Everything in me wants to go after them. But I know I can't. I have to get to Aiden.

I run to Aiden and grab him to help him up. His forehead is bleeding. One eye is nearly swollen shut. He tries to shrug me off, but stumbles and falls on the pavement again.

"Aiden? Stop! You need to sit down. I'm going to call the cops. You need to go to the hospital," I tell him, getting down on my knees beside him.

Aiden keeps moving away from my hands. "I need to get to her. I need to go to her. They took her! I don't know who they are or what they're going to do with her! I need her, mama!" Aiden cries to me. "I need her like the need to breathe."

Tears stream down his face now. It doesn't take long for my home to be surrounded by countless cars, first responders, my family, and Braxton.

"Oh, Braxton." My heart aches as I look at Aiden. He's fighting against the people trying to check him out. "Ace. Honey. I need you to let them check you out. We need to make sure you're okay," I try to tell him.

But he's not listening. He never listens to anyone besides Brooke. Braxton's arms slip around me. "What's going on? Where's Brooklyn?"

I reluctantly turn in his arms. "We don't know... Someone took her..."

Until Next Time...